P9-DLZ-105

All the Little Liars

ALSO BY CHARLAINE HARRIS

AURORA TEAGARDEN MYSTERIES

Poppy Done to Death
Last Scene Alive
A Fool and His Honey
Dead Over Heels
The Julius House
Three Bedrooms, One Corpse
A Bone to Pick
Real Murders

LILY BARD MYSTERIES

Shakespeare's Counselor
Shakespeare's Trollop
Shakespeare's Christmas
Shakespeare's Champion
Shakespeare's Landlord

SOOKIE STACKHOUSE / TRUE BLOOD NOVELS

After Dead
Dead Ever After
Deadlocked
Dead Reckoning
Dead in the Family
Dead and Gone
From Dead to Worse
All Together Dead
Definitely Dead
Dead as a Doornail
Dead to the World
Club Dead
Living Dead in Dallas
Dead Until Dark

HARPER CONNELLY MYSTERIES

Grave Secret
An Ice Cold Grave
Grave Surprise
Grave Sight
Cemetery Girl Trilogy (with Christopher Golden)
Inheritance
The Pretenders

MIDNIGHT, TEXAS NOVELS

Night Shift
Day Shift
Midnight Crossroad

All the Little Liars

CHARLAINE HARRIS

Minotaur Books
New York

This is a work of fiction. All of the characters, organizations, and events portrayed in this novel are either products of the author's imagination or are used fictitiously.

ALL THE LITTLE LIARS. Copyright © 2016 by Charlaine Harris. All rights reserved. Printed in the United States of America. For information, address St. Martin's Press, 175 Fifth Avenue, New York, N.Y. 10010.

www.minotaurbooks.com

Designed by Omar Chapa

The Library of Congress Cataloging-in-Publication Data is available upon request.

ISBN 978-1-250-09003-4 (hardcover)
ISBN 978-1-250-09005-8 (e-book)

Our books may be purchased in bulk for promotional, educational, or business use. Please contact your local bookseller or the Macmillan Corporate and Premium Sales Department at 1-800-221-7945, extension 5442, or by e-mail at MacmillanSpecialMarkets@macmillan.com.

First Edition: October 2016

10 9 8 7 6 5 4 3 2 1

This book is for the people who asked me what Aurora was up to in the years since I wrote about her. I might have never attempted another book about my favorite librarian if it had not been for all of you.

Acknowledgments

I welcomed the help of my teacher cousin, Cathryn Harris, my long-suffering continuity maven, Victoria Koski, George Fong (former FBI agent, now Security Director for ESPN), and my fellow writer Jeff Abbott, who agreed to be Robin's best man at the wedding. If I have misused or misunderstood any information given to me, it's my fault.

All the Little Liars

Chapter One

Aurora Teagarden Bartell and Robin Hale Crusoe were joined in holy matrimony on December 8 at Saint James Episcopal Church. Officiating at the ceremony was the Rev. Aubrey Scott. Providing music was Emily Scott.

The bride, in an ecru lace dress, carried a bouquet of bronze chrysanthemums. She was attended by Angel Youngblood of Lawrenceton. Mr. Crusoe was attended by his friend Jeff Abbott, of Austin, Texas.

Following their honeymoon in Savannah and Charleston, the couple will reside in Lawrenceton. The bride is employed by the Lawenceton Public Library. The groom is a noted fiction writer.

Ms. Teagarden and Mr. Crusoe request that in lieu of gifts, well-wishers make donations to the Salvation Army or the Sparling County animal shelter.

"They only made one mistake," I said, reaching over to the butter dish. I applied butter liberally to my scone. Yum. I had gotten crumbs on my bathrobe sleeve, and I shook it off over my plate. This was a good morning. I was keeping everything down.

"What's that? Oh, the 'Bartell'?" said Robin. He was reading the Atlanta paper, which made the local paper seem pretty puny. Robin looked like he was about to commute to work, in khakis and a long-sleeved shirt. In Robin's case, that meant he'd walk from the kitchen to his study. "I guess they wanted to establish your status as a twice-married woman."

I'd never taken my first husband's name. We'd been married three years before I'd become a widow. "I guess I'll always stick to Teagarden."

"Better than Crusoe," Robin muttered.

I smiled. "Matter of opinion."

"How are you feeling?" He looked over the top of the paper.

"Like I'm not going to throw up." It was a moment-by-moment thing, for me.

"Hey, the day is looking good already." He smiled back at me, but he seemed anxious. Robin had never dealt with a pregnant woman before, and I could tell he wanted to ask me six times a day how I was doing . . . if his good sense didn't tell him that would drive me crazy.

I'd never been pregnant before, so we were even.

My phone buzzed. I glanced down at my messages.

"It's tomorrow afternoon when we go to the OB-GYN?" Robin knew that, but he had to double-check. "And if we don't like her, we're going to look elsewhere, right?"

"Absolutely," I said firmly. "We're going to Kathryn Garrison, to check her out. Listen, I just got a message from her office. She had a cancellation! I can get in this afternoon." I was pretty excited. I gave my new husband a thumbs-up gesture. "She comes highly recommended."

"By whom?" Robin was nothing if not suspicious; since he was a mystery writer, that came naturally.

"Melinda used her for both pregnancies, and she said Dr. Garrison was great. Angel went to Dr. Garrison, too." Melinda was my stepsister-in-law, and Angel had been my bridesmaid. They were both sensible women.

"Define 'great.' " Robin was all about the information.

I raised my hand so I could bend the fingers down as I ticked off points. "She took all Melinda's worries seriously. She took enough time at each appointment to make sure Melinda knew what was going on with the baby. Angel said she was low-key and calm. And Dr. Garrison served her residency in a Miami clinic specializing in threatened pregnancies. That's good, right? I'm not a young mother, especially to be having a first child." I made an effort to sound matter-of-fact. Rather than scared.

"Honey, you're going to be fine," he said. "It's so important that we both trust this doctor. I don't want you to have a moment's worry."

"Well . . . that ship has sailed," I said ruefully. "That's why I haven't wanted us to tell anyone. I've been waiting for [illegible] doctor's exam. I just want to be sure everything is okay."

"I understand," Robin said.

And I knew he did, though we hadn't been married three weeks yet. But we had dated before my first marriage, and we had picked up where we left off when Robin had returned to Lawrenceton after my widowhood.

"So we can tell your mom tonight." Robin grinned, his smile looking large in his narrow face. "How do you think she's going to react?"

"Half of her is going to be saying 'You *had* to get married! Oh, Aurora!' and the other half is going to be saying, 'A grandchild of my own at last!' "

Robin laughed. "My mom's going to be doing cartwheels. She'd given up on me contributing to the grandchild tribe. Ours will be her fifth." He laid the paper on the table and carried his dishes to the sink. I knew when I got home from work the dishwasher would be loaded and the coffeepot would be washed. Yet another reason Robin was going to be a better husband and father than my own dad. Dad had cheated on my mother, and she'd told him to leave. He'd married again, and now he lived across the country in Los Angeles. The best thing my dad had done after he'd left was father my half brother, Phillip, who was living with us now.

Thinking of Phillip, I noticed there was still silence from his room. "Listen, has Phillip said anything to you about his grades?" I asked Robin. "He should have taken all his semester tests but one."

It had taken many, many e-mails and phone calls before we'd finally come to an agreement with Phillip's private home-schooling network. I'd never before heard of such a thing. I'd been aware my younger half brother didn't go to a brick-and-mortar school, but that had been the limit of my knowledge.

I had discovered that this system of home-schooling classes was nationwide. The California division had agreed to let him finish the semester online, though Phillip was in another geographic location. Our father had at least done some of the work on the California end, which was only right and proper. Frankly, I'd been a little surprised.

"I don't think Phillip's ecstatic about sitting in his room with his laptop," Robin said. "But he's definitely been listening to the classes, and he has his last semester test today. Tomorrow's the start of the semester break, just like the local high school."

"You don't think going to a public school will be a shock for him?"

"I think he's looking forward to January so he can go to high school with his new friends. And he knows that with his mom gone, and Phil being a—well, a careless father, staying here is the best choice for now."

"Phil" was always my father, and "Phillip" was always my brother. Otherwise, it got too confusing.

"I can tell you for sure," Robin continued, "that Phillip

hasn't said anything about wanting to see his dad." Then he reverted to our favorite topic. "So tonight, I can call my mom and my sisters?"

"Okay," I said, half-scared and half-thrilled. "If Dr. Garrison says everything is fine, we'll tell everyone tonight."

I looked down at my bathrobe. "Pretty soon, we won't have to tell them, they'll just look at me and know." I was amazed, excited, and anxious about the changes in my body. Bigger boobs, yay! Thickening waist, boo.

"What was your birth weight?" I asked.

"Gosh, I don't know. We'll ask my mom when we tell her. Tonight," Robin said pointedly.

"Okay, okay." While it would be fun to share our happy news, we would not be in our little bubble any longer. We'd have to listen to all the input and speculation other people would offer: about what gender the baby would be, about whether a birth was safe for a first-time mom over thirty-five, about what we should name the baby. I looked forward to the excitement of sharing this happiness, but I was reluctant to let go of our secret joy.

Just at this moment, I had to pick out something to wear to work on this cold, brisk morning.

It was a little less than two weeks until Christmas. If ever I was going to wear my new red sweater, a gift from my mother, today was the day. It would only fit for maybe another month. I felt seasonal and bright in the sweater and some gray slacks as I pulled on my coat.

As I passed by Phillip's room, I could hear him talking on his phone. "Bye, little brother," I called. "Good luck on your test!"

"See you later," he called back. "I'm not worried about the test. Hey, can we have some chili tonight?"

"I think we have some in the freezer. It's labeled. Just get it out to thaw." I'd been close to Phillip when he was a child, but when my father and his wife moved to California it had become harder and harder to keep connected, until Phillip got old enough to e-mail me. Just a couple of weeks before, Phillip had hitchhiked from California to Georgia when he'd grown too angry at his father to stay at home. (I was still recovering from the retroactive fear.) Most guys wouldn't be too pleased to have a new wife's little brother living in the same house, but Robin had been totally cool about it. He really seemed to like Phillip.

Robin had gone back his office, a big room at the back of the house lined with bookshelves. As I paused to pick up my purse in the living room, I could look down the corridor to see him peering intently at his computer. He was already in the work zone. Robin was a best-selling writer, and he'd just gotten his editorial comments on his new book. His work ethic commanded my admiration.

I said "Good-bye," but quietly. I wasn't surprised when I didn't get an answer. When Robin was with me, he was all the way with me, but when he was working, he was just as absorbed in that. I was learning about living with a writer. I had loved Robin's crime novels long before I'd ever met the man and loved him, too. I left through the kitchen door into the carport to get in my Volvo for the fifteen-minute ride to work.

A few years before, it would have taken me eight minutes, tops. Growth equals traffic. Lawrenceton, once a shady small town, had been annexed into the urban sprawl of Atlanta.

There'd been a fender bender on my usual route, and I was delayed for several minutes. By the time I turned in to the employee parking lot behind the library, I was almost late. I hurried to the staff door, wishing I'd worn gloves and a scarf when the cold hit me. I had my keys in my hand, because this door was always kept locked.

I stepped right into the large room that had been added onto the library a few years before. It encompassed a small kitchen, a break area, and the book-mending area. On the other side of the hall lay the glass window through which I could see the desk intended for the secretary of the library director, and beyond that the door to Sam Clerrick's office. Right now the outer office was empty and bare, and the door to the director's office was firmly shut.

I put my purse into my little locker before I stepped out into the hall, heading for the door leading into the main floor of the library. Two women were between me and the door, and they were deep in conversation. Janie Spellman, the computer librarian (as I thought of her), was chatting with Annette Russell, the new children's librarian. Since I'd been substituting in the children's section for some months while the position had been advertised, I'd been delighted when Annette had been hired.

Annette and Janie were both in their early twenties, and they'd become friends quickly. Janie was vivacious and had a quick smile and vivid coloring, while Annette had a more relaxed personality. Her hair was in short dreadlocks with touches of platinum. She looked like a dandelion. I liked it.

They both said "Hey, Roe!" with varying degrees of enthusiasm.

Janie said, "Roe, I read the paper this morning. Is it true?" She looked almost hurt, which I found odd. She'd made a big play for Robin, but now she seemed to feel that I should have confided in her.

"That I got married? Yes, it's true. Robin and I got married."

"That's why you took a long weekend off?"

"Uh-huh. We had a little honeymoon." I smiled at them brightly, and Annette smiled back. Janie looked less . . . beneficent.

"So are you Mrs. Crusoe now?" she asked, as if she meant to be a bit insulting.

"No, I'm sticking with Teagarden," I said. I could not figure what Janie's beef was. She had known, even when she flirted with Robin, that he and I were dating.

"And you got married at the church?" Janie said, her voice even sharper.

I finally thought I understood. Janie wanted to know why she hadn't been invited.

"We did," I said agreeably. "Just family and one attendant apiece. My second wedding, you know." Plus, we'd been determined to get it done quickly and as low-key as possible.

I wasn't sure Annette did know that I'd been married before, and Janie had clearly forgotten. They both nodded, looking a little abashed. "That makes sense," Annette said.

"Anything new and wonderful happening?" I asked, to change the subject. I wasn't especially interested in whether Annette thought my private arrangements made sense or not. Perhaps I was being overly touchy.

"New, anyway," Janie said, looking excited again. "Sam's interviewing some women who've applied for the secretary job today."

"Wonderful." I meant that from the bottom of my heart. "He feels so much better when he's got a filter between him and the public."

"Well, the downside is, one of them is Lizanne Sewell."

I'd been on my way out to the main floor of the library. I stopped and turned back to face Janie. "What's wrong with Lizanne?" I said. I hoped my eyes weren't actually shooting sparks.

"She's not the brightest tool in the shed," Janie said, as if that were well known and should be obvious to me. There was a moment of silence.

"I didn't know Lizanne was applying for this job," I told Janie. "But she's a longtime friend of mine. Sam could hardly do better. She could handle his schedule very easily."

I left through the door into the library, so I wouldn't be obliged to wrestle Janie to the ground and deal out some hurt.

Perry Allison was working the checkout desk, and though he was busy with a patron, he gave me a nod in greeting. Perry's mother,

Sally, was a friend of mine, though she was at least fifteen years older than me, and Perry was becoming a friend, though he was younger. He'd had a hard life, and it was going to get harder. Sally was ill.

I went behind the counter to the employee computer area, and prepared to send out overdue notices. This was automatic to a certain extent, since the miscreants' names and addresses popped up when the books or other materials had not been checked in. But some people didn't have e-mail addresses, and those people had to be prompted by a phone call or a letter, whichever they requested.

There were few people who didn't have a phone *or* an e-mail address. My task was to notify those people. Naturally, there was a form letter to plug in that would take care of it. All I had to do was actually type the patron's name in. I'd heard Janie laughing about this backwoods method. She was proud that you could apply for your library card over the Internet. Proud.

The library had always been an unofficial community center, with books, magazines, newspapers, and all kinds of reference sources available to everyone. Free! I had always been amazed at how fortunate people were to have a public library, though almost every citizen took it for granted. But now, with a roomful of computers available to everyone, Lawrenceton Library had become even more vital. There was a constant flow of patrons from the moment the doors opened to the time they were locked. The computer have-nots used the public system to check out the help-wanted sites and for-sale sites. They looked up breaking news. They read the classified ads. They took their online courses, like my brother was doing at home this very minute (I hoped). Of course, the haves didn't even need to come into the building any longer. They could check out e-books and audiobooks online.

I appreciated the fact that the library was so relevant to the lives of the people it served. Just because you couldn't afford a computer shouldn't mean you couldn't access all this amazing information, right? And if you were elderly or disabled or just super busy, it only made sense to offer books in the easiest way available.

But I'd always been a printed-word person. I loved holding an actual book. I loved turning the pages. I loved carrying a novel around with me, getting it out of my purse at lunch to read for a few minutes in the break room. I had never been able to fathom what people did with their free moments, if they didn't read. But I'd become increasingly aware that this attitude aged me, made me more like seventy-six than thirty-seven.

And there were also plenty of actual, physical books that needed to be dealt with right that moment. I finished the overdue notices before I arranged the checked-in books on the cart in the order in which they'd be shelved. I popped a stool on the bottom shelf of the rolling cart. Though stools were available throughout the stacks, I found it was quicker to simply take one with me. When you're barely five feet tall on a good day, you have to think ahead.

I steered the cart carefully. The library was busy. Most of the patrons were adults, since school was in session—though in two more days it would be Christmas break. I took my time, and said hello to everyone, because I thought that was part of my job and I enjoyed it.

About halfway through shelving, I felt the sudden necessity to rush to the bathroom. A pregnancy book had told me this was a common occurrence, though I was entering that phase more quickly than I'd estimated.

I didn't have time to make it to the employee bathrooms in the back, so I dove into the closest ladies' bathroom and into a stall. A couple of minutes later, I emerged feeling a lot better. As I approached the sink, I saw Perry's mother staring into the mirror.

"Sally?" I said. I hadn't talked to Perry lately about what the doctors had said after he'd taken her to her long-awaited appointment. Sally had turned fifty-one only a month earlier.

"Roe, I haven't seen you in a year," Sally said brightly.

While I was standing there, nonplussed, Tiffany Andrews came out of another stall. I didn't know Tiffany very well. She had a daughter named Sienna, I remembered, and she owned and taught dance at one of the local studios. Tiffany was wearing a white sweater and a black skirt, and my first thought was that she looked like a hostess at a nice restaurant.

She gave Sally and me a casual nod and washed her hands. I'd hoped she'd leave, but she began to root around in her handbag for makeup, and then to do repair work to her face.

"Sally, you saw me at the Carriage House about two weeks ago," I said gently. Robin and I had been celebrating our secret good news. Sally had been sitting across the dining room with Perry and his boyfriend, Keith Winslow, a financial adviser.

"The Carriage House?" Sally said uncertainly.

"The restaurant," I said, maintaining my smile with some difficulty. Sally was worse, clearly.

"Um-hum," she said, clearly deciding I was making this up. "Well, see you later." She looked at me with suspicion.

I risked another question. "Are you here to see Perry?"

Sally looked at me blankly.

"Okay, see you later!" I said, trying not to sound too bright, too cheerful. Tiffany Andrews was looking from me to Sally.

I left the ladies' room to search for Perry. I was relieved to see him returning to the check-out desk. I took a deep breath or two as I went behind the counter to talk to him. "Perry," I said, trying to be very quiet and very calm.

It was clear that Perry was used to getting shocks now. "What is it?" he said, whipping around to face me, his voice equally low.

"Your mom is in the ladies' room. She's confused," I said, not knowing any way to make it more palatable.

"Why didn't you bring her out?" he asked.

"She didn't seem to trust me," I explained. I'd been scared that if I tried to steer Sally into a course of action, she would rebel and cause a scene. I felt like a coward. I was a coward.

Tiffany Andrews emerged from the ladies' room and walked briskly to the staff door. She breezed by the STAFF ONLY sign on the door. Maybe she was also being interviewed for the secretary's job? But the next moment, I forgot all about her when I saw how sad Perry looked.

Perry went into the ladies' room while I stopped a twenty-something who'd been about to enter. I asked her nicely if she'd go to the other ladies' room, on the second floor, and she flipped me off. Even ten years earlier, that would never, ever have happened. At least she walked away in the right direction.

It didn't take Perry long to coax Sally out the door.

It was like someone had flipped a switch. Sally seemed perfectly all right.

"Son, I cannot believe you came into the ladies' room," Sally said, smiling but startled. "What did you think could happen to me in there?"

Vastly relieved, I turned around to go back to the desk while Perry dealt with his mom. But Sally said, "Roe Teagarden! I haven't talked to you since Moses wore diapers!"

"Sally, good to see you. I have to get back to work, but I'll give you a call." And I cast a smile over my shoulder and sped away.

Yep. A coward.

Forewarned, I intercepted Lizanne when she came in for her interview. To my relief, she was dressed just right, in wool slacks that fit her (which meant, not too tightly) and a blouse that also was not too snug. Sam didn't like women who emphasized their femininity. Tiffany had been on the wrong track with her heavy makeup.

"Roe?" she said when I bore down on her right inside the front door.

"You want this job?" I said in a low voice. I looked up into her gorgeous brown eyes.

She nodded. Lizanne had always been beautiful, and motherhood hadn't changed that, though of course she'd matured . . . we all had.

"Then dodge into the ladies' room and blot your lipstick," I said. "And when Sam's asking you questions, just assure him that you can do everything he asks, and that you will only disturb him when there's something really urgent. Be balm on the waters. What he wants is a barricade."

She nodded. "I can do that." And it was true that Lizanne had always been the most relaxed person I'd ever known, and quite capable.

I had a lot of questions I wanted to ask my old friend, but her glance at her watch told me she was worried about the time, so I pointed to the staff door. Lizanne was in the process of ending her marriage to a local lawyer and budding politician, Bubba Sewell. The pending divorce had caused a flurry of gossip, almost none of it accurate.

I didn't see Lizanne again, though I ate my salad lunch in the break room in the hope of catching her when she left. I worked for another two hours. Then it was time for me to go to my doctor's appointment, finally. As I gathered my coat and my purse, I texted Robin to tell him I was on my way. I saw I had a text from Phillip. *I nd to tlk to u,* he said. I texted him back, *Great. See you back at the house in an hour, or hour and a half?*

MayB, MayB not, he answered. *Josh coming by after school.*

Josh Finstermeyer and his twin sister, Joss, had become instant friends of Phillip's. They lived a short distance from my house. The twins went to the public high school, and they were both bright kids. And as a bonus, since they were sixteen (a few months older than Phillip), they were both able to drive without an adult in the car.

K, see you later, got news, I said.

He answered with a surprised emoticon.

Pretty typical message exchange with a fifteen-year-old, I thought, and then concentrated on what the doctor might say.

Chapter Two

As Robin and I filled out a million forms in Dr. Garrison's waiting room, I whispered, "This is definitely blowing my cover. We have to go directly to my mom's house from here."

Robin nodded. "You'd think they'd told people we were going to be here," he muttered back.

I'd already seen three women I'd gone to high school with, though they'd all been a few classes behind me. In fact, there weren't any women my age in the waiting room. They were all either five to ten years younger or twenty-plus years older. It was almost embarrassing. Luckily, I got to look down a lot to the clipboard in my hands. I'd already completed some paperwork online; I hadn't realized those had been only the warm-up forms.

At last the nurse, whose name tag read "Jennings, R.N.," called me back. Robin went with me as a matter of fact. Blood pressure, height, weight, more questions. It was a lot of work, going to a doctor. I felt like I'd passed some kind of test when Nurse Jennings showed me into an examining room.

There was a little curtained cubicle with a tiny bench in one corner, and I climbed out of my clothes and into the rose-colored paper robe. All of a sudden, I was absolutely terrified. What if all the pregnancy tests (I'd ended up taking three) had been mistaken? What if I had some disease that made my boobs swell and hurt, instead of having a baby inside? What if something was wrong? I came out to perch on the end of the examining table. I tried to smile at Robin. I was actually relieved that Robin looked just as anxious. I couldn't have endured his trying to tease me out of my apprehension.

After about a year, Kathryn Garrison came in and shook my hand. She was a solid woman in her forties with short blond hair and some truly hideous black-rimmed glasses. She wore very little makeup. And she was wearing Nikes. Well, okay.

"Ms. Teagarden," she said, taking the rolling stool at the little counter. "And Mr. Crusoe, I take it? Hey, you wouldn't be related to the writer?"

Robin said, "I'm the writer." He assumed his public smile.

"Well, a celebrity! I love your books!"

I usually took this in my stride, because I loved Robin's books, too. But today was not the day to admire his talent.

"I'm glad you do. But today we're a little anxious, and we'd like to be sure everything is fine and normal," Robin said.

"Sure, I get that!" Dr. Garrison said, and turned to me. "Let's go on and have a quick examination. Now, you've taken some home pregnancy tests?"

"Three," I said. "All positive."

"And this is your first pregnancy."

"Yes." I'd put that on every form that had passed through my hands.

"We'll just check you out," Dr. Garrison said. "Mr. Crusoe, can you step out a minute?" Reluctantly, he did. "Aurora, you slide down to the end of the table and put one foot in each . . . okay. Relax, please."

I wasn't sure I could, but I tried. Dr. Garrison looked off into the distance while she examined me, as if she could see a ghost in the corner. She gave me a hand to sit up, and called Robin back in. "Oh, my goodness, yes," she said, smiling. "Pregnant for sure. Congratulations, primigravida!" That meant I was a woman having her first pregnancy, I remembered from one of the many booklets in the waiting room.

I'd let out the breath I'd been holding. I was grinning like an idiot, and so was Robin. Tears rolled down my cheeks. Our baby was official.

When I felt more in command of myself, Dr. Garrison resumed her seat on the rolling stool and asked me some very personal questions. "Let's do an ultrasound," the doctor said. "That way we'll have more information before I give you a due date, since you're not sure about your last menses."

"Okay," I said, feeling things were moving very fast.

"So just lie back again, and I'll ask Nurse Jennings to wheel in the ultrasound." She put the stirrups away and extended the footrest. Apparently, Robin did not have to go outside for this phase.

"Will we see the baby?" Robin asked, as if he hardly dared to know the answer.

"Oh, yes," Dr. Garrison said, smiling. "You sure will. But you won't think it looks much like a baby."

Getting ready for the ultrasound took a little longer, but then I had cold gel on my stomach and Dr. Garrison was gliding a sort of disk thing over it. Robin and I watched the screen, terrified and riveted. He gave me a wild look like a horse that's going to bolt. I probably looked equally nervous.

"There's your baby," Dr. Garrison said, smiling.

Our baby seemed to be two faintly connected blobs. Friends had told me how disconcerting that was, and now I got to experience it for myself. Then the baby wiggled. It was alive!

"It can *wiggle,*" I said, and began crying again.

Dr. Garrison said, "Let's see," and moved the device around some more. Suddenly, there was a rhythmic swishing sound in the room. "Yes, I'm getting the heartbeat."

"Our baby has a heart," Robin said proudly, and I didn't even think this was strange.

"It sounds so swooshy," I said. I'd always imagined heartbeats as sounding like drums or hooves, but this sounded more like water sloshing in a bucket.

Dr. Garrison nodded. "Perfectly normal," she said. She let us continue to listen and look while she sat with her laptop.

"So," she said. "The baby is approximately ten weeks old."

"Our baby," Robin said reverently.

"Yes, Mr. Crusoe. You and Ms. Teagarden will be having a baby right around July twenty-first."

As we went to my car, I realized I didn't remember anything else about the visit, though Robin clutched a big envelope containing a prescription for prenatal vitamins, an appointment slip for four weeks later, and about a ton of material about baby development, labor and delivery choices, and how to take care of myself during my pregnancy. A quick peek had told me that not only was I a primigravida, but I was an elderly primigravida. Horrors. (I was over thirty-five.) But Dr. Garrison had assured me several times that my age didn't necessarily mean I'd have any trouble at all carrying and delivering our baby.

Our house was on the way to my mother's, so we dropped off Robin's car there.

We didn't go inside. We didn't check on Phillip.

I didn't even think about it.

When Robin climbed into my car, again carrying the big envelope, we sat looking at each other: stunned, excited, terrified. Then we leaned sideways to hug each other, awkward in our coats. This baby had suddenly become very real. We were too flustered and excited to have a coherent conversation. We threw out remarks at random, though.

"My next book is due July fourteenth," Robin said. "I've got to make a schedule so I can turn it in early."

"Good idea," I said. "I have to find out if the library has

maternity leave. And I guess we have to decorate the room by Phillip's?"

"Has to be that one," Robin said. "Thank goodness we've got the study."

"Yeah, I'd hate to move again," I said.

"Ohhhhh . . ." Robin thought about that. "Maybe wait till he's older, ready to start school. There might be a school district we ought to be in."

"School," I said, overwhelmed. "Let's just think about getting her here safe, okay? We can worry about school in a few years."

"You're right, of course," Robin said, with the abstracted air of a man who was wondering if his child should go to Harvard. "Do you think he might have red hair like mine?"

I laughed, and then Robin was laughing with me. "I don't think I've ever been this happy in my life," I said, and started crying again. This seemed to be a pattern.

"Let's go see your mom," Robin said, and looked as if he might get teary, too.

My mother and her husband, John, were surprised when we rang the doorbell at four thirty in the afternoon. My mother was her usual well-groomed self, correct down to the last hair on her head—still dressed as though she were going into the office, though she was now semiretired. I automatically scanned John, and he was looking good, too. He'd had a heart attack a few years before, and I still worried about him.

Mother said, "Have you come to eat supper with us?" She glanced down at her watch. "I can stand you some grilled cheese sandwiches and minestrone."

"No, no, we just dropped by to tell you some news." I fidgeted around for a minute. I glanced up at Robin. I braced myself and I also smiled hugely. "Mom, I'm pregnant."

I had *finally* impressed my mother.

Her mouth open, she sank onto a handy couch. John practically leaped forward to shake Robin's hand.

"Really? You've been to the doctor and everything?" My mother had never trusted home pregnancy kits.

I nodded. "We just left Dr. Garrison's. My due date is July twenty-first."

"Oh," Mother said breathlessly, and I swear she had tears in her eyes. "This is wonderful news." Then after a moment of silent absorption, she said, "Thank God you got married already." Then she sat up. "Wait. Is this why you got married?"

I'd been waiting for that. But I didn't know quite how to answer. Luckily, Robin was prepared. First he pulled me over to the couch opposite Mother's, while John buzzed around aimlessly, beaming.

"No," Robin said, smiling. "We would have gotten married anyway. But we got married a little sooner and a little more quietly because we were pretty sure we had a baby on the way."

I'd figured Robin and I were in a serious relationship and were headed for an even more serious one. But I hadn't been sure how he'd react to finding he was going to be a father. To my profound relief, he'd had the ring in his pocket before he'd even discovered I was pregnant. I hadn't even imagined he was going to propose.

My mother's delighted smile morphed into something more like gloating. I knew she was thinking about Arthur Smith, a police detective I'd dated for a few months . . . until I'd gotten an invitation to his wedding and noticed the bride was pregnant. The next words out of Mother's mouth were, "I wish that Arthur Smith was still in Lawrenceton. You'd show *him*."

"Beating a dead horse, Mother," I said. "I didn't even know he'd gone. Where to?"

"He got a job as sheriff in a town in northern Arkansas," she said.

"Well, I don't have enough brain to spare to think about him," I said. And it was lucky Mother didn't know that Arthur's marriage was the least of his offenses. I'd never tell her or John that Arthur had had an affair with my now-deceased half sister-in-law, John's son's wife.

"Are you going to find out if it's a boy or a girl?" John asked. His smile just wouldn't go away. He had three grandchildren, and I could tell he'd been hoping my mother would have one of her very own blood to spoil—though she'd been doing a fine job on her step-grandkids.

We looked at each other. "Are we?" Robin asked me.

I shrugged. "I don't know. What do you think?"

"We might need more time to talk about that," Robin said, which sounded good to me.

After thirty more minutes of hosannahs and a lot of questions we couldn't answer, we were in the car and driving back to our house. My mother's excitement, and John's, had made our own the keener. We were moving out of the stunned phase (which we'd pretty much been in since I'd taken the home pregnancy test right after Thanksgiving) and into the joyous phase. We'd given my mom the green light to tell John's family—John David, a widower and the father of a toddler, and Avery, married to Melinda. Avery and Melinda had two kids, a little girl and a toddler boy.

While I heated up the chili Phillip had put out on the counter and made corn bread to go with it, Robin called his mother, Corinne. Corinne had other grandchildren, but she'd given up on Robin producing any since he'd turned forty. She was very happy, too, and asked to talk to me directly. She had all the same questions my mother had had, and I still didn't know the answers to all of them.

When dinner (such as it was) was ready, I called my brother Phillip, who emerged from his room. My half brother is blond, a look he enhances, and he has blue eyes. I'm brown and brown. He's much taller, at least five foot nine to my five foot nothing. Phillip's a good-looking guy, no doubt about it. But I like to think that we have a certain similarity; maybe in the shape of our faces, the set of our eyes. "Corn bread?" he said, surprised. Evidently corn bread and chili did not go together in Southern California.

"You'll like it," I promised. "We have something else to tell you."

"Yeah, I need to talk to you, too," he said. "But you go first. You look pretty excited."

"Phillip, we're going to turn the bedroom next to yours into a nursery."

"Yeah? Why?" he said, his eyes on the pan of corn bread. I deduced that he wasn't really listening to me.

"Phillip. Why would we need a nursery?" Robin said.

My brother's jaw dropped and he flushed red as a multitude of ideas and images seemed to be hitting him broadside. "For real?" he said in a choked voice. "For real?"

Robin nodded.

For one moment Phillip looked very happy. He pumped Robin's hand enthusiastically, and came around the table to give me a hug. But then the joy collapsed. "So I guess you'll need me to move back to California?" he said in a very subdued way.

That hadn't been my intention at all. "No, you kidding? We need a babysitter," I said. "Don't you dare go off and leave us." (I hoped that was how Robin felt, too, because we hadn't talked about it; our list of things to talk about grew longer and longer.)

After supper, while he was loading the dishwasher, Phillip asked if he could tell his friends. After a glance at Robin, I nodded. I was impressed that my brother had enough friends here in Lawrenceton to tell. He'd lived with us a very short time. Maybe he meant his friends in California, too. He'd probably just put it on Facebook. Oh, God.

Phillip went off to his room again without having told me what it was he needed to talk about.

I called Amina, my best friend in high school and college, who now lived in Houston with her husband Hugh and their child. Amina started crying, she was so happy. "I saved all my baby clothes," she said between sobs. "If you have a girl, you're all set!" I called my friend Angel Youngblood, and though Angel's emotional range was not as wide as Amina's, Angel, too, sounded glad. She, too, offered me baby girl clothes. We were covered for pink.

Robin called his best man, Jeff Abbott, another writer. Jeff, who'd been a father for many years, told Robin, "You won't know what hit you." From what I could hear, Jeff sounded pretty pleased with what had hit him. I noticed that Robin looked relieved after he hung up.

There were more people we could have called, but abruptly, we circled our wagons and spent the rest of our evening reading. Phillip wandered through to get his after-supper supper, which consisted of a bowl of grapes and some fruit dip. "What's the due date?" he asked. "People want to know. Is that when the doctor guesses you'll be having the baby?"

"It's a little more scientific than that, but close enough," I said. "July twenty-first." Robin had turned on the television so he could check the progress of a basketball game, and he and Phillip had a conversation about the score. Phillip vanished again.

At halftime Robin lowered his book to say, "We're going to need stuff."

I nodded. "And we need to have a long talk."

"Ah-oh."

"No, we just need to bring up some things and develop a couples policy."

"How we feel about something, as opposed to how you feel or I feel?"

"Right."

Robin looked apprehensive, but he nodded. "When you get off work tomorrow?"

It was my turn to nod.

The next morning, I slept late and had a little trouble with nausea. I finally managed to eat some dry toast and drink some juice, and I got ready for work very deliberately.

I only caught a glimpse of Phillip before I left. He was staggering toward the kitchen to get his bottle of juice, and he gave me a hug as I was going out the door. "See you later," he said, and I remembered he wanted to talk to me about something.

"Okay, we'll have a heart-to-heart," I said.

On my way to work, I stopped by Lizanne's house. I hadn't seen a lot of Lizanne since she'd served Cartland (Bubba) Sewell with divorce papers. I'd known Bubba for a few years; but I'd known Lizanne my whole life.

When she opened the door, I could hear screams from the back of the house. "Breakfast," she said. "They slept late." She was in a heavy robe, but barefoot, and she led the way to the kitchen briskly.

Brandon was doing the screaming; he was a little over three, if I remembered right, and his little brother, Davis, was less than a year. Brandon was protesting some great injustice, and Davis was fascinated by the bellowing. Davis was making a huge mess with some sliced banana and Cheerios.

Lizanne remained calm. I couldn't remember ever seeing Lizanne agitated, except the day her parents had died. "Brandon," Lizanne said, "you need to be quiet."

"I want chocolate milk."

"You can have plain milk, or juice."

"Chocolate milk."

"Then, nothing," Lizanne said sternly.

"Juice," Brandon said, his lip stuck out as far as physically possible.

I sat down across from Brandon and looked at him.

"So, I hear you'll have one of these next summer," Lizanne said as she poured the juice.

"I knew I couldn't beat the news here," I said, disgusted. "I even came by extra early."

"You could have come by even earlier," she said. "These two are up at the crack of dawn."

"Are you glad you had 'em?"

"Oh, yes," she said fervently. "The minute Brandon popped out, I was a different person. The love hit me like a hammer."

"And . . . Bubba?"

"I think he's more in love with the way they round out his picture of himself as a man," Lizanne said with unexpected acuity. "Bubba loves having them to make pictures with, and he loves taking them to the park so people can see him with his kids and think he's a great guy."

"Daddy?" Brandon asked.

"You'll see him tomorrow," Lizanne said. In a quiet aside, she told me that Bubba had gone back to his widowed mom's house. "The kids love Bubba," she said. She sounded sad about that.

"How did the interview go yesterday?"

"Pretty well, I thought," she said. "That Sam is a sweetie, isn't he? Doesn't want to talk to anyone, just wants to do the work."

"That pretty much sums Sam up," I agreed.

"Did he interview someone else?"

"Yeah, that Tiffany who owns Gotta Dance? Teaches there in the evenings?"

"The one who wears all the makeup."

"Yeah, her."

Lizanne smiled. "Then I bet I get the job."

"I know the library doesn't pay much," I said doubtfully. "Will it cover the day care fee?"

"It must be nice not to have to worry about money," Lizanne said.

Everyone in town knew I'd inherited money from Jane Engle, a spinster librarian. That was the good thing and the bad thing about Lawrenceton. Though it was changing in character every year, at its core it was still a small town. In ten years, I was sure even that would be transformed.

Lizanne continued, "Bubba's sister offered to keep the boys if I found a part-time job. I really need to get out of the house."

Lizanne had managed to stay on good terms with Bubba's family while preparing to divorce Bubba, which was quite a feat. I complimented her.

"It's not so much my wonderfulness as the fact that Meredith loves the kids," Lizanne told me. "And her little guy is just the same age as Brandon." Lizanne's cell phone rang. She looked a little surprised, but she answered it. For a wonder, the boys were quiet while their mother talked. Lizanne turned to me with a grin, her thumb going up in a universal gesture of triumph. After a brief conversation, she hung up.

"So you got the job?" I'd poured Brandon some dry cereal, and I'd refilled Davis's bottle.

"Yes. I think I'm going to enjoy working at the library," Lizanne said, smiling.

"I'll get to see you more often." I was really pleased. "When do you start?"

"I go in to get the lay of the land this week, but I don't start keeping regular hours until the New Year," she said. "Mr. Clerrick was really understanding. Christmas with the kids is pretty hectic, and this year it'll be complicated." Bubba had extended family in Lawrenceton, and Lizanne had an aunt and uncle with accompanying cousins and nieces and nephews.

I looked at the clock. "I gotta go, Lizanne."

We hugged each other and I left for work. The last time I'd had a talk this long with my friend, she'd told me she'd been able to see that the writing was on the wall for her marriage, and she'd been laying the groundwork for the divorce by taking the kids to church every Sunday (by herself), squirreling away some money, and visiting a financial planner to develop a way to use her inheritance from her parents' estate to create an allowance that would help her weather the financial storm. She'd also hired a lawyer who had a great track record and didn't like Bubba or support his run for state representative.

Lizanne was a lot smarter than most people gave her credit for being.

As I drove to the library, I thought about my first marriage. I wondered if it would have lasted, if Martin had survived his heart attack. It wasn't the first time this question had crossed my mind, and I supposed it wouldn't be the last. I'd had a sizzling passion for Martin Bartell, and we'd had some great times and moments of true happiness during our marriage. He'd been romantic, thoughtful—and more domineering than I had cared to admit to myself. While it had been flattering and sometimes comforting to be treated like a china doll, it had also been disconcerting. Maybe unhealthy.

As I always did, I made myself put the speculation away in mothballs. I was someone else's wife now, and I'd be a mother. I loved Robin; he loved me. It was going to be fine. We had some newlywed bumps ahead, I was sure, but I had faith we'd weather them. We would not end up in a divorce court, like Lizanne and Bubba. Like my mother and my father.

After I'd stowed my purse in my locker, I passed through the empty secretary's office to knock on Sam's door. Sam looked up from the pile of papers on his desk. He seemed relieved that his caller was me.

Sam was younger than his wife, Marva, who had quit teaching school this past May. Though their daughters were young adults, Sam was in his early fifties and Marva five years older. Marva was a social woman with a flare for doing anything in the craft line. She'd decided to travel on the weekends, selling her merchandise at festivals and craft fairs. She painted coatracks, she made aprons, crocheted scarves, and made signs. In fact, one of hers was hanging on Sam's wall now. "My job is secure. Nobody wants it." I shuddered.

Sam's desk was neat and orderly, as always. He had a cup of coffee at his elbow, a radio tuned to NPR, and a list of things to do that day. Sam loved his job as long as he was left alone to do it.

"What do you need, Roe?" he asked. (Note the graceful way he led into it.)

"I need to know about the maternity policy here, Sam."

"It's in your employee booklet." He looked annoyed.

"I'm sure it is. I figured if I asked you, you'd understand that I needed to know that policy."

"New mothers or fathers get three weeks," he said, still oblivious.

"I know you'll enjoy working with Lizanne," I said, changing tactics.

"She has two boys?" he said.

"Yes, little boys," I confirmed, wondering why he'd brought up her family.

"I like little children," Sam said.

I had to remember not to let my mouth hang open. That seemed so random, and frankly, so atypical. "Then you'll be delighted to hear that I'm having one," I said.

"You? You're having a baby?"

"I am. In July."

"The summer," Sam said, clearly displeased. Everyone wanted vacation time in the summer.

"Yes."

"Well, we'll have to make do somehow," he said, and that was that. Sam bent back to his paperwork.

I don't know what I'd expected. A handshake? A pat on the back? Tears of joy? I couldn't help but smile as I left Sam's office. I'd worked for Sam, off and on, for fifteen years. I should have known.

My priest and friend Aubrey Scott came in that morning. He was in his civvies, as he called them. No clerical collar, no black. He was doing some research for a series of sermons he planned on the conditions of life in the time of Jesus, and he had visited the library several times to consult some sources.

When Aubrey stood at the check-out desk, I figured I'd better ask him when he and his wife Emily were going to take their vacation. "When school gets out in June," he said. "We'll probably be sorry later in the summer, but Elizabeth—no, *Liza*—wants to go to Disney World for her birthday. It's a big vacation for us moneywise, but Liza has had a hard time at school lately." He'd adopted Elizabeth, Emily's daughter, soon after they'd married, and he adored her. This year, Elizabeth had announced that she wanted to be "Liza," and her parents were trying to comply.

I didn't want to ask about the hard time, not today. "Disney World will be fun," I said. "Maybe it won't be horribly hot then."

"Is summer on your mind for some reason? Have you and Robin been planning a vacation?"

"We'll be ready to have a baptism in August," I said.

Aubrey's gaze dropped directly to my waistline before he self-consciously looked up at my face. "But that's the most wonderful news, Aurora! Give Robin my best wishes!" There was no doubt he was sincere.

"I will," I said, grinning back at him.

There were several people within earshot. To my surprise, Perry gave me a hug, and to my even larger surprise, so did Lillian, an older librarian who'd always had it in for me. Baby happiness, apparently, was universal.

Lillian made the rounds of the other librarians with the speed of light (much more quickly than she did her actual work) and during the morning all of them tracked me down to congratulate me.

All in all, it was a very happy morning; and I hugged it to myself to think about in days to come.

I would need that memory.

Chapter Three

The next day Phillip vanished, though I didn't know that until hours afterward.

My half brother had spent a lot of the evening on Facebook in his room. He hadn't mentioned the conversation we were supposed to have. He'd only emerged once to heat up a bowl of leftover chili and corn bread. Robin and I had read, and talked about some important things sporadically. We'd been in our own little world. I was sure sooner or later we'd start taking the baby's arrival for granted, but not now.

Since I wasn't due in until noon, Robin and I had taken an hour this morning to talk. We'd settled in his study with the door shut, so Phillip wouldn't hear, since part of our conversation would be about him.

"I assured Phillip that he could stay here. I hope I wasn't just speaking for myself. Do you object to his living with us?" I asked my husband. "You didn't sign on to support stray half brothers."

Robin took a deep breath. "I wouldn't mind if he went back to his dad or his mom at some point in the future," he said carefully. "But I'm sure not going to vote for throwing him out. He's had a rough time, and he's a good kid."

Though I'd hoped that was what Robin would say, I hadn't been certain. I relaxed; I hadn't realized how tense I had been, though the two males got along well. Robin loved to help Phillip with English composition.

"And it's okay to bring the baby up Episcopalian?"

"Sure," Robin said. "Did you think I'd suddenly decide we should be Mormons?"

"I guess that was silly," I admitted. "But I wanted to be sure we're on the same page."

"I was talking to Angel a couple of days ago," Robin said, to my surprise.

"Where'd you run into her?"

"At her work," he said. Angel had recently gotten a part-time job at a big-box sporting goods store halfway to Atlanta. Shelby was able to take the baby to the child-care center at Pan-Am Agra, a program my first husband had instituted while he was head of operations there.

"You went there why?" Robin, though fairly fit, was no workout fiend.

"To buy a Christmas present for my sister," he said. "You know how she loves to go to Pilates. I got her an outfit that Angel promised me was what women want to wear."

"And what else did Angel say?" I knew advice about exercise clothes was not Robin's point.

"That hospital nurseries all have different ratings, according to what level of emergency they can handle."

"Wow." I was aghast at my ignorance. "We'd better check into the rating of the nursery at the Sparling County Hospital."

"Yeah, I don't want to drive into Atlanta unless we have a really good reason," Robin said.

We looked at the Lamaze class schedule and picked out a

start date that would allow us to complete the course with a comfortable margin of time.

When I told him the library policy allowed me three weeks' maternity leave, Robin was not happy.

"That's not long enough," he said. "I know you like your job, but we don't have to depend on it for the income. You may not feel like going back that quickly. Of course, that's up to you."

I'd thought three weeks was generous. But I understood his subtext: I was old for a first-time mother. "Would you take care of the baby if I did go back to work?" I asked.

Robin looked startled. He ran his fingers through his already wild red hair. "Sure," he said stoutly.

"Are you as scared as I am?"

He looked rueful. "Maybe more."

"Let's not talk about names for a while," I said. "That's going to be a delicate process."

"Oh, God," he said, closing his eyes in horror.

So Robin and I had a productive, but anxiety-ridden, discussion. I got ready for work, feeling tired and as if I should be going back to bed.

So, I have a lot of excuses . . . but the fact was, I never tracked down Phillip to find out what he had wanted to talk about. And I didn't miss Phillip the next afternoon. And I had no idea anything was wrong, until the evening.

Phillip wasn't in the house when I got home from work at three forty-five. Robin had left a note. *Gone to post office back soon.* I looked for a note from Phillip, but I couldn't find one. We had some rules about Phillip keeping us current on his whereabouts, and I wasn't happy. But when I checked my phone, I was glad to see that he'd texted me. *With Josh,* it said. He'd sent it at three thirty. Josh Finstermeyer came by almost every day after public school let out, to pick up Phillip. The two ran errands for Josh's mom, or went to Sonic, and Josh usually picked up his sister Joss after basketball practice or soccer lessons. Joss was a busy girl.

Just the day before, I'd seen Phillip with Josh and Joss and two other teens, all crammed into Josh's car. They'd been laughing. I'd felt warm and reassured about this glimpse of Phillip's new life. Phillip was fitting in and making friends.

I glanced at the clock. I figured that by five or five thirty, Josh would drop Phillip off, and we'd have dinner together an hour or so later, which had become the frequent pattern of our evenings . . .

But that didn't happen.

My cell phone rang about five o'clock. I noticed the time, because I'd been trying to imagine what we could have for dinner that night, and so far I hadn't come up with anything. I was exhausted, after a very mild day at work. Would this be the norm until the baby was born? That would be a real pain.

Supper had to be ready early, because Robin's writers' group was meeting tonight at the new Community Center, at seven.

Right after I'd come home I'd gotten a load of clean clothes out of the dryer to fold. Then I'd collapsed on the living room couch to read for a few minutes. When those minutes were up, I tried to summon up some energy. Either this exhaustion was a result of the pregnancy, or an energy-draining vampire was sneaking in at odd moments.

Maybe we could have bacon sandwiches with fruit salad?

When the phone rang, I answered it without much enthusiasm.

"Roe," said Beth Finstermeyer brightly. "Listen, the kids wouldn't happen to be at your house, would they?"

"I'm sure they're not, but just in case they slipped past me, I'll check Phillip's room," I said. A finger of dread tickled my spine.

I knocked, and when I didn't get an answer I opened Phillip's door. Either thieves had ransacked his room, or a very localized tornado had swept through.

"No, it's just like he left it," I said to Beth. I looked at my phone. "And he hasn't texted me again, since he told me he was going out with Josh."

There was a moment's silence. "I am sure I'm just being a silly mom," Beth said, "but would you try to call Phillip? I can't get either Josh or Joss to pick up. There are a million reasons, of course. . . ."

"Sure," I said promptly. "A million. Of course I'll try him, Beth, and I'll call you after I talk to him."

"Thanks," she said. "Oh, and congratulations on getting married. I never said anything, but Robin's so much fun. I know you two will be really happy together."

"Thanks, Beth," I answered. I could tell she was really anxious, and I found it was contagious. "I'll let you know about the kids the minute I hear."

I called Phillip the instant after I'd pressed End Call.

My call went directly to voice mail.

"Yo, leave me a message, and I'll get back with you," Phillip said in a tough-guy voice.

"Phillip, it's Roe. Please call me back the second you can. I really need to talk to you." I heard the front door open and hurried back into the living room. Robin was taking off his coat and hanging it on the old rack just inside the front door. Then he started riffling through a small stack of envelopes, probably from his official Robin Crusoe mailbox. But when he looked up, he dropped the letters and came to me.

"What's wrong?" Robin had radar for trouble. He put his big hands on my shoulders and looked down at me intently.

"Beth doesn't know where Josh, Joss, and Phillip are," I said. "They're late getting home."

"Worrisome," Robin said, instead of trying to soothe me with possible explanations: Phillip's phone could have gone dead or he could be in one of those areas out in the country that had no bars (why?), or he could be away from his phone (as if! he slept with it), or he could be simply avoiding me. If he was, it was the first time he'd transgressed to such an extent, and I found it unlikely he was doing something so heinous at exactly the same moment his friends were.

I called Beth. "No answer," I said, in the brightest voice I could manage. "I'll keep trying."

Robin had pulled his coat back on. He had mine over his arm. "Let's go look," he said.

That was such a perfect thing to do that I felt a flood of reassurance. I'd often doubted my wisdom during my time with Martin; but now I felt a rightness and a surety that we had done the right thing when we got married.

"Yes," I said. "Let's go."

We'd driven all around the high school, the baseball practice field, the soccer field, and the basketball gym. We'd even checked the football stadium. Then we'd cruised past the Dairy Queen, McDonald's, Burger King, and every other fast food place where kids hung out. We'd checked out the Finstermeyers' house, just in case. We'd gone past the Cinema Super Six. We'd even checked out the nearest mall, ten miles closer to Atlanta, which I avoided like the plague after Thanksgiving Day.

We didn't see Josh's car, a black 2010 Camaro, anywhere.

I'd dredged up the names of a few of the kids Phillip had brought home or talked about, and we'd been by their houses; I knew where most of them lived.

And we didn't find the kids or the car.

On our way home, I called Beth and told her what we'd been doing and that we'd found nothing. Beth was still at home with her thirteen-year-old, Jessamyn, and she had given up any pretense that everything was normal. "I've called the police station," she said, a hitch in her voice. "They haven't had any accidents reported this afternoon. And I called George, he was already on his way home from the office."

George Finstermeyer worked for the federal government in downtown Atlanta, and he took an express bus both to and from his job, leaving his car at the bus station most days so Beth wouldn't have to fetch him. That was the extent of my knowledge about George.

"Good," I said. "If he knows of any other place to search, we'll be glad to go there. I guess now we'll head back to the house. We've looked everywhere we can think of to look." I hesitated, realizing I was about to cross a line. "Could Jessamyn suggest any places we might check out?" I asked. That was the nicest way I could think of to ask if Jessamyn knew where her brother and sister were, or if they'd told their sister to keep a lid on that knowledge.

"I would put bamboo slivers under her nails if I thought she knew where they were," Beth said frankly. "She talked to Joss, but only about Joss's hair appointment. But when I can be calm, I'm going to have a heart-to-heart with her."

"Of course," I said, though privately I was wondering where I could find some bamboo slivers. "I'll talk to you soon. I am so going to ground Phillip for the rest of his life."

"Me, too, when I see them," she said, and started crying. We both hung up.

I called the police myself. I explained the situation to the officer who answered the phone. She advised me that teenagers often didn't let their parents, or their half sister, know what they were doing. I reminded her that three teenagers were missing, not just one, and they were all reliable kids with no history of causing trouble. I may have been a little forceful.

"Your brother's name is Phil Teagarden, have I got that right?" she said in a long-suffering tone.

"No," I said through gritted teeth. "His name is Phillip. Phil is our father."

When Robin and I walked into the house, it was six forty-five and had been dark for a long time. Robin's meeting was at seven, and I told him he should go. The group wouldn't meet again for a month because of the holidays, and he was president and founder, so he needed to be there. After some debate, he agreed, but made sure I would call him if I heard anything. Of course, I said yes. He made himself a sandwich and ate it standing, and then he was out the door.

If I'd asked him to stay home, we would officially have had a crisis. I still had some hope that Phillip would walk in the door at any moment, looking abashed and with a simple explanation for his absence. Flat tire in an area with no bars? Something like that.

So I sat on the couch and watched the front door. I wasn't hungry at all. Robin texted me every twenty minutes to let me know he was thinking about me.

Truthfully, it was almost a relief to have him gone for a while, because I was trying to grasp the whole situation. While I brooded, Moosie came to sit in my lap. Half-Siamese and declawed, Moosie was a relic of my sister-in-law Poppy Queensland, who had died a few weeks earlier. No one had wanted Moosie, even me, if truth be told: but I had not-wanted her the least of anyone. Now I was glad for her presence.

I used the landline to call Aubrey Scott. He answered immediately, his voice tense.

"Aubrey, it's Roe," I said.

"Have you seen her?" he asked, his voice desperate.

"I was going to tell you that Phillip is missing, along with Joss and Josh Finstermeyer," I said. "Are you telling me . . ."

"Liza is gone," he said. "Do you think they're together?"

"But . . . she's so much younger than Phillip and Josh and Joss," I said. "I was hardly aware they knew each other?" I'd only been able to get Phillip to go to church with me twice since he'd shown up on my doorstep.

"She's been completely nuts about Phillip since she saw him come in the church with you," Aubrey said, sounding both fond and exasperated. "She's at that age. It's like he's Justin Bieber." And then his voice broke in a sob.

I had had no idea Liza felt like that. If Phillip had known this, he'd been too self-conscious to bring it up. I didn't remember his ever having mentioned Liza's name.

"Aubrey, call the police now. I already have. I know the kids will show up, but it won't hurt to have as many eyes looking as we can."

He hung up, unable to speak. I sat with the phone in my hand, thinking so many thoughts, all of them horrible in varying degrees.

The least important was that Emily, Liza's mother, had never cared for me, and now she would hate my guts.

The most important was that people might say that Phillip, who'd only been here for a short time and was therefore an unknown factor, had abducted Liza. And Josh and Joss, presumably.

I would swear on a stack of Bibles that this was unthinkable. But I didn't know if everyone would believe me.

Chapter Four

Robin hurried into the house a little after eight, his face asking a question without any words. I shook my head. "The only development is bad," I said. "Liza Scott is missing, too. And she's only eleven."

He was as stunned as I'd been. "That has to be a huge coincidence," Robin said. "What could they have to do with each other?"

"According to Aubrey, when I took Phillip to church, Liza fell into crush at first sight," I said. "But I would swear Phillip wasn't the kind of guy to take advantage of a kid like that. And I know he likes girls his own age." I simply could not believe that Phillip was such a creep as to make a pass at a child. At the same time, as a mystery reader, I knew that no one else ever felt that way about their loved ones. At least not in books. Surely, in real life, you'd have a clue?

"Aurora. Don't even think that. Phillip and I are nowhere close to the same age, but from Phillip's conversation when we're guy-on-guy, I'm sure he's completely oriented to females of the appropriate age."

"You don't think he was blowing smoke?"

"I don't think so. I'm not a psychologist, but I'm not dumb."

I nodded. This was not conclusive, but it was comforting. "I don't know what else we can do," I said. "We've been everywhere we can imagine. It's not like we have the old family cabin in the woods, like they always have in books."

"Where people always suddenly remember, 'Oh, yes, as a child he used to go there whenever he was upset,' " Robin said. "Nope, in his case I guess we'd have to go to California."

"And I don't think he's gotten to pick where he is," I said. "He'd never just leave town without telling me. And Joss and Josh would hardly go with him! Much less Liza."

There was a knock at the door. I sat up so suddenly that Moosie was dumped off my lap. She vanished into our bedroom. Robin launched himself at the front door. "Phillip!" he was saying as he pushed it open.

But it was not Phillip. It was the police.

"Have you found him?" I asked, aware for the first time of how accurate the description "my heart was in my throat" was. "Have you found the car?"

"No." The woman who entered first said, "Roe, do you remember me? I'm Detective Cathy Trumble. We want to ask you some questions." I did remember the detective. We'd met before. The uniformed patrolman with her was Levon Suit; I'd gone to high school with Levon. We nodded to each other.

"Sure," I said. "Anything to help find Phillip."

"When did you notice he was missing?" Trumble, middle-aged and solid, sat down on the couch opposite my chair. Robin sat on the ottoman, holding my hand.

"I knew he was with Josh and Joss, and I expected him home by five or so. They usually drop him off by then, but I figured, the last day of school before Christmas, maybe they did some extra shopping or celebrating. So I wasn't really worried until Beth called me."

"Bethany Finstermeyer."

"Right."

"And what have you done since then?"

"We've tried to call him many times. We've driven around town looking at all the places we imagined he might be."

"You haven't called his mother or his father?"

"I was so hoping that he would come home and I wouldn't have to," I confessed. "But I'm going to have to do that soon. They're out in California, you know, and they've separated. So calling them with news like this . . . if there's any way around it . . ."

"Mr. Crusoe, what about you?"

"What about me? What do you mean?"

"You just got home? Your car was warm."

"Yes, I had to leave Roe for a little while to go to a meeting, and as soon as I could leave it, I came home." Robin's tone had chilled considerably.

"Despite the fact that her brother is missing?" Detective Trumble could not raise one eyebrow, but she could hike them both. And she did.

"I told him to go," I said, not believing the left turn this conversation was taking. "It was his last meeting before a month's break, he's the leader, and he needed to be there. Plus, I figured it was better than sitting here worrying."

"Is this the first time your brother has pulled a stunt like this?" Cathy Trumble looked like a pleasant middle-aged woman, but I abandoned any view of her as pleasant the minute the words left her mouth.

"Pulled a stunt? I don't think he's *pulling a stunt.* I think something has happened to him, and it's not going to be anything good!"

"But he ran away from his home in California to come stay with you. How do you know he hasn't run away to somewhere else?"

I took a deep breath, trying to keep levelheaded. "Because

he wouldn't take an eleven-year-old girl, and the Finstermeyer twins, with him!"

"But if they weren't involved, you might be thinking he'd left for home?"

I struggled with that one. I wanted to categorically deny it, but I would have been less than honest. "I don't think he'd hitch-hike back to California," I said. "He had a scary thing happen on his trip here, and I think he'd be very leery of repeating that experience. And he's happy here, already making friends and looking forward to going to public high school next semester. A little concerned about changing classes and teachers, sure. But Phillip is smart, and I don't think he was anywhere close to scared about it."

At least Cathy Trumble was listening to me. She nodded, and wrote something on a little tablet, which she'd pulled out of a pocket.

"Can I look in his room?" she asked, out of the blue as far as I was concerned.

"You mean search it? If Robin is in there with you," I said.

Robin glanced at me, startled, but then he nodded. We'd been together long enough for him to understand that I'd chosen him for a reason.

"All right," Trumble said, and Robin led the way to show her to Phillip's room. Levon went along to help.

The minute they were out of earshot, I called Bryan Pascoe.

"Aurora," he said, sounding a little startled. "I'm glad to hear from you, of course, but very curious."

Of course he was. I'd met him when my sister-in-law Poppy had been murdered, and he'd been pretty frank about being interested in me personally.

"I guess you read my marriage announcement," I said.

"I did, and of course I'm very happy for you," he said smoothly. "To what do I owe the honor of this call?"

"Bryan, it's about Phillip," I said.

"Phillip. Oh, your brother. He answered the phone the last time I called."

"My half brother," I said. I filled him in very concisely on Phillip and the current situation.

"How can I be of service?" Bryan asked, which was really polite of him considering I was calling him at night and I was not a regular client of his.

"I hope you will agree to be Phillip's attorney," I said. "Because this isn't looking good, right now. And even if we find him, and he's okay . . ." And here I had to speak very fast to leap over the abyss. "It's clear that the police are way more concerned about Liza, and the fact that Aubrey's certainly told them about her infatuation with Phillip. Which I understand, okay? *I get it.* But Phillip is a good kid. No saint. But a good kid. And smart."

"Do you have a power of attorney giving you the say in what happens to Phillip?"

"Yes, in case of emergency. My dad did give me power of attorney. Medical and legal." Robin had thought of that when we'd agreed Phillip could live with us, God bless him.

"Then I'm hired," Bryan said. "Call me when I'm needed."

"You'll be in town for the holidays?"

"At least for another week and a half," he said. "And longer if I need to be."

"Thank you so much," I said. I couldn't think of any other way to express my gratitude.

"Thank me after I've done something for you," he said. "Good-bye."

I felt better, as if I'd really accomplished something. That was hardly the case, but at least I'd been . . . proactive.

When Robin and Cathy Trumble came back into the living room, Cathy looked dissatisfied (yay!) and Robin looked relaxed (also yay). Levon Suit, trailing behind, shook his head at me. They hadn't found anything incriminating in Phillip's room.

Okay, that was one tiny step forward. Robin looked relieved.

I asked Cathy Trumble to please let me know the minute they heard something, and she assured me she would.

Robin walked her to the door. The second she was outside, I texted Phillip with Bryan Pascoe's phone number. I told Phillip that this was his lawyer and he must call Bryan as soon as he could. I had no idea where my brother was or what had happened to him, but that was essential information.

I really didn't have a good grasp on what I was doing or what I imagined might happen, by that time.

I sank down on the couch. I was comforted when Robin put his arm around me. *This is my husband,* I said to myself, and the idea still seemed a little odd.

"Let's think," Robin suggested.

"I wish I could quit thinking," I said. "But I know we have to try to figure something out."

"Okay, the first thing Trumble asked me when we were out of your earshot is if Phillip had been acting any different lately."

"I don't think so. But—maybe I don't know Phillip well enough to be certain, especially since I've been caught up in the pregnancy excitement."

"Me, too. But I'll tell you, I had a thought. While we were gone on our honeymoon? We left Phillip with your mom and John."

"Which he didn't want to do, but the Finstermeyers were out of town."

"And he also went to church with your mom and John."

"So he did."

"So we need to know if anything happened then that might have a bearing on this."

We'd just been gone a week. But that was the only time something could have happened to Phillip that we didn't know about. Of course, he could always have gotten a phone call, or a text . . . but I found it very hard to imagine that someone would pursue Phillip from California because he'd dissed a girlfriend or something like that. Something I would think was trivial.

So I called my mother. She answered on the second ring. "Hi, honey!" she said, the smile in her voice very evident. I hated to bring her down.

"Mom, the pregnancy is fine, and everything is all right with me," I said. "But Phillip is missing."

"You mean he's late?" She must have known it was worse than that, but she was hoping.

"No, it's more serious. The Finstermeyer twins are gone, too, and Liza Scott."

"Father Aubrey's daughter? Oh, Roe . . . that's *horrible.*"

"Yes, it is. Of course, the police are asking all kinds of questions, and we're trying to fill in all the blanks we can. Did anything happen while he was staying with you, anything out of the ordinary that you can recall?" My mother had never been completely comfortable around Phillip, since he was the product of my father's unfaithfulness to her, as she saw it. But she was fair enough and well-balanced enough to see that wasn't Phillip's fault, and she'd offered to give him a berth while Robin and I were gone. John, her second husband, was the soul of hospitality, and he'd raised two boys of his own during his first marriage. He was really pleased to have Phillip in their house.

"Let me think about it and call you back," my mother said. "I'll ask John, too."

"Thanks, Mom," I said.

So that was that. Another "wait and see."

In thirty minutes Mother called back. "John and I have racked our brains," she said. "Neither of us can come up with anything. I'm so sorry, Aurora. Please keep us posted."

So that was that.

It was a miserable night.

Chapter Five

The next morning was cold and raining, as dreary as you could imagine.

No one had had any news about anything.

The Finstermeyers called us to commiserate, and I asked them if the police had searched the twins' rooms. "Yes," Beth said. "And they didn't find anything that would indicate where the kids were."

She wished they had, I could tell. "Did they look on the kids' laptops, or whatever they have?" I asked. "Phillip's is still here."

"No, not yet," she said. "But I'm sure they will."

We really had nothing to talk about, and after a few more minutes, we gave up on the conversation to go be miserable by ourselves.

"We could try to check Phillip's laptop ourselves," Robin said.

It was a new one, since the one he'd had in his old backpack had been left in a truck on his hitchhiking trip across the U.S. to reach Georgia.

I agreed to invade Phillip's privacy without a moment's hesitation.

The laptop was password-protected, but I happened to know the origin of his password, because we'd talked about it. Phillip was a huge *Walking Dead* fan, and we'd been watching a recording of the show when he'd told me how cool he thought Carol was. "Carol's what I think my mom would be like if she went through the zombie uprising," he'd said, and I'd laughed. I'd only seen Phillip's mom once or twice in the past few years, but the idea of Betty Jo as the originally downtrodden Carol, who'd turned into a ruthless survivor, was kind of funny.

I typed in "Carol," and that didn't work. So I tried "Carolscookies" and that didn't work either. "CarolsCool" did not open the laptop. But "Carolkills" did. I was in.

Robin was quicker with computers than I was, so I ceded the laptop to him. He opened the e-mail program. "He's heard from friends in California," Robin said. "He's gotten a few e-mails from that girl who gave him a ride when he was hitchhiking from Memphis to here. I can tell you that 'ride' was not just in a car." Robin scrolled down. "His father e-mailed him."

"He did? Phillip didn't say anything to me." On the other hand, why wouldn't my dad be e-mailing his son? "What about?" I asked, out of sheer curiosity.

"Mostly asking if Phillip's heard from his mother. Phillip always says no. He tells Phil that he enjoys living here," Robin summarized. "Phil says a few uncomplimentary things about Betty Jo. Way to go, Phil. Phil goes on to say that he's not totally happy that Phillip's with you, but he's also glad that Phillip's not with his mom."

"Can't have it both ways," I muttered. "He needs to be with some adult related to him, and I'm the only one left after my dad's escapade."

"There's some talk back and forth between Phillip and his teachers in California," Robin said. "Okay, none of that is pertinent. I'm going to check his browsing history." After a minute, I could tell he was trying not to be amused. "Okay, about what

I would expect from a kid his age. I'm not surprised that Detective What's Her Name didn't find any porn in his room."

"Oh, it's all there on the Internet?"

"Yep," he said. "And if the sites he visited are any indication, I was right about Phillip admiring adult women."

"I assumed that was the case," I said. "But I realize that I really don't know everything about Phillip."

"I didn't find any suspect activity," Robin said. "I checked his e-mails and his history. I checked his Facebook page. In a minute, I'll check his Word files."

"I don't think Phillip is a bad kid at *all,*" I said. "Oh, I'm sure he takes a drink now and then if it's available. I'm sure he'd be glad to have sex with a girl who was willing, in fact I know he would. Maybe he'd take a joint if one was going around at a party. But I don't think he goes out looking for trouble. And I am sure that Phillip is brave. And I know he has a lot of charm; he got that from my dad. And he's practical; he got that from his mother." I thought hard. "I don't think he's ever lied to me, either when he was a kid or since he's come here. And I don't think there's anything—sick, or tainted—in my brother."

"Then why is he missing?" Robin, his hands still resting on the keyboard, was giving me his full attention.

"Phillip's new here, really new," I said. "I think Cathy Trumble, if she's an accurate representative of the police position, is looking at this as something Phillip made happen. He's the unknown kid. Maybe they think because he's a newcomer from wicked, evil, California, he's brought a taint with him. What they don't get is that he lived in a suburb a lot like the ones here. It's just that there were palm trees."

"Good point," Robin said. He scanned the Word files. "Nothing even remotely suspect," he told me. "What else? I can tell you're not finished."

"The way I see it, they can't be missing because of Phillip.

It has to be one of the other three, who've lived here—well, forever, in the case of Joss and Josh, and for years, in Liza's case."

"That makes sense," Robin said. Robin has a quirky face, with his bony nose and crinkled mouth and bright blue eyes. But right now you could see the intelligence written large on it. "If I were putting this in a book, my story line would be that someone followed Phillip from California because Phillip had witnessed some criminal action. The other kids tried to save him but were swept up in the same net."

"But," I said.

"But that's ridiculous. What do you know about the Finstermeyer kids?"

"I don't know Joss as well as I know Josh. She's a jock, I understand, and very talented. She plays basketball and soccer for LHS. She makes good grades. Josh is more of a reader. He's in and out of the library at least once a week. He's a good student, he's always on the honor roll. He's pretty popular. He runs track. Phillip was thinking about trying out for the track team. He didn't make the cut at his old school."

"Have you heard any rumors about either of them?"

"Not a one. Phillip was mildly interested in Joss as a girl, but when he didn't say anything about trying to move the relationship along, I asked him about her. He said she was gay."

Robin looked startled. "He didn't feel angry about that?"

"He was totally nonchalant about it, not like a spurned suitor or a bigot. Just, 'Oh, I don't think it'll work. I'm pretty sure she's gay.' "

"Liza," Robin said. "Any rumors about her?"

"You know, it's strange," I said slowly, "but when Aubrey was in the library a couple of days ago, he said that Liza had had a hard year."

"In what way?"

"He didn't elaborate, but I got the impression that it was

more a social situation than making bad grades, or not being able to grasp geography."

"But he reinforced that she had a crush on Phillip."

I shrugged. "Robin, she's just so young. Eleven is still a little girl, especially to Phillip and Josh. I can't help feeling that there's something more to know. And now, while I think about that, or try not to, I have to call my dad." I'd been dreading this.

The phone call went just as badly as I'd anticipated. My father accused me of ignoring Phillip, of neglecting him, of not protecting him. I had known he'd be upset and angry—and I'd figured he might aim that anger at me—but it was like he'd forgotten that I was his child, too. There was no way I was going to tell him he'd be a grandfather while he was this upset with me. I had tears streaming down my face when I hung up in response to Robin's furious hand signals.

"You don't have to listen to that," Robin said, wrapping his long arms around me. "You don't have to take that abuse."

"I knew he was going to go off the deep end," I said. "Who wouldn't? But I took the best care of Phillip I knew how to do!"

"At least you weren't having sex with me on the couch when he walked in the door," Robin said. That was the incident that had pushed Phillip to leave his parents. My dad had been doing the nasty with a young woman on the living room couch when Phillip had returned home from school one day. Phillip had felt he had to tell his mother, and he'd developed a wild plan to hitchhike to my place because he couldn't stand the arguments and recriminations that ensued. After Phillip left, Betty Jo had packed her bags and vanished.

"Yes, at least that," I said, trying to smile. I calmed down and dried up. "I'm lucky to have one good parent," I said. "What was your dad like?"

"We'll talk about him some other time," Robin said. "Let's keep on track here."

I nodded. I went to the bathroom to wash my face with cold water. I know how I look when I cry, and it's not pretty.

Just as I returned to the family room, there was a tap on the front door. If a tap could sound surreptitious, this one did. I went to the door, casting a *What the hell?* look at Robin while I did so. He stood, as if he was going to stop me, but before I could even process that, I'd opened the door and looked up.

She was tall, almost as tall as Phillip, about five foot eight. She was wearing blue jeans and a dark green T-shirt and a bright blue puffy coat. She had black hair and caramel skin and enormous amber eyes, and I had never seen her before.

"I'm Sarah Washington," she said. "Are you Phillip's sister?"

"Yes, please come in," I said. I could tell the intensity of my stare was freaking her out, but I couldn't help it. This girl had information.

"This is my husband," I told Sarah. "Robin, this is Sarah Washington. You're a friend of Phillip's, Sarah?"

"A new friend," she said, with a small smile. "We met when he and Josh picked Joss up after basketball practice a couple of weeks ago. I'm on the basketball team with Joss."

I nodded. And?

"Well, Phillip and me started talking," she said.

I knew enough teens to know that when two people started "talking" it was a prelude to actually going out on a date.

I cast an eye on Robin, who nodded very slightly. He knew this, too.

"In the course of our talk, he told me that Liza Scott was following him around, as much as she could, since she can't even drive yet."

"We had heard that Liza had a crush on Phillip," Robin said, his voice neutral.

"Well, it was really cute," Sarah said, as though she were in her forties. "But it kind of embarrassed Phillip. I mean, Liza's a cute kid, really, but she's a *little kid.*" Sarah looked at me as if to be sure I understood how hopeless that was. I nodded, with what I hoped was an understanding smile, and that turned out to be the right expression.

Sarah's face turned very serious. "I think Phillip was careful to be kind to her because of—you know, right, about Liza's situation at school?"

"I've heard a little." I was absolutely startled, but I didn't want to seem like a half-wit. This girl's calm assurance was kind of daunting. "Apparently, I don't know enough. Please tell me." I'd discovered from a stranger that my brother was kind . . . and that he'd had a "situation" of his own.

Sarah nodded, as if she'd confirmed a suspicion. "Bullying. Liza's mom and dad have been to the school several times. They've talked to all the parents. But these little bitches, excuse me, just won't leave Liza alone."

We'd been standing, but now I saw we were going to have a conversation, and I gestured to the couch and the chairs. Sarah sank into one of the armchairs, so Robin and I took the couch. Robin's big hand folded around mine. I was so relieved he was there.

"How old are these girls? What are they doing to Liza?"

"They're twelve or thirteen. And they're saying awful shit about her to her face. And on Facebook. And on every other place they can find to say nasty stuff."

"Why?"

"It's a long story." Sarah shrugged. "Liza tried to tell me about it, but I got lost in the pronouns, you know? Too many 'then she said this' and 'then someone else said that.'"

"So these girls ganged up on Liza."

"Yeah, it's all over the schools. 'Cause her dad's a minister, and because Liza is freaking out. When Liza's mom went down to the school, she asked to talk with each of the girls separately, with the school counselor present. The principal at Liza's school,

Mr. Carson, he couldn't let Mrs. Scott do that. So she went to their houses and talked to the parents."

"Good for her," I said. Emily might not be my favorite person, but she had a backbone and she loved Liza.

"Yeah, but it got worse after that. Like 'Little kid, sent your mommy to fight for you,' type thing." Sarah shook her head. "Anyway, that's why when Liza kind of latched on to Phillip, he didn't have the heart to shut her down."

Thank God, I thought. My brother was kind. I held that to my heart like an ember to warm it. "And that's why Liza was with Phillip and Josh and Joss? When they went missing?"

Sarah looked relieved. "See, I was standing right by them at the soccer field, so I heard what they said. I'd given a lesson to Harmony Davis, and Joss was working with Liza. But the little creeps had come over to the soccer field just to say nasty stuff to Liza." Sarah shook her head, her lips compressed in a look of disgust. "They were almost . . . jeering at her. And Liza's mom was late picking her up. Of course, Liza wanted to get away from them. She asked Joss for a ride home. Joss was on the phone with Tammy, but she said sure. Then Phillip and Josh came to get Joss, and they were all getting into the car when I left, myself."

"When did you last hear from Phillip? Or any of them?" Robin asked.

"I got a text from Phillip right around then," Sarah said. She messed with her phone, which she'd been clutching in her hand for the whole conversation, and showed us her initial text and the exchange it had initiated.

Where r u going?

Taking Liza home. C U later?

Could happen.

"So you had plans to meet later?"

"Well," Sarah said, waving her hands. "Maybe. We'd talked about going to the movies. But he wanted to let you know, and I had to ask my mom." Sarah looked embarrassed that she had to tell her mother where she was going. "Since my mom doesn't know Phillip, she'd have to meet him. And we'd have to go in my car."

At fifteen, Phillip didn't have a car, of course. He hadn't even gotten his learner's permit. I hadn't realized what a handicap that was going to be for Phillip's social life. But that wasn't important now.

"So Liza was taking a lesson from Joss, and when it was over, Mrs. Scott hadn't gotten there to pick Liza up, so Josh, Joss, and Phillip decided to take her home," I said, by way of recap.

"Yeah. I think normally they would have hung around for Mrs. Scott to get there, right? But the three witches were around, and Joss had to get to her hair appointment."

Beth had mentioned a hair appointment, but it hadn't really registered with me. "Where was that?" Robin said.

Sarah looked blank.

"Where does Joss get her hair done? We can drive the route they would have driven."

"Good luck, then, because I did and I didn't see anything," Sarah said rather unexpectedly. "Joss was getting her hair cut at Shear Delight on Pickett Street."

I found myself liking Sarah more and more, and not least because of her unpredictability.

"So you haven't heard from any of them since Phillip's text?" Robin asked.

"No," Sarah said. "I mean, no sir."

I saved that for later. Robin rated a "sir," which meant either he looked more formidable than I did, or he looked older than I did.

"Sarah, thanks so much for coming over and filling us in on the situation," I said.

"My dad didn't want me to," Sarah said. "But my mom thought it was only right."

"I can see both their points of view," Robin said diplomatically. "But I know when we get Phillip back, he'll be grateful."

She grinned. "Well, I hope so. On both counts. Oh, before I forget, I passed another car coming into the parking lot when I was pulling out. At the soccer field."

"Who was in it?" I asked.

For the first time, Sarah hesitated. "I'm not sure," she said slowly. "And I don't want to get anyone in trouble. Not with something this big."

I tried coaxing the information out of Sarah by telling her I wouldn't tell anyone else, but she had dug her feet in. She didn't want to implicate anyone who might have a legitimate reason to be at the soccer field that afternoon.

Sarah left, and I watched her go, feeling bleak. But better informed.

"So," Robin said, after the door closed. "Did this bullying of Liza have something to do with their disappearance, or not?"

"You mean, is that the right track or a diversion?" I shook my head. "I don't know, but it's all we've got. Do you think the police know all of this?"

"Why wouldn't the Scotts let them know?" Robin said. "But then, why didn't they explain it to us? Why didn't they let us know that Liza was actually with Joss when she got in the car? It seems to me that Phillip being there was simply random."

"I don't think I can call them up and say, 'Why the hell didn't you tell us all this?' right now," I said. I tried the idea on for size, and shook my head. "I just can't."

"They already feel as bad as they can," Robin agreed after a moment, and I couldn't tell whether he was hinting that such a phone call could not make them feel any worse, or that we should not add to their bad feelings. Either way, I wasn't going to make the call. I was definitely out of the school loop for gossip, and my mother was, too. She liked the Scotts; she would certainly have told me about the persecution of Liza.

I sat on the couch beside Robin and put my head on his shoulder. Poor Liza. The cruelty of children could not be denied.

They were pack animals, or at least some of them were. I remembered we were going to have one of these for our very own, and I promised myself that we would bring up our child to be better than that. It really bothered me that Phillip had a problem he hadn't had a chance to tell me about. Had it been Liza's crush? But I was so tired . . .

The next thing I knew, Robin was putting my feet up on the couch. And then, though I struggled to wake up, I sank back down into sleep.

It was daytime. The sun was just peeking through the front windows. My eyes felt glued shut, but I managed to pry them open and look around me. I was still in the same clothes I'd worn the day before, and there was a blanket spread over me. Robin was asleep in one of the chairs, and the house phone was ringing. I struggled to sit up, but Robin suddenly erupted from the chair as if a puppeteer had yanked his strings, and he grabbed the phone from the table between us. "Hello?" he said hoarsely.

"Yes, this is he," he said next. "What happened?"

Then something terrible passed over Robin's face, and all the sleep left me as if I'd never closed my eyes. I tossed off the blanket and sat up. A wave of nausea hit me so hard that I dashed into the kitchen and threw up in the sink, because that was the closest receptacle. I hadn't thrown up much with my pregnancy until now—mostly, I'd been queasy—and I'd been very, very lucky, I realized. I finished upchucking and ran the water full force, dashing it on my face. I filled a glass and drank it very slowly.

"Honey, are you okay?" Robin was right behind me.

"After I brush my teeth and eat something," I said, maybe optimistically. "What was the call about?"

"We have to go as soon as you do those things." His voice was so sad. "They found a body and they want to know if it's Phillip."

While I brushed my teeth and washed my face and Robin got a sleeve of saltines to take with us, I simply denied this discovery. They hadn't found a body: if they had, it wasn't Phillip's. It was someone else's. It wasn't even Josh. It was some completely unknown male person.

I was determined to eat some saltines so I wouldn't be sick again. Everyone had told me that was the best preventative. Maybe so, but we had to stop again halfway to the spot so I could vomit again.

I didn't even ask where we were going.

Finally, we came to a stop in one of the newer parts of Lawrenceton, a strip mall that currently housed a vapor shop, a manicure/pedicure place, an army recruiting station, and the haircut salon Shear Delight. There were police cars and civilian cars parked badly, and people everywhere. Robin helped me out of the car and put his arm around me. We made our way slowly through the throng to the driveway leading to the alley in back of the strip mall.

Robin said something to the first uniformed cop we saw, and we got passed up the chain. Each time we moved a little closer to the center of the activity. Finally, I could see that there was body lying almost concealed behind a Dumpster to the right of the salon's back door. I could see the feet, in tennis shoes. I could not remember what shoes Phillip had been wearing, or if he had any like that.

We moved around so we could see better. Though there was lots of activity around the still remains, I could see that a body about the size of Phillip and with golden hair like Phillip's had been hidden behind the Dumpster. I could see that the clothes were bloody, and the body was distorted by broken bones.

"You don't look well," Detective Trumble said, appearing suddenly at my shoulder.

"I'm three months pregnant and I wonder if my brother's dead," I said.

"We're just about to turn him over," she said.

"All right." I nodded. "Let's see." I had to know.

Robin's arm tightened around me.

A man in medical scrubs squatted by the body at the shoulders, and another at the feet. They each positioned their hands, agreeing on which way they would turn the body, and then they moved.

There was a gasp that came from no one and everyone.

The corpse was not Phillip; in fact, it was not even a male. It was a girl.

Even though I'd been pretty sure, I sagged. "Thank God," I whispered. And I turned sideways, so the body was not in my line of sight. I felt guilty for my thanks. This body had been a real person, loved by someone.

One of the scrubs-clad men said, "That's Tammy Ribble." His voice was hoarse and broken. It was clear he was trying not to cry. "I know her folks."

"Local girl?" Detective Trumble said.

"Yeah. Plays soccer at the high school. Runs track. She's gone to school with my boy her whole life. Gone to church with him."

With Tammy's short hair and athletic build, it was just possible to mistake her for a boy from the back, especially since she'd been wearing sweatpants and a quilted olive-green coat.

"What happened to her?" I asked.

"She was hit by a car, I think," Scrubs Guy said. He'd gotten his breathing under control.

I felt like I was living in the Twilight Zone. "Take me home," I said to Robin.

And no one tried to stop us as we left.

I wondered why the Ribbles hadn't reported Tammy missing. I wondered why no one had spotted her in that alley. "How long has it been?" I asked Robin.

"Two nights," he said. He'd wondered, too.

"It just seems like forever," I said.

He nodded. I felt somehow I should apologize to Robin. We

were newlyweds and expecting a baby. We should not have all this on our shoulders. The most serious topic for discussion should be whether or not we wanted to know the gender of the baby before it was born. It would have been nice to talk about this, to have something pleasant to discuss; but I just couldn't bear to bring it up.

"I wonder," Robin said, and then hesitated.

"What?"

"I wonder if Tammy was Joss's girlfriend?"

"Oh. I hadn't gotten that far. But it would sort of make sense. I mean, that she would be there."

"Because Joss was getting her hair cut, and she'd want her girlfriend there for that? Is that a girl thing?"

"Yeah, it could be." My best friend, Amina, had gone to the salon with me a couple of times when we were teens.

"So Tammy met Joss there, and then something happened. This may be the point at which they disappeared."

"Oh," I said, shocked. "So maybe Tammy's parents thought she was going to spend the night at Joss's house . . . maybe two nights . . ."

"I'll bet they haven't missed her yet," Robin said. "I'm surprised they didn't hear about the kids being missing, though. Since Joss is gone, surely that would alarm them."

When we got home, we trailed into the house. Robin pointed to the dining table and said, "Sit."

I slumped in the chair. "You're going to eat," he said. "If I have to spoon it into you. What do you think you can keep down?"

"Cereal, I guess," I said. "If we have any bananas, a sliced banana on the cereal?"

I ate slowly and carefully, because if it was coming back up I wanted to know in time to get to the bathroom. But it stayed down, and I could tell I felt better after about thirty minutes.

I was scheduled to work today, I remembered dimly. I called in to tell them I wasn't coming. Lizanne answered the phone in the director's office, to my surprise. For the past few weeks, Sam had been letting all calls go to voice mail. The minute she heard my voice, Lizanne said, "Oh, honey, don't worry. We all know how tough it is for you now. Just call when you think you can come back."

"Thanks, Lizanne," I said, surprised that Lizanne had identified with the library so quickly.

"You bet. Call me if you need me," she said.

"Roe," Robin said. I looked up. "Why don't you get in the shower," he suggested. "Fresh clothes. It would have to make you feel better."

"You're right," I said. I gathered up my energy to stand, and plodded to the bathroom off our bedroom. He gathered up my clothes and took them to the laundry hamper, while I got into the hottest shower I could stand. I washed my hair, I scrubbed my body, and I dried off thinking how exhausted I was, after a night on the couch. I pulled on the nightgown laid out on the bed. Wait! I had to get dressed in outdoor clothes!

I looked down at myself. Then I looked up. Robin. "Nightgown?" I said.

"You need to climb in bed for a while," he said.

"You're getting so bossy." But I didn't mind. I didn't feel that I was taking very good care of myself just now.

"You can be bossy next," he said, and turned down the unused bed.

So at nine in the morning, I went to bed, and at nine twenty, Robin joined me.

Chapter Six

My cell phone rang at ten thirty. Robin had plugged it into the charger and put it on my night table, so I groped for it. His side of the bed was empty.

"Roe, I'm sitting at the airport," my father said. "Who's going to come get me, or do I need to get a cab?"

"What airport?" I asked, bewildered.

"Atlanta," he said. "What did you think?"

"I didn't think anything. I didn't know you were coming. I've been asleep."

"I left a message."

"Where?" I didn't think I could bear to move. I patted Robin's pillow, which was cold. He'd been up for a while.

"On your answering machine," Dad said, clearly very irritated.

"I guess we didn't check it when we came back from the crime scene," I said, struggling to wake up. "We just showered and went to bed. Call Uber. You have that app on your phone?"

"Yes," he snapped. "What crime scene?"

"It wasn't Phillip," I said. "The dead person."

"What? What dead person?"

"The police asked us to come look at a body, but it wasn't Phillip," I said.

"You had to look . . . ?"

"Yes," I said. "I had to look."

"I'm sorry, Aurora," he said, in a more subdued tone.

"Right," I said. "So you're telling me that you're coming to stay with me while Phillip is missing."

"Yes. If you have room for me," he added, but without any real doubt in his voice. "I can get a hotel room, sure, but I am not that flush right now."

I covered my face with my free hand. "Okay, we'll do our best," I said. "You have my new address?"

"I do. Wait, I see your husband pulling up to the curb. Looks like the wedding picture. Tall, redheaded?"

"Yeah, that's him. In a Volvo or a blue Toyota Camry?"

"Camry."

"You're not being abducted. See you," I said. I ended the call and thought, *God bless Robin.* I forced myself out of the bed, pulled on some clothes, and brushed my teeth and hair, and ate more crackers, this time with a little cheese. I looked at the clock. I'd have to plan a lunch. I sighed. My phone rang again; it was Robin.

"I'm picking up some lunch at Hero Heaven," he said. "What can I get you?"

I loved subs from Hero Heaven. I picked a combination that would stay down . . . at least, I hoped it would. I looked at the clock in the living room. They'd be here in ten minutes, maybe more, depending on how long the line was at the drive-through. I did a little picking up, put some dishes in the dishwasher, and checked the computer for e-mails. I had a lot of expressions of sympathy, which I appreciated. I was glad people were letting me know via e-mail, instead of tying up the telephone.

I had a Facebook page that Robin had insisted I needed; I seldom posted to it or visited it. It seemed like a good time to check it. I had a lot of messages there, too. I managed to post a blanket response. Moosie came to sit on my lap at my little desk in the kitchen. I remembered to feed her.

And then Robin and Dad walked in the door, and I had a whole different set of problems. Robin's smile was weird and tight. My dad was clearly in a huff. I ignored that, and gave him a hug. He seemed smaller to me, and his face looked more lined. It had been a long time since we'd seen each other. He stood back from me and glanced down at my waist.

"You must like being married," Dad said, with a fake chuckle. He was a thin, short man with a pale complexion and an inexplicable allure to women. Dad's hair was still mostly brown, I noticed. Good. I hoped mine stayed brown for many more years. I had last seen Dad when Martin and I had been in California—I'd felt I should visit with him, if only to see Phillip. I had been hurt that he hadn't even come to my first wedding. Now he seemed diminished.

"If you're hinting that I've put on weight, you're absolutely right," I said. "I'll be putting on weight for the next six months." Might as well break the news.

It took him a minute to process that. "My Lord," he said. "I'm really glad for you, honey." That sounded just as artificial as the laugh.

"Thanks," I said. "I was going to call you and tell you but all this happened. And you were so angry with me on the phone."

"So what's the update on Phillip?" Dad asked. From the corner of my eye, I saw Robin shoot my father a look of intense dislike.

In all fairness, I couldn't blame Dad for being more concerned about my brother's absence, rather than my safe pregnancy, under the circumstances. While Robin stowed Dad's bag in the guest bedroom, I told him everything we knew about Phillip's disappearance. As I talked, I poured drinks for everyone and put out paper plates and napkins for the sandwiches. I didn't like eating off wrappers.

Robin came back looking more relaxed. Evidently he'd taken a few deep breaths while he was out of the room. As he distributed the order from Hero Heaven, I texted my mother to warn her that her first husband was in town.

It was good I'd done this, since they were on their way over. After ten minutes, Mom and John were ringing the doorbell.

My mother hugged me, smelling as she always did: linen-clean crisp, expensive, not overwhelming. John was with her, and I hugged him, too. Since John's heart attack, I never saw him without mentally evaluating how he looked. He seemed well today, and calm about meeting his wife's ex. Good.

Here, I have to say something about my father. It had broken my heart when he'd left my mother, or rather, when she'd told him to leave. But I had known, always, that it had been his mistakes that had caused his banishment, though my mother had never trash-talked him to me. I'd been old enough to understand what "unfaithful" meant. I had also been old enough to understand how deeply he had hurt and offended my mother. It must have been an odd marriage all along; my dad, aside from his inexplicable magnetism for women who should have known better, was so ordinary that marrying a standout like my mother must have surprised even him.

The woman he'd married next, Phillip's mother, had been a sharp contrast to the former Aida Brattle. Betty Jo had been plainer, shorter, less ambitious, more content; but he hadn't been able to stay faithful to her, either. My dad couldn't keep it in his pants, and though I hated to think such a vulgar thing about my own father, it was quite simply true. It wasn't a big surprise that when I'd dated Arthur Smith, the first man I'd gone with after college, he had turned out to be the same way.

I'd done some deep thought.

After that, I'd become very careful about my own judgment.

"Where is Betty Jo?" my mother asked, after she'd said hello and commiserated with my dad on the missing Phillip.

"Aurora didn't tell you?" My dad gave me an unreadable look.

"She doesn't talk about you," Mother said, with no expression.

"Betty Jo is taking a break from the marriage," my dad said. He smiled wryly.

"But she knows about this, right? I can't believe she's not here," Mother said.

"She's . . . actually, I don't know where she is," Dad said. "She might have gone off with another man." Hmm. He'd told me that was for sure. The truth and my father weren't best friends.

"I think you ought to tell the police," Mother said. "In case somehow she's asked Phillip to come to her. I know it doesn't seem likely." She held up a hand to forestall his protests, which I could see stacking up in his mouth.

"But it's possible," John said. He was doing his best to keep out of interchanges between my mother and her ex-husband, but he did have an opinion.

Dad shrugged, a martyr bearing up under unreasonable requests. "All right, I'll tell the cops," he said. "I want to go talk to them anyway." He turned to me. "Can I borrow your car, honey? I don't guess the police station has moved since I left."

"Actually, it has. They're out at the law enforcement complex, now." I told him how to get there, and rather reluctantly gave him my key ring.

"Pretty neat that we're going to be grandparents, huh?" Dad said to Mom on his way out the door. "But it's going to be a while before I can think about it."

"I understand," she said coldly.

And then he was gone. It was like I'd taken off a bra that was too tight. Everyone seemed to heave a silent sigh of relief.

"How are you feeling, Aurora?" my mother asked, and I knew that from now until the delivery, those were always going to be the first words out of her mouth.

And I was fine with that. "After I had a nap, I felt better," I said. "You know that Robin and I went to see the body in the alley?"

"You should not have done that," she said.

"We had to know if it was Phillip. And from the back, for a minute, I thought it might be. But it was Tammy Ribble, as I'm sure you've heard."

"I know her grandfather," John said. "He's devastated. His son, Tammy's father, and his wife had taken a weekend vacation with no media—phones or Internet. So he had to drive to the lake to tell them."

"I am glad it wasn't Phillip," I said. "But I'm really just sorry it's anyone. Mom, have you heard anything about Liza Scott getting bullied at school?"

"I did hear something about that," she said. Surprise, surprise.

"I haven't," John said. "Tell me."

My mother sighed. "Oh, honey, there's this little clique of girls, led by the daughter of that dance teacher, Tiffany Andrews. This Andrews girl is a—well, excuse me, all of you—she's a bitch in training, and her mom has given her some good lessons. Tiffany's child, Sienna, has these two buddies who think she's hot stuff. Anyway, Liza crossed them in some way. Since then, they've had it in for her. They've made her life hell, I hear, both at school and on the Internet. I told Emily how sorry I was and asked if there was anything I could do. I know some of the grandmothers." My mother's shoulders were squared in a way that said she would do her unpleasant duty if she was called upon to do so.

"I take it Emily and Aubrey said no." Robin had gathered up all the trash from lunch and deposited it in the garbage below the sink.

"They did. They were going to talk to the parents themselves."

I made a face. "That sounds absolutely horrible."

My mother nodded. "Yes, it does. I don't know if children have gotten crueler since you were growing up, or if parents don't have the control over them they used to have. A little of both, I expect."

If I found out our child was behaving like a savage, I would take steps. I wasn't sure what those steps would be, but I'd take 'em. I wondered if cruelty like that had to be sparked by some terrible parenting, or if some kids were just born that mean. I would ask Robin what he thought when we were alone and had no pressing crisis. If those two things ever happened at the same time.

And for a reason I can't fathom, at that moment I thought of something very important.

"The backpack," I said.

I became aware that there were three pairs of eyes examining me with varying degrees of curiosity and doubt.

"Where's his backpack? He always took it with him everywhere," I said.

"Why would Phillip carry a backpack?" my mother asked. "He didn't have to carry schoolbooks since he was homeschooled, and his cell phone would fit in his pocket."

"Phillip always carries that small backpack. He likes to sketch, and it holds his sketchpad, his pencils, his billfold, his phone, a bottle of water, a bag of raisins and some beef jerky, sometimes a pocketknife."

"He didn't like his pockets to be full," Robin said. "That's what he told me."

"And you don't think he has it with him?" Mother asked.

Why had I started picturing the backpack? "No. Josh would have come by after school let out to pick up Philip." Phillip was definitely looking forward to a new semester, being in a classroom with other kids. He'd felt very left out since he'd come to live with me. "I saw it after that. I saw it on the bench when I came home."

"It wasn't in his room when Detective Trumble searched it," Robin said.

"I have to go through that room myself," I said. "Otherwise, I'm just going to worry about it. But the backpack is here somewhere, I know."

So for the next ten minutes, we all searched the house. As it happened, Robin found it. Right inside our front door in the broad entrance hall was a coat stand mounted over a bench. In the summer, I hung decorations from the hooks, but in the winter, the hooks held useful stuff . . . like actual coats. The bench opened for storage. The backpack wasn't in the bench, but it was effectively hidden on the floor in a shadow between the bench and the front wall.

We surrounded it as though it were the Koh-i-Noor diamond.

"Shouldn't we call the police?" my mother said.

"I'm going to see what's inside right now," I said, and no one tried to talk me out of it. "Robin, if you would, please? Call them and tell them it's here."

When I had been a teen, there would still have been written notes in any teen's backpack. But in this age of cell phones, such things had fallen by the wayside. I sighed. No handy clues there, written on torn slips of paper. I pulled out a bottle of water, a paperback Jim Butcher novel, a sketchpad, and a small box of pencils. "He has his cell phone," I said.

There were some phone numbers in the backpack, written on odd things like a test schedule and a receipt. But I knew that most often Phillip entered numbers directly into his Contacts list. However, I'd check them out later. I flipped open the sketchpad.

Since the first drawing was me, I understood right away that this pad had been initiated since he'd moved here. Seeing my own face stopped me dead, and I felt tears flood my eyes. I looked prettier, smarter, and more skeptical than I'd ever imagined, at least in my own head. And I was smiling.

I'd never realized Phillip was so talented.

Everyone he'd met was recorded in the sketchpad. He hadn't been keeping it a secret, but he'd never volunteered to show me his work. I'd been waiting until we were really used to each other to ask him. I asked myself if I felt bad about invading his privacy.

No. I was sorry for the necessity, but it *was* a necessity, not a whim. I had to know who Phillip knew, what he'd been thinking. This sketchpad was the only clue I had. I examined each picture, hoping to derive some information from it. I learned that he thought Joss was strong and lovely. The dead girl, Tammy Ribble, was in one sketch with Joss. There was a drawing of them looking at each other, and it was almost romantic. Now it made my heart ache.

Phillip had done a sketch of Josh, too: Josh looked careless, happy, bold. There was even a drawing of Liza facing three other girls her age. It was clear whose side Phillip was on and what he thought of the girls. Phillip had studied *Macbeth* as a tragedy and *All's Well That Ends Well* for a comedy, when his class had had Shakespeare. I could see that Phillip had drawn the girls as the three witches from *Macbeth,* if I was interpreting correctly.

I knew one of the girls, though her face was distorted by meanness. Sienna Andrews, daughter of Tiffany. Then I recognized the other two: One was Marlea Harrison, whose family was very well off. The other was Kesha Windham. Her father was a dentist, and her mother did a lot of volunteer work and was a frequent library patron.

Identifying Marlea as one of Liza's tormentors was no surprise; I had never been impressed favorably by her manners while she was in the library, or the sly way she conducted herself. Sienna, I could take or leave. It seemed she had turned to the Dark Side. But Kesha Windham's inclusion in the group astonished me. Her mother was in the library all the time because she liked to read cookbooks, and the library had a huge collection of them. That seemed like such a wholesome hobby that I couldn't fathom her daughter's association with the other two girls.

"No doubt how he felt about the bullying," I muttered.

My mother and John recognized the girls, too. "Can this be true?" Mother said. "Can Sandra and Webster Windham know about this and still let it be going on?"

"I thought better of Kesha, too," I said. "The Windhams have always been so nice."

"If the police don't know about Liza's situation, they need to," Robin said. "I'm glad they're coming."

"But I don't see what the bullying could have to do with the kids missing," John said. "Three twelve-or thirteen-year-old girls aren't going to be kidnapping big kids."

"No," I said. "They aren't. But it's the only other extraordinary thing—at least, that I know of—happening in the lives of these kids. And it's only part of Josh and Joss's lives because Liza had—has—such a crush on Phillip, and she takes lessons from Joss. It's easy to see that Phillip likes the child, or at least sympathizes with her."

"Maybe we should remove the picture of Joss and Tammy together?" My husband asked this, but he sounded very uncertain of his ground. That was not like Robin.

"Why? Because it implies they were a real couple?" I let my astonishment show.

"I don't care what they were," he said immediately. "But what I care about is the willingness of the police to go every extra inch in finding them. I hate to say this, but do you think they might not care quite as much if they know Joss is gay?"

"That's horrible," Mom said. One of the realtors who worked for my mother was gay, but I hadn't known Mom knew that. Of course she had. My mother wasn't naive.

"It is horrible, but it may be realistic," I said. After a moment's hesitation, I removed that page. I put it in a folder and tucked it away in a drawer. I might be maligning our police, and I hoped I wasn't, but I did it anyway.

Surely the police knew all about the bullying situation by

now. Aubrey and Emily must have told the police about it. What would Tiffany Andrews say if I asked her why her daughter was persecuting Liza Scott? Any parent would get defensive, even a very fair-minded parent; and I couldn't say that Tiffany Andrews was a very pleasant person even when you weren't saying hard, but true, things about her daughter. I knew Marlea Harrison's parents, but only in a superficial way. I'd always thought of Kesha Windham as a pleasant child, and Sandra and Webster were good people. Maybe I could talk to them, see if they had any insight.

I had to start somewhere. I wanted Phillip back, I wanted to know Liza was safe—and if I was scared for my brother, I couldn't even imagine how the Finstermeyers felt, missing two precious children.

While we waited for the police, I called Beth. "No news, but I wondered if you'd talked to Jessamyn yet?"

Beth said, "That's coming up next. You want to sit in?"

I realized the generosity of the offer. "Yes, I do," I said. "I have a couple of ideas that may steer us in the right direction."

"Then come on over," Beth said. "We're getting out the thumbscrews and the bamboo slivers." God bless her, she was tough.

I had to explain to my family where I was going and why. Robin wanted to go, but I asked him to stay at the house to answer the phone and give the sketchpad and backpack to the police. He nodded, reluctantly. Mom and John said good-bye and went home, but not until I'd asked my mother to put her real-estate brain to thinking of properties any of the families involved might own. I know, that was looking for the old hunting cabin again, the one everyone in mysteries seemed to have tucked away. But the kids had to be somewhere.

If they'd been in a car accident, the car would have been found by the road now, with all the people out searching.

I left Robin sitting on the couch with a book, the phone beside him and Moosie on his lap.

If it hadn't been so cold and miserable, I could have walked to the Finstermeyers' house, which was only a couple of blocks away. It was very much like my house: thirty or forty years old, renovated, sitting on a quarter-acre lot with large trees. There were lots of cars in the driveway, because the Finstermeyers belonged to a large family through Beth, who'd been a Coggins. George was an import—Beth (or Bethany; her family always called her by her christened name) was a local girl. She'd met George while they were in college, and though at first George's job had taken him to the North, after a few years the family had gotten transferred back to Atlanta.

I finally found a parking space on the street, and walked back. It was misting, and the wind picked up. I thought of how careful I would have to be if we had ice this year. What if I fell and hurt the baby? Even this reminder of my pregnancy made me happy for a moment, until I had to knock on the Finstermeyers' door to deal with more sadness.

Chapter Seven

It was warm inside. I felt almost claustrophobic in a couple of minutes. The Finstermeyer house was crowded, and all of the people were talking at once. There was a golden retriever padding through the maze of well-wishers, and a miniature poodle who liked to bark. It was kind of overwhelming. And it bore an unpleasant resemblance to a wake.

"Let me tell Bethany you're here," said a tiny gray-haired lady. "You probably don't remember me, Aurora, but I'm Bethany's mother Martha."

"It's good to see you," I said automatically. "How are you holding up, Miss Martha?"

"I'm hanging in there, Aurora. This is the worst thing that's happened in this family since my great-uncle Farris went on a bender and drove a John Deere tractor into the lake."

I was startled into laughing. "Excuse me," I said immediately. "I know it must not have been funny then."

"No, John Deeres are expensive," Martha said, with a hint of a smile. But then the upcurve vanished. "And our twins are not replaceable like the tractor was. Beth's down the hall, second doorway to the right."

I knocked lightly before stepping inside. I knew instantly I was in Jessamyn and Joss's room. It was large, but full of furniture and girls' clutter and three tense people: George Finstermeyer, Beth, and Jessamyn. Jessamyn was thirteen, and she was both defensive and sad in the way only teenagers can seem to manage.

"Roe, glad you're here," Beth said. "You can shut the door behind you."

I did, and sat in the rolling office chair that was the only available seating. Beth was sitting with Jessamyn on one bed, and George was sitting on the other; I was sure it was Joss's. "George," I said, "I'm Aurora Teagarden, Phillip's sister. We've only met once before, I think."

He nodded. George, a short and stocky man in his forties, was blond and had a reddish complexion. He obviously needed sleep. His fists were clenched. "You're married to the writer fella?" he said.

It was my turn to nod.

"Phillip told Josh you're gonna have a baby," Jessamyn said.

"I am," I admitted. "I was counting on Phillip babysitting for us, but until we find him, I'm just going to worry about him. Can you give us anything to go on, Jessamyn?"

She sighed, as if the world was on her shoulders. And maybe she felt like that at the moment. She said, "I already told Mom and Dad. You know Liza Scott, the minister's daughter?"

"I go to that church," I said.

"Well, you know those little—excuse me, b-asses, are just being mean to her. There's nothing wrong with Liza except she's a little too holy."

"You're not the first person to tell me about her situation at school. So?"

"So," Jessamyn said, just this side of sarcastic, "Liza had this huge crush on Phillip. Like a little lapdog. Anyway, Phillip felt bad for her after Joss told him what was happening to her at school, and he was nice to her, when he should have just shoved her away. So the afternoon . . . the afternoon they went missing . . ." For the first time, Jessamyn lost her composure. Her eyes filled with tears. "Well, that day, Joss called me from the soccer field. She was really happy because it was the last lesson of the year and she'd get nearly three weeks off from school and teaching soccer lessons."

"And Josh and Phillip came to pick her up."

"Yeah, 'cause they're like best buds ever since Phillip moved here." Jessamyn went on to relate the story of Liza's unwillingness to stay at the soccer field until her mother came, since her tormentors were present. Joss had called Jessamyn (evidently before she'd called Tammy) to remind her that Joss was going to have her hair trimmed before she came home. Joss had wanted to make sure Jessamyn had a way home from her piano lesson. "So I told her I'd gotten a ride with Lynn McManus, and that I'd remind Mom about Joss's haircut," Jessamyn said by way of roundup. "Joss said she and Tammy would get here later than they'd thought, because she was a little behind to her hair appointment."

This was not as familiar to the Finstermeyers as it was to me, and they asked several questions. Jessamyn couldn't answer most of them.

"I wonder why the boys didn't drop Liza off on their way to Shear Delight," I said. I looked at Jessamyn inquiringly.

"I don't know," Jessamyn said. "Maybe there was no one at the Scotts'. Liza wouldn't want to be there alone." The scorn was apparent in her voice.

"A lot of eleven-year-olds wouldn't want to go into an empty house," Beth said sharply.

Jessamyn had the manners to look a little abashed. "Anyway, Joss said good-bye then. She just wanted to be sure I had a ride, since Josh was taking Liza home. This was a real short phone call, because she had to call Tammy."

"Why did she have to call Tammy?" Beth said.

"They were supposed to meet at Shear Delight. Tammy's sister was dropping her off there. Tammy was going to come over here to spend the night."

"I didn't know that," Beth said. "But then, Tammy is over here a lot, if Joss isn't at her house!" She smiled fondly, but then remembered why we were having this conversation, and her face crumpled. "And now poor Tammy is dead! And she was Joss's best friend!"

"Mom." Jessamyn looked away, clearly exasperated.

Oh, not now! I thought. *Don't dump this on Beth now!*

George said, "Beth, the girls are—were—a couple."

Beth's mouth dropped open. "No," she said, more as if she was testing the word than as if she actually believed it.

"I'm sorry, Mom. She was going to tell you. She was so scared you'd be mad," Jessamyn said.

Beth looked from one face to another, stunned into silence. "How could she ever imagine I wouldn't still love her? Oh, my child." She closed her eyes and took a long breath, trying to get a grip on herself. Finally, she said, "Roe? You knew, too?"

I was profoundly embarrassed. I just nodded. I started to tell Beth I'd only found out hours ago, but that really didn't make a difference. Beth had had the rug pulled out from under her, and she had to have a little time to get back on her feet.

"Well," said Beth in an unsteady voice. "Well. Okay. I'll have to deal with that later. But I love my daughter, no matter what."

Jessamyn was subdued, now. And maybe to point out the fact that she was a daughter, too, she said, "So if it hadn't been for Lynn and her mom, Josh would have come to get me, too, and I'd have been in the car."

"Thank God for Lynn's mom," said George. "Thank God."

Jessamyn looked at him as if she were seeing her father for the first time. Then she shyly took his hand, and he clenched it so hard that her fingers must have ached, but she didn't say a thing.

I said, "Jessamyn, do you know *anything* about what might have happened to your brother and sister? Do you know of any other problems they might have been having with other kids, or with a grown-up?"

"Nothing big. Josh wanted to ask Heather Sissley for a date, but he hadn't worked himself up to it," Jessamyn said. "He and Phillip were talking about throwing a party during the Christmas break. But that's it, that's all I know." I was leaning forward, prepared to getting up, when Jessamyn said, "You saw the post on Facebook, right? The one from yesterday?"

"Show us," George said.

I was liking George Finstermeyer more and more.

Jessamyn grabbed her laptop and clicked on a few buttons, brought up a posting by Marlea Harrison. Her icon was a cartoon of a caped woman with a mask. The post read, "Does anyone on the planet miss LS? I don't think so! Now, Josh and Phillip r hot. Their a loss, for real!"

Beth's face froze. She pulled a cell phone out of her pocket. She called up a listing in her address book and punched it. We heard the buzz of a voice on the other end. "Karina? It's Beth. No, no news yet. But I think you need to go on Facebook and read your daughter's latest post. It was brought to my attention." Beth's voice was as frosty as her face. "No, I don't want to read it to you. I'm very upset. I'm sure you can get Marlea to take it down. Talk to you later." And she pressed End.

The cruelty of children is more shocking than the cruelty of adults. Not only was I shocked, I was angry. But it felt somehow wrong, unhealthy, to be so furious with a child. I closed my eyes, knowing that if Marlea had been in front of me at that moment, I would have been tempted to slap her across the face. I still felt like tracking her down and giving her a "Come to Jesus" moment.

Jessamyn seemed a bit pleased at having dropped such a bombshell. I tried to feel more sympathy for a girl who was caught in between her sibs' age group and Liza's age group. Instead, I wanted to turn her upside down and shake her in the hope that something useful would come out of her head.

"Thanks, Jessamyn," I said, working hard to sound grateful. "We needed to hear everything you knew."

"I miss them," she said, and I felt like a heel. At that age kids seemed to revolve from one side of the emotional coin to another with the quick flip of the cosmic wrist. "I wish Liza had never been born. Then none of this would have happened."

"Jessamyn," her mother said, and in that one word was a weight of censure that made the girl cringe.

"It also would not have happened if Marlea, Kesha, and Sienna had not been born," I said. "Don't blame the victim for the crime." In this case, Liza was literally the victim.

There had always been a certain amount of sound coming from the rest of the house, with so many people talking, moving. Now there was silence. We all turned our heads to the closed door.

Aubrey and Emily came in. I had never seen such a drastic change in two people in such a short time. They looked as though they'd lost ten pounds in two days, and they looked shattered. Though Emily and I had never been soul mates, I never felt sorrier for anyone in my life. Since Aubrey and I had dated for some time, he'd confided in me that he couldn't father a child. When he'd married Emily, who was a widow, he'd adored Liza and adopted her. So Liza was the only child, for both of them.

"We came to ask Jessamyn . . ." Emily said, and then she seemed to realize who was in the room already. "Oh, then we aren't the first ones to think of this." She even managed a faint smile.

For the first time, Jessamyn looked stricken by the pressure of being the sister of the missing twins. She might be able to keep up a facade in front of her own parents and me, but in the presence of such overwhelming anguish she could not. I liked her better.

"I told my mom and dad, and Miss Aurora, that I really didn't know much of anything else," Jessamyn said. "I'm sorry. Liza asked them to drop her off, and they were going to do it."

"I was late," Emily said, and she began to cry. Silently. "I was late because the women's Bible study ran late, and I had to pick up the Christian education room, no one else seems to think about that, and then I looked at my watch and it was just past time to pick up Emily from her soccer lesson, and by the time I got there she had gone. I figured someone else had given her a ride, and that she'd borrow a phone and call me. We were going to give her her own phone for Christmas. She's too young to have one, I think, but with her situation at school and the rough year she's had, we . . ."

She stopped herself with a hiccuping sob. Aubrey put his arm around her, and something about the gesture told me that Emily had said this many, many times in the past few days, and that Aubrey had tried to console her just as often. "Ten minutes cost me my daughter," Emily said.

There was nothing to say to rebut that. We were all missing children, too. I guess it seemed worse for Emily and Aubrey since their child was so young, so unable to defend herself. Against whom? We didn't know. No one knew why they were missing. No one knew why Tammy Ribble was dead. Why hadn't Josh and Joss's car been found?

"I am so sorry," I said, and I got up to leave. My stomach twinged, and I put my hand to it.

"Are you all right?" George asked.

"I'll be fine," I said. It wasn't the time to talk about my pregnancy.

Had Jessamyn told us everything she knew? I wondered. Ordinarily, I would not have spoken, because her parents were there and knew her best. But this wasn't an ordinary time.

"Jessamyn," I said, my hand on the doorknob. "You know how crucial it is that you tell us every little thing."

I could see the panic in her eyes. She looked down, and I thought she was steeling herself to say something. "I just remembered that while we were on the phone, me and Joss, Joss said something about Clayton."

"Who?" Emily said, blank-faced.

"Clayton," Jessamyn said, the impatience back in her voice. "Clayton Harrison. Marlea's brother."

I didn't blame Sarah Washington for not wanting to cast any suspicion Clayton Harrison's way, if his was the car she'd seen turning in to the soccer parking lot.

Everyone knew Clayton Harrison.

Chapter Eight

Every town has a boy like Clayton, I suppose. His parents, Dan and Karina, had money, both earned and inherited, and they let it flow down to Clayton without attaching any responsibility to it. Clayton was handsome, reckless, and constantly in trouble . . . when he wasn't leading the high school baseball team to victory, or being elected to the homecoming court. He'd wrecked his first car, only to be presented with another one. He drank and ran into ditches. Dan Harrison had bought Clayton's way out of a drunk-driving charge, a persistent rumor had it. Even worse, Clayton was reputed to be the father of a child whose fifteen-year-old mother had given the baby up for adoption . . . after Clayton had broken up with her in a text message. That couldn't be considered entirely Clayton's fault, exactly—but it didn't add to his virtues, either.

Clayton was a charming liar. This was his senior year in high school, and he was definitely Lawrenceton High's alpha male. His girlfriend of the past year, Connie Bell, was a beautiful, timid girl, also from a well-to-do family. She'd always seemed overshadowed by her boyfriend.

And Clayton was the big brother of Marlea, whose nasty Facebook message we'd just read.

This new piece of information stunned us all into silence. Jessamyn looked both scared and relieved of a burden. George spoke first. "Did Joss say if Clayton was in the car with him? Or did Clayton follow them? Or maybe he met them by chance? What did she say, exactly?"

"I don't know," Jessamyn said. She was about to cry. "Joss just checked that I'd gotten a ride home, and then she said Clayton was there. Something like, 'There's Clayton, yuck,' or something. She doesn't like him."

"Why didn't you tell us this right away?" Beth said, trying as hard as she could to sound calm.

"Because you told all of us never to hang around with Clayton," Jessamyn said. "And we didn't. I figured he was in his own car. Connie's always with him."

The Scotts looked blank.

"That's Connie Bell," I said. "Clayton's girlfriend. They're both seniors."

They didn't look enlightened.

"Clayton's dad owns Harrison Timber and Land," I explained. "Connie's dad is the president of State Pride Bank."

"And why should this matter?" Aubrey said.

The atmosphere felt too thick in the small, crowded bedroom. If I'd thought the living room was packed, now I knew it hadn't been. I wanted to throw open the door and gulp in air. "It matters because those are both families with a lot of money and power and you can't go poke them with a stick," I said. "First thing, we need to be sure that Clayton is home, that he's safe and sound."

"I'll call Karina again," Beth said, but you could tell the idea didn't sit well.

"No, let me," I said. "She's already defensive, with you."

Beth nodded.

I looked at Karina's number on Beth's Contacts list and punched it in.

I switched the phone to speaker as it rang.

"Hello?" Karina Harrison said. I could recognize her piercing voice, from the occasions she'd come into the library. She was on the citizens' advisory board for the library. She'd tried to get the Harry Potter books banned.

"Karina," I said, "this is Aurora Teagarden. Phillip's sister. How is Clayton?"

"Fine," Karina said cautiously, after a significant pause. "Why do you ask?"

"Because I just learned Clayton met up with our missing kids on the day they vanished," I said bluntly. "And I want to know what happened, straight from Clayton's mouth. Or maybe I could talk to Marlea, since she was at the soccer field, too."

This time the pause was longer.

"Marlea's gone to stay with my mother in Savannah," Karina said. "I just talked to her about her Facebook posting. I'll ask Clayton about who he saw that afternoon when he walks in the door. I'm not sure where he is at the moment."

We all looked around at each other. Really?

I said, "I find that hard to believe. Everyone is in an uproar about our missing kids, and you don't know where your son is *at the moment*? Bull. We need to talk to him, Karina. Now, or at the police station."

That tripped a wire. "No," Karina said, and she was clearly panicking. "You don't understand. If you tell the police, my son is in danger."

"What do you mean?" I said.

"He's been kidnapped. And since your brother and the Finstermeyer kids are missing, maybe they're the ones who did this! Did you think about that?"

I don't know how anyone else in the room felt, but I was beyond stunned. George spoke for the first time. "Karina, our kids have also been kidnapped. You can't seriously believe Josh and Joss, not to mention Liza, and someone new to town like Phillip, plotted and planned to abduct Clayton in broad daylight and ask you for ransom. They're victims, too. You need to call the police, so they'll know to look for Clayton's car."

"Who's that? George?" Karina asked. "You've been listening in?"

"Yep."

"No, no, no. Clayton will be lost if we bring in anyone. The kidnappers told us so. We're paying soon. We'll get him back. I'm begging you." She was pleading from her heart; at least, it sounded like that to me.

"We'll think about it." I hung up.

Beth was incandescent with rage. "She didn't tell the police. Clayton's gone too, and she didn't tell the police."

"I can understand that," I said slowly. "They've gotten a ransom demand. It's their son's life. But none of you have gotten a ransom demand, right? I sure haven't. My father hasn't."

All the adults shook their heads. "But we hardly have as much money as the Harrisons," George said. "No sane person would take our kids and expect to be paid any big sum."

Jessamyn looked from face to face, terrified, and began to cry out loud. The sound was almost unendurable.

Beth said, "Jessamyn, do *not* say anything about this, either in person or on social media. Not to your best friend. Not to anyone." She hugged her daughter to take the sting out of her words.

"Okay," Jessamyn said. "But all the people who are looking for my brother and sister . . . shouldn't they know about this?"

Beth thought hard. "I don't see that it'll make any difference," she said finally. "The kids are still missing. But . . . it would make more sense, wouldn't it, if all of us had gotten demands? I know the Harrisons are rich, but the rest of us have at least some money, too."

None of us knew what to make of Karina's news. It seemed Lawrenceton had one more missing kid.

Was this a kidnapping? Or was this a voluntary disappearance? Though I didn't believe it for a minute, Karina ostensibly thought it possible that Joss, Josh, and Phillip had conspired to kidnap Clayton and hold him for ransom. If I swallowed that, and I really couldn't, what about Liza? How could she possibly be a part of all this?

On the other hand, how could three vigorous and active teenagers (possibly four, with Clayton's being included) and an eleven-year-old girl be abducted? Wouldn't it take a lot of people to coerce them or force them?

Phillip was not a brawler, but he was also not one to stand down from a challenge. I might not know Phillip as well as if we'd grown up together, but I knew my brother well enough to be sure I was right about that.

I left the Finstermeyer house both baffled and depressed. I felt like I'd been in Joss and Jessamyn's room for a whole day, but in fact it had been only an hour and a half.

And I felt very queasy.

On the way home, I had to open the driver's door at a stop sign and lean out so I could throw up. I was glad no one was behind me, but by that time, it was not a major consideration.

My father had parked my car right in the middle of the carport, so I had to park on the driveway. I walked to the front door, feeling as though I were a hundred years old.

Robin, looking unhappy, was sitting at the kitchen counter with my dad. A row of casserole dishes cluttered the table. Friends had brought food. That proved we were in a crisis.

Dad was writing in a little notebook. Robin looked up as I

closed the front door. He said instantly, "Roe, you're going to lie down." I didn't protest, but went to stretch out on the couch. Robin brought me some peanut butter crackers and water. I ate slowly, and drank the water sip by sip. Gradually, I felt better.

"What did the police tell you?" I asked my father. "You sure were there a long time."

"Turned out they wanted to ask me some questions about Phillip," Dad said. "About him running away. About his mother." He snorted.

My father looked angry and uneasy. That wasn't good. There was something he wasn't telling us, but at the moment I hardly cared. I wondered if he'd expected the police would give him a rundown on all the information they'd gathered. I felt too despondent to respond to his indignation or to figure out what he was hiding. Robin sat on the floor beside me and took my hand. Poor Robin. I was willing to bet that few couples had so much drama so early in their marriage. He was weathering it well.

When my father went back to the guest bedroom, Robin said, "What happened at Beth's?"

I told him what Jessamyn had said, but I had to hold back a few things. With Dad within eavesdropping distance, I couldn't tell Robin about the ransom demand for Clayton Harrison. My father would go straight to the police with it, and I wasn't convinced that was the right thing to do. Karina had seemed so desperate. In my opinion, she genuinely believed Clayton's life was in peril.

"And now I have to think about supper," I said. Drearily.

"We can go out."

"No, we've got so much food in the refrigerator. It will be easier to heat it up."

After asking if I needed help, Robin told me that he was going into his office for a while to answer e-mails. He'd had enough real drama for a while, I suspected, and needed to refresh himself with some fictional drama. I didn't blame him.

I loaded the dishwasher and checked the refrigerator for an evening meal. It seemed ridiculous to think of such a thing when we were all so anxious, but it had to be done. To my huge relief, I found a pan of lasagna crowding the second shelf. And I had lettuce and tomatoes for a salad. And some garlic bread in the freezer? Yes. There, supper was determined. I turned on the oven to preheat.

Collapsing onto the couch, I felt as if I were a million years old. I dragged myself to my feet after a few minutes to feed Moosie, who rubbed against my legs in a way that said, *Notice me!* Poor cat. She hadn't gotten her quota of attention in days.

My dad popped out of the guest bedroom after ten minutes of peace. He threw himself in the chair across from me. He said, "The police have no idea at all what they're doing."

"Surely you don't think they're dragging their feet," I said, perversely determined to defend the local law enforcement contingent. "You know they want to find Phillip and Josh and Joss and Liza as much as we want to."

"*No one* wants to find Phillip as much as me."

"Uh-huh," I said.

"You doubt that?" He was incredulous.

If I hadn't been so tired, I would have said, "You love Phillip so much you let him walk in on you cheating. You love him so much that you made his mom crazy enough to run away."

But I was too tired to say all this, though I thought it. Probably I wasn't being fair to my father in some way. Dad hadn't planned Phillip's unexpected arrival during Dad's little sex party, I suppose, and Dad hadn't actually forced his wife to leave.

"Have you heard from Betty Jo?" I asked, instead. "Can you get in touch with her? Can you tell her about Phillip?"

"You know she ran off with some man. We don't exactly talk."

"I wonder why she hasn't let Phillip know where she was, before this?"

"She just told me to tell him she'd call. She didn't tell me where she was going," my father pointed out. "Just like when Phillip lit off. We didn't know where he was until I heard from you. And now I don't know where he is, again."

I didn't know how to respond to that, so I didn't. Instead, I got up to put dinner on the table, and I called Robin to eat. My father washed his hands and took his place at one end. After a long silence, my father decided to make conversation. "So you're going to have a baby, you and Robin."

"Yep," Robin said.

"When is it due?"

We talked about that, and Dad said he'd like to come for the baptism. I gave that the weight it was due. He hadn't even come to my first wedding.

I found I was actually hungry. The lasagna was warm and bubbling from the oven, and the salad balanced out the heaviness of the noodles and cheese. My father told us he'd never had lasagna like that. He thought the meat sauce tasted "funny." Neither Robin nor I responded to this.

As a long and unpleasant day drew to a close, I felt something close to despair. And I admit there was a little resentment mixed in. The week had started out so happy, with the confirmation of my pregnancy and the excitement of telling my family and Robin's. We should be discussing bottle vs. breast, and debating whether the nursery would be themed Winnie the Pooh or Jungle Creatures. We should be thinking of where we were going to register—Babies R Us? Target?—since we needed everything. I had a vision of soft baby blankets and diaper bags, plastic rattles and pacifiers.

I knew how selfish my resentment was, and I didn't think it meant I loved my brother the less. I was just clinging to my hope, instead of to my despair.

At least I got to be alone with Robin after dinner, though it was already late. Dad retired to the guest bedroom without offering to help with the dishes or clearing the table, and in about thirty seconds I heard the little television come on.

The day had been so emotionally exhausting that I climbed into bed with profound relief, and I was asleep within a few seconds. I didn't dream about anything more frightening than a bake sale.

Chapter Nine

In the morning, Dad reemerged from his room to ask directions to the alley behind Shear Delight where Tammy's body had been found. I told him the route. I don't know what he hoped to find, since the police had searched it very thoroughly, but I would love having him out of the house. Besides, he was too fidgety to sit still for long. He borrowed my car again. I reminded him to check the gas level.

When he'd left, I told Robin everything I hadn't been able to tell him the day before about Clayton's abduction. Robin was as baffled as everyone else. How could anyone take so many people hostage?

It was a puzzle we couldn't solve. We talked about it while we ate and showered and dressed.

Every theory we came up with had a snag. The Harrisons said they'd sent Marlea off to her grandmother. But if Clayton had stopped by the field, and Marlea had been there, surely she would have something interesting to tell the investigators? If Clayton had been snatched, his car was missing, too. And what about Connie Bell? What had she seen? Where were the two cars? Why hadn't they been found? Clayton's red Trans Am was hardly anonymous.

"If Connie Bell is gone, too, why haven't her parents said anything?" Robin said. "They surely wouldn't let Karina Harrison persuade them to keep it quiet. Not if their child was missing."

"I don't know, and I can't think of a reason in the world to call her house. I don't know the Bells at all."

"Well, let's settle that." Robin looked in the Lawrenceton phone book and tapped a number on his cell phone. It rang. When someone answered, he said, "Hello. This is Robin. May I speak to Connie?"

In a few seconds he said, "Sorry, I just realized I called the wrong Connie," and hung up.

"That was Connie's mother," he said. "She called Connie to the phone. Evidently, the girlfriend is fine. But if she was with Clayton, how come she hasn't told anyone what she knows?"

"Maybe the Harrisons asked her not to?"

"If they did, she must know something. Why didn't they take her to the police? Or even . . . would the FBI be involved? In a kidnapping?"

"I think it depends on the age of the child," I said. "And I'm pretty sure Clayton is almost eighteen, since he's a senior. Could Phillip be considered kidnapped, rather than vanished? Because we don't know what happened?"

"I have no idea. I wish we could kidnap Connie and make her talk," Robin said morosely. "I wonder what she's told her family."

"If no one knows that Clayton is gone, she wouldn't have to tell them anything."

"True."

"She can just sit on her hands and hope everything will be all right."

"Would she?" Robin asked incredulously.

"I don't know Connie personally, but maybe so. All the kids seem to think that where Clayton went, Connie was with him. She must know something. But as long as she stays silent, it didn't happen. No one is asking her questions, or angry at her."

I brooded over ethics and morality. I balanced Connie's rights against my desire to see my brother again. And I decided, *To hell with her rights.* I would have interrogated the girl if I could have thought of a way to do it without getting accused of terrorizing her. I wondered if the Harrisons had paid the ransom yet, and I wondered how much the kidnappers had asked for.

Late in the morning, the phone rang, and Robin reached out to answer it. "Hello? Oh, hi, Perry."

Then he said, "Where?" At the tension in his voice, I sat up, and my heart thumped.

"We'll be there." He hung up. "Perry Allison was listening to his mom's police scanner. They've found Josh's car."

"Where?"

"Not too far from your last house."

Robin meant the Julius house, where I'd lived during my marriage to Martin Bartell. It would never be called the Bartell house; the Julius family had greater claim. They had been killed while they lived there.

"Let me go to the bathroom, and then we'll leave," I said. "Would you call my dad and tell him? He should know."

Robin nodded without enthusiasm.

"I know you're doing all the heavy lifting with Dad," I said. "I'm grateful. I realize he's a pain in the butt. And he seems to be getting worse."

"He is," Robin said, smiling just a little. "At least he lives all the way across the country. I have that to be thankful for."

In a few minutes I was bundling up again, and we were on our way in Robin's car.

As we took a familiar route, I tried not to think of all the times I'd driven from work to the Julius house during my first marriage. Memories flickered, no longer vivid. I'd loved Martin, I had no doubt about that. And I was sure he'd loved me. I'd sunk into a miasma of grief when he'd died.

But it was also true that we hadn't had a trouble-free relationship. Martin had been a man with a lot of secrets.

I sighed, and put that behind me. The present was painful enough.

After we passed my former home and went another half mile, we saw all the police cars. We pulled over at a discreet distance, and got out to walk the remaining yards in the bright clear light. The wind blew across the open fields, which stretched over the rolling hills around us. There was a grove of trees in the middle of a field, around a tiny old cemetery; and in that grove I caught a flash of light, glinting off something shiny. Josh's car. The black Camaro.

I felt as if I could hear a bell tolling in my head. Robin put his arm around me as my steps faltered.

We got up to a highway patrol officer, a woman I didn't know. She said, "You have to stop here. No farther, please."

"My brother Phillip is missing," I said, forcing the words out of my throat, which felt constricted. My eyes burned with unshed tears. "Is there . . . anyone . . . in the car?"

She hesitated. Finally, she said, "There's no one in the front or back seats. They're opening the trunk now. Why don't you go home and let someone call you?"

There was no way I was going to leave this spot. I glanced up at my husband.

"Who found it?" Robin asked, taking my cue to stall. We were going to stay until the trunk was opened. I had to know.

"I did." Trooper Allen didn't mind telling us that. "I was returning from an accident site at an intersection two miles north, and I caught the sun bouncing off the hood. When I went to investigate, I recognized the license number. We've been looking for it."

"Was there anything inside?" I held my breath before she answered.

She hesitated. Then, out of mercy, Trooper Allen said, "There were just a few spots of blood in the car, if that's what you're asking. Nothing significant."

I sagged against Robin. I closed my eyes and said a silent prayer. This was beyond terrible. We stepped to the right of Allen so we could see more clearly, though with the car in the grove, and the weeds that had been allowed to choke up the ground, it was hard to tell what was happening.

"The trunk is opening," Robin said quietly. "No one's jumping back or . . . anything. I think we're okay."

There were both Lawrenceton deputies and highway patrol clustered around the car. "It's empty," called one of the uniforms.

I deflated with relief. "Whose land is this?" I asked Allen, who had turned to look.

"I don't know that," she said, turning back. She looked almost as relieved as I felt.

Aubrey and Emily ran from their car to join us.

"It's empty," Robin told them instantly.

Emily collapsed, sobbing, and Aubrey was crying, too. I expected the Finstermeyers to show up any second. But the Harrisons could hardly show an interest, since they were harboring such a great secret. I thought about Tammy's parents, whom I only knew by sight. They knew where their child was: lying on a cold metal table. Uncertainty was better than that.

I called my father myself, and told him not to come out to the site. There was nothing to see or discover, at least nothing we'd have access to.

"Did you see the front of the car?" he demanded.

"No, it was facing the other way," I said.

"See if you can have a look at it."

"Why?"

"To check if there's anything that indicates that was the car that hit the girl."

I felt the cold to my bones. Robin and I began walking back to his car. When we were out of earshot, I told Robin what my father had suggested. Robin was disparaging. "We're not standing out there in the cold to see if there's any damage to the front of the car," he said firmly. "We don't know how long it'll take for them to be ready to move it. How would we know what any damage came from? For all we know, the car hit a tree in the grove, or an old headstone."

"True." I was relieved to be talked out of that chore.

"Home?" he asked, as he maneuvered the car into a U-turn.

"I want to stop at Shear Delight on the way."

"Again? Why?"

"I need to go inside," I said. "And I think I'd better go alone."

The parking lot of Shear Delight was not crowded. Robin pulled out an *Ellery Queen Mystery Magazine* to while away his wait in the car. I went in through the front door, and a bell chimed to announce my arrival. A quick glance around told me the place was like almost all the other hair salons in Lawrenceton. Walk-ins were welcome, a sign told me. There was a rack of hair products and one of bright flowered handbags for sale. A little Christmas tree was up in one corner. Carols were playing on the sound system.

I had almost forgotten about Christmas.

A middle-aged woman was getting highlights put in her hair by a slim, pretty girl in a smock decorated with poinsettia appliqués. Another hairdresser was sweeping the floor around her station. A woman in her sixties was sitting at the reception desk filing her nails. She looked up inquiringly. "Did you need to make an appointment?" she asked. "With Laurel or Debra?"

"No," I said. "My brother is one of the kids who is missing."

I had the undivided attention of all four women after the

words left my mouth. "I'm so sorry for your trouble," said the sweeping woman, and they all nodded. Suddenly, tears stung my eyes. I hadn't braced myself for compassion.

"I just wanted to know what happened in here, since the police haven't told me anything. I know Joss had an appointment. Was Tammy here long, waiting for her? I'm Aurora Teagarden," I added belatedly.

"I'm Laurel," said the girl giving the highlights. "Joss had an appointment with me. Like we told the police, she didn't come in the shop. Her friend Tammy was here. Someone had dropped Tammy off, I don't know who. Tammy got a haircut and highlights just a week ago from Debra, there." Laurel nodded toward the woman with the broom. "It looked so cute, short."

Debra said, "Tammy was just waiting for Joss to show. She was supposed to go home with Joss afterward. She was telling me how much she was enjoying having short hair. Most girls can't wear it that way." A tear rolled down Debra's cheek, and she pulled a tissue out of a pink box and dabbed at her face.

The woman behind the desk nodded. "Short, but feminine," she said. "I'm Daisy. I do manicures and pedicures."

I nodded at her. "So she went out the back door?" I asked.

"She was texting," Laurel said. "And she started laughing. She told us, 'They're behind the shop, I need to go out and rescue them,' but not like anything was really wrong. I swear! If I'd thought something was really wrong, I would have called the police."

I nodded again. I believed Laurel. "But she didn't come back," I said, nudging the narrative along.

"No," Daisy said, shaking her head. "She never came back."

There was a moment of silence.

"The cops wanted to know why we didn't go outside to look for her," Laurel said. "Honestly, after five minutes, I got kind of peeved with the girls. I thought Joss had called Tammy outside because she was going to blow off her appointment. I was steamed.

It wouldn't have cost her but a minute to come in and tell me she didn't want to get her hair cut. Actually, it would have been a relief, because she was my last appointment and I could have gone home." Laurel shook her head sadly. "Now I feel so bad about that. If I'd had any idea what had happened, you can bet I'd have done something. Maybe . . . maybe she was alive, and if I'd gone to look, I could have helped her."

In a ragged chorus, all the women told Laurel she couldn't have known, that she wasn't a psychic, that there had been no sound to indicate anything was going on outside the shop.

"I know you would have," I said.

That seemed to be that. More information that I didn't know what to do with. Tammy had not expected any danger when she left the salon.

After thanking all of them (including the customer, whose name I never knew), and receiving many assurances that they were *just so sorry,* I went out to the car. I told Robin what the ladies had told me, which didn't amount to much. "But Tammy said she needed to rescue Joss," I said thoughtfully. "From what? But she was laughing, Laurel said. Apparently, Tammy didn't fear there was a serious threat, but she was concerned enough to walk outside."

"Whatever happened, it was then," Robin said. "Otherwise, the kids would have gotten help for Tammy. So their communication was cut off then."

"I don't know why Clayton would have been following Josh," I said. "But maybe the kidnappers were following Clayton? And our group of kids got caught up in that drama."

We drove the rest of the way in silence. Kidnappers in Lawrenceton? A popular teen left dead in an alley, not found for two days? It all seemed so unlikely, and yet *something* had happened to them all.

After I'd made my bed, and started some laundry (dirty clothes stacked up no matter how dire life got), I could not think of one more thing to do. I sat with my feet on the floor and my hands on my thighs, letting my burdens float away. I was by myself in a not-unpleasant way. My father was out prowling around the town, and Robin was checking his e-mail in his office.

Gradually, I began to pick up my worries again. I wondered who had jurisdiction over Josh's car. And the entire case. Tammy had been killed, and the other kids had disappeared, within the city limits. The car had been found in the county, which would indicate the sheriff's department would handle it, but it had been found by a state trooper. I hoped, for the sake of the investigation, that they were cooperating.

My mind drifted to the windy countryside, the hood of the car concealed in that small cluster of trees and tombstones. I had been past that little grove a hundred times. The old cemetery had not seen a new burial for a hundred years, as far as I knew. The historical society went and cleaned it up once in a while. There were, at most, twenty graves there. It was not a place that jumped to my mind when I imagined dumping a car. I wondered: did that mean the dumper had knowledge of the land? Maybe. On the other hand, the grove was visible from the road and there was a rutted track leading across the field to it, so its existence wasn't exactly an esoteric piece of knowledge.

I wanted to know more facts. They were in scarce supply.

Then my father came in the front door, which meant he hadn't put my car away. He tossed the keys on the counter, and made himself a cup of coffee in the Keurig. "So nothing in the car," he said. "Did you get a look at the front?"

"No, they hadn't started towing it out of the field," I said. "And I couldn't wait there forever." I don't know how the conversation would have gone after that, but the doorbell rang. To my surprise, it was a group of ladies I knew, and their visit was to assure me that they were very sorry about my half brother . . . and the minister's daughter! And those Finstermeyer twins, thc cute ones who were so active in the school and their church.

I would have considered this torture the day before, but now I let their voices wash over me like stream water over stones. Their intentions were good, and their faces were kind. My father stayed to be introduced to them all—one of the ladies remembered him from when he lived in town, and he had to talk to her for a few minutes. My stepfather's daughter-in-law, Melinda Queensland, had come, and I was really glad to see her. She gave me a warm hug and told me how happy she was for my good news, and how sorry she was for my bad. Marva Clerrick had come, which was a bit of a surprise, and Teresa Stanton, Bryan Pascoe's ex-wife. I realized, after some conversation, that they'd stopped at Emily and Aubrey's house first, and my house second, and the Finstermeyers would be third. Sort of a trifecta of the stricken.

Dad escaped as soon as he could, but Robin heard the voices and ventured out to be polite. He could have claimed he had to work (which he did), but he put himself out.

All the ladies wanted to help, and I wished I could have asked them to fold my laundry; probably they would have done it in a flash. But that hardly seemed appropriate or necessary.

After a half an hour, they were on their way, leaving trays of cookies and seasoned pecans and cheese straws, as if Robin and I were going to throw a party. Well, I never turned down a good cheese straw, and I was glad to have the snacks. They reminded me that I hadn't eaten breakfast and that it was almost lunchtime. I made myself eat a pear first, but then I gave myself permission to dive in. I sighed with happiness, and didn't even mind when I caught Robin grinning.

"Eating for two," I said defensively.

"I have no problem with you eating," he said. "I'm just glad to see you keeping it down."

My dad came out and ate a huge ham sandwich, and Robin had one, too. Then Dad announced his intention to go see a couple of old friends who still lived in Lawrenceton, and I could hardly agree with him fast enough.

When he was out the door, I said, "Robin, I was figuring that the Harrisons would pay the ransom last night, and that today we'd hear Clayton had been released. I've been thinking any minute we'd hear that . . . and that the kids were all free too."

Robin said slowly, "I don't see why we can't call the Harrisons. We know that Clayton's being held already. Why can't we ask if they've paid the ransom?"

I was startled by the idea. "Hmm. Well, when I think about it . . . why not?" For the second time in two days, I called Karina Harrison.

"Yes?" she said, sounding strung as tight as a guitar string.

"Hi, it's Aurora. Karina, we've been thinking about you, and wondering if you'd paid the ransom, if you knew when you were getting your son back."

"Aurora, for God's sake, leave us alone. No, you can't get that kind of cash instantly! We'll do it soon. That's all I can say. I'll let you know, okay? When we know anything else. Don't talk about this! Now I need to get off the line. We're expecting to get instructions any moment."

"Sorry to bother you," I said. "We're all very anxious." I hung up, feeling embarrassed at intruding on the Harrisons' anxiety, but also feeling that it wasn't an outrageous query.

Robin just shrugged when I relayed the conversation. "Worth a try," he said, and headed for his office. I had no idea if I could focus on a book, but the habit was so strong that I got a book from my TBR pile and opened it to the first page. The phone rang. I hoped Robin would pick up, but he seldom did when he was in his office, so I answered.

My classmate, Levon Suit, was on the other end of the line. "Levon," I said, my heart beating faster. "What's new?"

"I just wanted you to know that Josh Finstermeyer's car is not the car that killed Tammy," he said.

I hadn't known how worried I'd been about that until the

tension was relieved. "I'm really glad to know that," I said. "Thanks, Levon."

"It's not classified information," he said. "And I figured after wondering if the body in the alley would be your brother, and wondering if he would be in the trunk of the Josh's car, you deserved a little good news."

I thanked him again, probably not very coherently, and put my head in my hands. I stayed that way for a long time. My father came back, dropping the car keys on the counter and getting himself a drink. "Any news?" he asked.

"Yes. Josh's car wasn't the one that hit Tammy Ribble."

Dad's shoulders sagged with relief. "That's something," he said. "Roe, do you think there's any way at all that the kids could have decided to . . . just run to Mexico? Teens are impulsive."

I hadn't been. But then, he hadn't been around to know that. I told myself to let it go. "If it wasn't for Liza, I'd have to consider that a possibility . . . if I didn't know any of them," I said carefully. "But I do know all three of them, if not very well, and I don't think that would ever cross their minds. And Liza's presence would prevent it, anyway."

"Phillip might've gotten a wild hair," Dad said. He shrugged.

Phillip could be reckless. But not with someone else's life. Time dragged on, every hour seeming twice the normal length. People called to show concern. Robin worked, or at least he stayed in his office. Dad paced and watched television, and asked me a dozen questions I couldn't answer.

I couldn't have told you what we had for supper, but Robin did the dishes and cleaned everything away.

Dad retired to his room early, which was a relief. I read the same chapter over and over. Finally I put my book down. Robin was sitting opposite me, with a book in his hand.

I couldn't stand sitting in the house any longer. I felt the urge to do something, anything, to feel like I was helping to find

Phillip. "Let's go stake out the Harrison place," I suggested. "If they didn't pay the ransom last night . . . and there's been no news that Clayton's been found . . . let's see if they pay any ransom tonight."

My husband looked at me like I was crazy. "How do you know it'll be at night? And are you sure she was telling us the truth?"

"I'm not. But let's say we believe her. And paying ransom at night makes sense to me. What else have we got to do?"

"I don't know about your schedule, but I have to finish working on the editorial changes for *Cricket Courts Death*," he said righteously. But then he smiled. "Sure. Let's go spy."

It wouldn't have been unpleasant if it hadn't been so cold. We bundled up and took lap robes. The Harrison place was halfway up the steep (and only) hill which comprised Fox Creek Hills subdivision. I couldn't see the house very well, but it was obvious someone was home. Most of the lights were on, including the one at the grand front entrance, and once I saw Dan Harrison moving across a window. The garage was at the back of the house, so we didn't know if all the Harrisons' cars were in place. After thirty minutes, I realized my plan was ridiculous. But it was comfortable enough, with a thermos of hot chocolate, to sit together. And we weren't moping at home.

We were parked above the house, facing downhill, so we could see whatever happened. We'd pulled in behind a pickup parked in front of the next house up, trying to blend in with the scene. Of course, in Fox Creek Hills, it wasn't a battered old truck, but a Raptor.

Robin was telling me about a plot issue in *Cricket Courts Death* when the car swept up the sloping driveway from the back of the house. I thought it was Karina's Mercedes, but I might be wrong. It was black, and gleamed in the streetlights.

"I don't believe it," Robin said. "You called it." He started the car and we followed the Mercedes down the hill and through the quiet streets. Lawrenceton does roll up the sidewalks pretty early; that aspect of being a small town still sticks. I felt we might be conspicuous. But the driver of the Mercedes, and from the glimpses we caught of his head I was pretty sure it was Dan Harrison, didn't seem to take fright. He drove slowly and steadily to the center of town.

"Is he going to drop it off?" I said, unable to be quiet any longer. This was big drama for a librarian. Robin seemed to be pretty excited, too. We were now in an area of small businesses, each with its own parking lot.

"We'll see in just a minute," he muttered, and turned left when the Mercedes went straight.

"What are you doing?" I was trying not to sound like I thought he was crazy. I spilled hot chocolate (by this point, it was lukewarm chocolate) all over my lap.

"I just think if we keep on right behind him, he'll have to notice, especially considering what he's out here to do," Robin said. Since I thought this was a very bad policy and we might lose him, I had to clamp my mouth shut before I said something I'd regret.

And it turned out Robin was right. We turned right and went up two blocks, and then we turned left to intersect the road we'd been on. To my relief, the Mercedes was pulling into a parking lot in front of a tire store. The adjacent businesses included a Dairy Queen, a pancake house (which immediately made me feel hungry), and a nail salon. None of them were open.

We had to drive by. No way we could stop. I said some unladylike things.

"I think if we go to the next street, where the businesses back up to these, we'll be able to see what's going on," Robin said. At least most of these places were well lit.

Again, my husband was right, which both pleased and aggravated me. We drove into the parking lot of a Krystal, and its drive-through backed up to the rear parking lot of the pancake house, though there was a low concrete barrier between the two. We were able to park in a shadowy area in one corner of the lot, right beside the large trash receptacle. We could see the Mercedes moving through the parking lot opposite, at first only in a slice between the tire store and the pancake house. In a moment, the car emerged from the paved area between the stores, then turned behind the tire store. Leaving the Mercedes idling, he got out of the car, and looked around. Robin and I ducked down for a minute.

Then we sat up enough to see, and what we saw was something curious. Dan Harrison opened the rear door, reached inside, and pulled out a duffel bag. Then he carried it over to large heating and cooling unit installed close to the rear wall of the store, and he dropped the bag behind it. With another look around, he climbed back in the Mercedes.

And he left.

"Huh," I said. "Okay. Let's see what happens."

"Hmmm," Robin said. We sat in silence for a long moment, which turned out to be a good thing, because here came the Mercedes again, and down we ducked, which was a lot harder for Robin than it was for me.

Dan's headlights swept over the car and vanished. We stayed down this time, but after five long minutes he hadn't returned.

"That was totally unexpected. So was that a real ransom drop?" I asked Robin. "Why'd he come back? Did he suspect we were watching?"

"Maybe he noticed our car and thought he'd catch whoever was in it while they were picking up the money," Robin said. "And when the car hadn't moved, he figured it was empty. If you look around this area, what do you notice besides the silence?"

I looked around, and then I looked up. "I don't see any security cameras," I said.

"Exactly," Robin said. "So this place was well chosen by the kidnapper."

I yawned, jaw-crackingly. "We might have a long wait for the money to be retrieved."

"I think we should go home," Robin said. "I don't have a good feeling about this. We're sure the ransom was delivered. If we stay, we might spook the kidnappers. That would be awful. Maybe now Clayton will be released tomorrow, and the other kids with him. Let's retrace his steps before we go." We drove around the block, turning in to the parking lot of the next store. Parking in a shadow, he got out the binoculars, which we'd brought but never used. He adjusted them for a long moment. I realized he could see in the little space between the heating and cooling unit and the store wall.

When he lowered the binoculars, I couldn't read his expression.

"What's up?" I said. In an eyeblink, I was terrified we'd somehow ruined everything in our attempt to verify the Harrisons' story.

But Robin shook his head. After a moment, he said, "It's not there."

"What? The bag?" I gaped at him.

"Yes. It's not there."

Chapter Ten

The landline rang in the morning just after I'd finished talking to my boss at the library, on my cell phone. Sam had been more compassionate than he usually was (not at all). He'd told me he'd call in one of the substitutes until I felt I could come back to work.

"I'm so glad you hired Lizanne," I remembered to say.

"Yes," he said, with immense relief. "She seemed like she could handle the job."

"She handled all the irate customers at the utility company. She should be able to handle this job with one hand tied behind her back." (And Liz was calm and beautiful. That never hurt.)

"She'll be full-time right after Christmas," Sam said happily.

I was glad to talk to someone who was pleased with the way things were going. Frankly, it was reassuring to know the library was running along as usual, waiting for me to come back and do my work there. That was something I understood. I didn't understand what had happened last night. Someone had grabbed the bag, quick as a wink, or it had vanished into another dimension. Would we hear about Clayton's release today? The suspense was exhausting.

My father got up late. I had some cinnamon rolls on the table—just Pillsbury. I wasn't up to baking from scratch. He was glad to eat two.

"I have to go to the store," I said, to change the subject. "Do you need anything in the way of groceries? A favorite cereal or something?"

"Anything you get is fine," he said, more graciously than I'd expected. He must have done a little reflection, alone in the guest room. "Last night I realized that I haven't said anything since I got here. But thanks for keeping Phillip these past few weeks, and helping with the school transfer, and buying him clothes, and everything else."

There had been quite a lot else, but I had been glad to do it.

"Okay," I said. Frankly, I was surprised that Dad had thought of thanking me. "By the way, Robin's at work, so please don't go back there." I nodded toward the hall that led to the back of the house and Robin's office.

"I don't know how he can do it," Dad said. I didn't know if he meant actually write a book or work while things were so fraught.

"He's on deadline. And work is his escape. There's nothing else for him to do, really." I got my keys off the counter where Dad had left them, bundled up, and went to the grocery. I passed up Piggly Wiggly in favor of the new Walmart superstore, not because I liked it better—I didn't—but I thought I would see fewer people I knew.

Not so.

Since it was the Christmas season, the store was packed with shoppers buying all sorts of last-minute items. Since all the kids were out of school, most of them were there with their mothers, full of excitement and therefore acting out. Or crying. There was a lot of crying. Especially from the little ones in the shopping carts.

I maneuvered my own cart with grim resolution. Despite the

generosity of the cooks of Lawrenceton, I had to pick up basic supplies. I needed toilet paper and paper towels, dishwasher detergent, Bounce sheets. I turned in to the appropriate aisle and came face-to-face with Connie Bell's mother, Katy.

Katy Bell looked like walking death.

After she tossed a package of facial tissues into the cart, she looked up and her eyes met mine. She turned white as a sheet. I thought she was going to faint. This was a very extreme reaction.

"How are you, Aurora?" she said, when she could manage to speak. Miraculously, we were the only people in this aisle at the moment. I stopped right beside her.

"Not good. You don't look so well, either."

"Well, it's been . . ." Her eyes couldn't meet mine. Her voice trailed off, and she started to push her cart by mine.

"Katy, was Connie with Clayton the afternoon he vanished? Did she see the other kids right before they went missing?" I felt cruel, but I had to ask.

Her face hardened. "No," she said. "Absolutely not. Clayton dropped Connie off at our house right after school. And she *never heard from him again*. She's been really upset because she hasn't heard from him." I could tell this was her bottom line, and she would not budge.

I couldn't tackle her and bring her down to the floor. I couldn't put her in a hard chair and shine a light in her face. But this woman knew something, and it was eating away at her. In one of the most frustrating moments of my life, I had to let Katy Bell walk away, because I was a civilized woman. I regretted that. To her back, I said, "I know you're going to be sorry you didn't tell someone what she saw. Please tell me what you know." For a second, she hesitated. I felt a surge of hope. But then Katy's back stiffened, and she was gone. I watched her until she turned a corner and was out of sight.

I didn't think Katy's behavior was simply that of a mother defending her daughter. I saw it as a clear admission of guilt. But what kind? Survivor guilt? *Your brother was abducted, but my child wasn't?*

I didn't even entertain the idea that the Bells had taken my brother. But Connie Bell knew something, something crucial. In the middle of the busy store, I stood stock-still, my hands on the push bar of my cart, and *thought.* A harassed mother with two toddlers was kind enough to ask me if I was all right, and I produced a smile and began moving forward. But I wasn't seeing the goods on the shelves, or the holiday decorations, or the crowd around me. I was trying to break down the events of the past few days. There were so many component parts.

I must have paid for my groceries and wheeled them to my car, because the next thing I knew, I was sitting in the driver's seat, and the car was running. But I didn't pull out of the parking slot.

There was so much I didn't know. But I did know a list of facts: Liza Scott had been bullied. Three older girls were hounding her at school. She was miserable. One of her tormentors was the little sister of Clayton Harrison.

Liza had a crush on Phillip.

Phillip was a nice kid who would not take advantage of her feelings.

Dan Harrison had dropped off ransom money the night before. And then, apparently, he'd picked it up again. Or had we missed something crucial while we were ducked down in the front seat?

My phone rang. I didn't recognize the number, but I answered it.

"Mrs. Crusoe? Hi, it's Sarah. Sarah Washington?"

The girl who'd come to the house and been so kind. The girl Phillip liked.

"It's Roe Teagarden," I said. "I kept my last name. What can I do for you, Sarah?"

"I just wanted you to know, today I told the police I'd seen

Clayton's car," she said. "They wrote that down, but I don't know if they really believed me. If I'd been able to give them something really definite, maybe . . ."

"Joss mentioned him when she was talking to Jessamyn, too," I reassured Sarah. "So it's not just you, bringing up the subject of Clayton." Though Jessamyn had probably not told the police, since Karina had pled to keep Clayton's predicament a secret. "Have you seen Connie Bell since all this happened?"

"Ms. Aurora, Connie and I aren't friends. She's always with Clayton. They're joined at the hip. It's weird, she made a point of saying on Twitter that she hadn't been with Clayton that afternoon."

I could see Katy Bell's hand at work.

"And all Marlea's posts have been taken down." Sarah said. "That's a relief."

So Karina had followed through. "Thanks, Sarah."

"You're welcome. Call me if you need anything. Or, you know, if you hear anything about Phillip. I'm going to Tammy's visitation tonight."

I'd seen that in the paper, but I'd almost forgotten, I thought as I hung up. I should go.

So Connie was very publicly denying she'd been with Clayton. However, she was staying in seclusion, and her mother looked like hell warmed over. The police might not even have talked to Connie. After all, they didn't officially know that Clayton was missing. And that was wrong.

"I just don't believe her," I said. Out loud.

There were too many questions. I had no answers.

Was it remotely possible that *all* these kids were in on some scheme?

I couldn't imagine that, either. (But then, I didn't want to.)

I drove to the hair salon again and parked at the rear. The whole strip of shops backed onto it. Each area behind a shop had parking spaces, garbage bins, wooden pallets. Employee cars.

Large trash bins. Piles of cardboard boxes broken down for recycling. The usual things that might be behind any business. Nothing spoke to me. I got no psychic emanations. I felt no enlightenment, no "eureka" moment. To my left was the back of an apartment building. Parking must be provided in the front, because there wasn't enough space back here. There was a wooden fence, and beyond it I could see a toolshed (for the super, presumably) and trash bins there, too. I was sure the police had thoroughly searched them, and I wasn't about to duplicate effort. I was equally sure the apartment renters had been questioned. But at four thirty in the afternoon most of them would not have been at home when the event took place. Whatever it had been.

I found myself reluctant to leave the last place Phillip had been; but I had groceries to unload and people to feed. There was no point whatsoever in breaking down. I had to believe that soon this mystery would be solved and my brother returned. I couldn't do otherwise. I put the car back into drive and went home.

Robin had finished working by the time I got there, and he helped me with the bags. My father was not there, to my relief. I realized that if Dad hadn't had been poormouthing since he landed, I would have suggested that he go to a motel. Though Dad had told me he had a decent job selling advertising for a real-estate magazine in California, he didn't look prosperous. And he was constantly fidgeting. Since his son had vanished, I could excuse that; but the fact of the matter was, he made me more anxious than I could stand.

Robin and I put away the food and paper supplies in a companionable silence. "How did your work go today?" I asked. I'd left out the ground beef to make hamburgers. Robin chopped some bell pepper and onion to fold into the meat.

"Not bad," he said, in a subdued voice.

"What's up?" I didn't sound very happy. Robin had something unpleasant to tell me. We'd been married just long enough for me to recognize subtext. He paused, holding the knife in his hands. I enjoyed looking at him. The beaky nose, the crinkly mouth . . . I loved him. But at the moment, my love object was having difficulty phrasing what he wanted to tell me, and from a man who lived with words every day, that wasn't a good sign.

"I'd rather talk about anything else, too," he said. "But I was thinking today . . . what if none of this is linked?"

"What do you mean?" This might be a long discussion, so I pulled the kitchen stool out from under its place at the counter and sat.

"At first, I thought this had something to do with the girls bullying Aubrey's daughter," he said. "By the way, I hope a lawyer finds a way to prosecute them. I came in for more than my share of mockery when I was a kid. I was imaginative, and I was smart, and I read all the time, and I had a big nose and a weird name. The other kids made sure I realized how different I was."

"I didn't know that." It made me angry. "But you had the last laugh," I said. "You're a best-selling writer. That's a great achievement. Plus, you have the Hollywood fairy dust thrown on you." A movie had been made about a series of killings here in Lawrenceton, based on Robin's nonfiction book. I hadn't liked the end product, but Robin's sales had soared and remained even higher than before.

"I wish I had known that was in my future at the time," Robin said, with a rueful smile. "It was really awful. Bullying is recognized as evil, now, but it wasn't then. My parents were at a loss as to how to handle it. Mom was afraid if she went to the school to complain, the kids would say I was hiding behind my mama, and it would get even worse. My father wanted to beat up everyone involved. While I appreciated the sentiment, that wouldn't have done me any good in the long run."

"So your parents did nothing?" I tried not to sound judgmental, but I fear I failed.

"They called the parents of the kids who were the worst."

"Did it help?"

"In two cases, yes. In two cases, it became worse."

"What happened?"

"Time happened. Also, my dad suggested instead of hiding behind a book, I try out for a sport. I liked to read a lot better, but I could see it might help. And thank God, I was okay at basketball."

"Really? You played basketball?"

"Yep. In junior high and high school."

"Did that make the bullying go away?"

"Actually, it did help. It never really stopped. But it kind of morphed into heavy-handed locker room teasing. I could handle that."

"I'm glad you told me," I said. "I'm really sorry that happened to you. I'm like your dad. I wish I could retroactively beat them up."

He looked down at me, and one of his wonderful smiles broke out. "I would have liked to see that. But I'm straying from the point."

"Which is?"

The doorbell rang. I said something unprintable.

Robin went to the door while I began forming the burgers. When Robin returned, he was accompanied by (of all people) Tiffany Andrews, mother of Sienna.

Tiffany was probably five years younger than I, and since she owned a dance studio and taught classes daily, she'd maintained a taut figure. Her face was a bit older than her body. I didn't think much of Tiffany, and I was sure she returned the sentiment, if she ever thought about me at all.

"Let me just turn on the griddle to preheat, Tiffany," I said. I washed my hands in the kitchen sink. "Please come sit down. Would you like some coffee or tea?"

She looked surprised. "No, thank you." With some hesitation, she took a seat in an armchair. Robin and I took the couch.

"I guess you're not teaching dance classes during the holidays," I said, utterly at loss. Why on earth had she come here?

"You should understand that I didn't want . . . that coming here is really hard for me," she said abruptly, as if the words had been ripped out of her throat.

"I don't understand at all," I said. I wasn't giving her a hard time. I meant it.

"Because of Liza," she said.

I made a "continue" gesture, trying not to look as impatient as I was feeling. Robin took my hand and squeezed it gently. He was telling me to calm down. I took a deep breath, let it out. "You want to talk about the situation between your daughter and Liza? The persecution?"

The word struck her like a slap. But she owned up to it. "Yes," she said.

"And why are you telling me this? Shouldn't you go to Aubrey and Emily?"

"I know you and Father Scott were . . . good friends," Tiffany said. I tried not to look indignant at her bringing up ancient history. "And you go to his church. You'll tell him what I say. I don't think I could face them now."

That did her credit, but I realized it would sound patronizing to say so. "I understand," I said.

"I want Aubrey and Emily to know that I've reviewed everything Sienna has done, for the first time. I've read her posts on Facebook and Twitter. I've seen the pictures. I know how far it went, way too far, without any interference from me. I know my daughter was very wrong to be so mean to Liza," Tiffany said. Her back was stiff and her face, too. She was doing her best not to cry. "I can only say I didn't know it was so . . . extreme."

I nodded, since I couldn't think of anything to say. I pitied Tiffany Andrews, which was something I'd never imagined I'd do.

"Sienna isn't a bad girl," her mother said.

All evidence to the contrary. But of course I didn't say that out loud. The woman was trying to do the right thing. Tiffany fell silent for such a long time that I was trying to think of how to prompt her. For one thing, I had to finish the supper preparations; but most importantly, this was excruciating to listen to.

"I guess that's all," Tiffany said. She met my eyes squarely. "Please tell them what I said."

Profound relief that this conversation was over. "What are you going to do about Sienna?" I asked, before I could stop myself. Sienna's punishment wasn't really my business. "I'm sorry, scratch that." I mimicked erasing a blackboard with my hand.

"No Facebook. No computer. No cell phone," she said. "And if she ever sees Liza again, she has to apologize to Liza's face."

Wouldn't that make Sienna even angrier at Liza? If a child was insensitive enough to torment another one, would she ever understand the damage she had done? But I'd never raised a child, and I figured Tiffany was doing the best she could. And a lot more than I'd ever expected.

"I'll tell them," I said. "And thank you for coming."

Tiffany, looking vastly relieved, stood to depart. "I hope you get your brother back," she said, as an afterthought.

"Me, too," I said. Exhausted, I heaved myself to my feet and walked her to the door.

I waved as I watched her back out of my driveway, and I pondered anew the fact that people can act directly contrary to your knowledge of their nature. Before I could chicken out, I called the Scotts. To my relief, Aubrey answered. As thoroughly as I could, I related what Tiffany Andrews had told me: her contrition, and her determination that Sienna would not do such a thing again.

Like me, Aubrey was surprised. But he seemed to take heart that Tiffany was stepping up to take responsibility for not stopping Sienna's cruelty sooner. "I didn't expect that," he said. "I'm really glad about it. And I'll tell Emily. Thanks, Roe, for receiving her apology. That must have been really uncomfortable."

Yep.

While I was still standing at the window, my phone in my hand, my father returned in Robin's car. My heart fell with a thud. I was ashamed that my father made me so unhappy, but it was a fact.

He didn't soften that resolve any by his nonstop bitching during lunch.

"I don't think the cops are doing *anything,*" he said, loading pickles onto his bun. "They're eating doughnuts at Krispy Kreme instead of looking for my son, and they won't tell me what they're planning to do."

I knew a lot of the men and women of our local law enforcement contingent, both city and county, and most of them were hardworking and sincere. But I didn't bother to interrupt the rant. He wouldn't listen. I laid my napkin by my plate, my appetite having fled.

Robin interrupted him. "Phil, I understand that you're upset about Phillip, and that you want to blame someone. But your attitude isn't helping us cope, and we'd rather not listen to this."

I had to stop myself from clapping.

Of course, Dad got offended. "Phillip's my son," he said angrily. "And he's missing! I'm scared he's dead! Can't I vent to my own family?"

"Aurora is scared of those things, too," my husband said.

And Dad said, "Are you feeling guilty, Aurora? Because you didn't watch your brother close enough?"

There fell a dreadful silence, while my brain tried to make my father have said *anything* but what he'd said.

"You can have the gall to say that to me? After you made him so upset he hitchhiked across America to find a place to stay rather than remain with you?" I was literally shaking with rage. "You can spend the night here, but in the morning you're gone.

I don't care where you stay or how you get around. I am done with you."

Dad rose from the table and stalked back to the guest bedroom, slamming the door behind him.

I had never been so angry. I had foreseen putting up with him until this situation was resolved, despite everything. Now I didn't have to.

"Roe?" Robin said anxiously. "Honey? How are you?"

"I can't believe I said that," I told him. I was stunned at my own words. "You wouldn't believe how good it feels. But I can't stop shaking, now."

He smiled with relief. "You'll relax in a minute. That's my girl. Go get 'em."

"If you had asked me if I would ever talk to either of my parents like that, I would have called you a numbskull."

"You were justified."

"I'm trying to stop a backlash of guilt," I confessed.

"No guilt necessary," he assured me, with a smile. "Now, can you please finish your dinner?"

The food tasted better now that my father was not at the table.

Later that afternoon, I told Robin I had to go to Tammy's visitation at the funeral home. He quickly volunteered to plan supper and do all the dishes if he could skip going. I thought he was getting the better part of the deal, but I agreed.

I was right.

And though we waited that night, we never heard anything about Clayton Harrison coming home.

Chapter Eleven

At some point during the night, after I got back from the visitation, someone left an anonymous letter under the windshield wiper of my car. Getting an anonymous letter is not a pleasant experience.

My father was gone when Robin and I got up the next morning. Apparently, he'd called a cab and crept out of the house in the early hours of the morning, and that meant he'd left the front door unlocked. At least our nameless visitor had not tried the door handle and visited us in our sleep.

Robin was holding the letter between his thumb and forefinger as though it were a dead mouse when he came back in the house with the newspaper. He'd gone out to move his car into the carport because it was supposed to rain, and also to make sure my father had left it in good order.

"Look," Robin said. He laid the piece of paper on the kitchen counter. I was still in my fuzzy bathrobe, trying to keep down a piece of toast and some cranberry juice.

I leaned over the sheet of white computer paper. It had crinkled in the damp air and felt moist to the touch. But the typed words were still legible.

They are still alive. Find them.

My first reaction was profane. "Why the hell didn't this person just tell us where they are?" I said. "This is useless!"

"I guess we'd better call the police," Robin said glumly, and soon he was talking to Detective Trumble. She came over right away; she didn't blink at me being still in my robe and nightgown. She'd brought a plastic sleeve for the paper, which she gently waved in the air with tongs so it would be dry when she inserted it.

"Interesting," she said. "Either a really nasty person is jerking you around, or someone connected to the disappearance has a big sense of guilt and responsibility."

"I wish that sense had been a little more helpful and specific," I said.

"Me, too." She looked at the message as if she hoped to find invisible writing below the typeface.

"Maybe whoever wrote it will crack under the strain and confess," Robin said. He was determined to be upbeat.

"That would be wonderful." I sighed. "But I'm not going to count on it."

"You'd tell me, wouldn't you?" the detective said. "If you had a good idea who had put this on your car?"

"I sure wasn't looking out my window," I said. Though I did have a suspicion. But that wasn't solid enough to tell Cathy Trumble.

"Aurora, when did your dad come into town?" Cathy Trumble asked casually.

It felt like forever ago. "Ah . . . three days ago?" I said.

"Is he still here? I mean, in your house?"

"No. We had some words last night, after which I told him to leave. Why?"

"Did you know that he's in trouble in California?" Trumble said.

Stunned, Robin and I gave each other a wide-eyed look. He

shook his head, and I shook mine. Neither of us had heard that. "No," I said. "Please tell me about this."

"He lost his job last month," the detective said. "His employer said it's because he's been gambling. He was getting threatening phone calls at work, and neglecting his duties."

"He never did that before," I said, startled, but then I paused. What did I really know about my father's life? I knew my mother had suffered from his infidelities; had he also had a gambling problem when he lived in Lawrenceton? "At least that I know of," I added, with much less assurance.

"Gambling where?" Robin asked.

"Illegal games," Detective Trumble said. She looked matter-of-fact. I realized she often had to tell people unpleasant truths. It was not a job I wanted, so I respected her for undertaking it.

"So. . . ." I waited for the rest of her facts. I knew there was more, or she wouldn't have brought it up.

"So he owes a lot of money," Trumble said. "He needs cash badly, or he's going to be hip-deep in the worst kind of trouble."

I said, "Wow." That was a lot of unpleasantness to absorb. "Like, knee-breaking and stuff?"

Trumble shrugged. "The people he's lost to, they don't like nonpayment of debts."

"That really happens?" Robin said, giving in to professional curiosity.

"Yep. It's not just in the movies." From the expression on her face, she would have liked to have told us something different.

"Are you thinking that Phillip could have been snatched to force Dad to pay up?" I was startled by this new scenario, and not a little skeptical.

"We have to consider it," she said. "On the other hand, what loan shark would abduct a whole bunch of other kids? That just doesn't make sense."

From the concentration on his face, I knew that Robin was trying to construct a plot in which Phillip's being taken would be feasible. I wanted so badly to tell Cathy Trumble about the missing Clayton and his ransom that it made me almost sick, but when I remembered Karina Harrison's plea, I just couldn't do it, not without warning her. But I was teetering on the edge. I glanced at Robin, but he was still absorbed in his thoughts.

"So there are possible scenarios that would account for one or the other of the kids being taken, but not one that would account for all of them," I said. "This is just crazy."

Trumble nodded. "It is. But we're working on it. Had you ever considered that Phillip might have left you voluntarily?"

"No, of course not. Why would he?"

"He left his parents' house without telling them where he was going," she reminded me. "Why wouldn't he do that again?"

This was not the first time Phillip's adventure had led someone down the wrong path. "But he had a *reason* to leave," I said. "There were big problems in that household, and a lot of marital discord." That was the nicest way I could think of to put it.

"He's been happy here?" Trumble said. She sounded skeptical, but I thought it was a reflex.

"He was," Robin said, unexpectedly. "He likes being in a calm household. He likes making new friends. He likes being away from the drama."

"Did he tell you anything about his father's problems?" the detective asked.

"Not in any detail," Robin said, to my surprise. He caught my look.

"Sorry, Roe, Phillip asked me not to tell you this because he knew it would upset you," Robin said. He looked a little guilty.

"Well, he was right. I'm upset."

"He knew you already didn't think much of your father, and he knew his mother hadn't acted very reliable."

"You mean when she vanished?" Trumble leaned forward. If she'd been a dog, I would have said she was on point.

"Phillip caught my father cheating on Phillip's mother," I said. "Phillip got so freaked out by the resultant quarrel, he felt he had to leave. He got here, and I called Betty Jo and Dad to tell them where he was. Betty Jo was so angry that a few days later she left my dad for another man . . . unless he was lying about that too, lest I get *upset.* Do you know anything about that that I don't know, Robin?"

Robin looked at me unhappily, but he didn't say anything besides, "No."

We would discuss this later. For sure.

"Have you talked to Betty Jo?" Trumble asked.

"Not since I called them to tell them Phillip was here," I said. "Before Thanksgiving."

"Her son is living with you. Wouldn't you expect to hear from his mother, from time to time?"

"I didn't think anything about it until now," I said honestly. "I figured Betty Jo just couldn't take any more of my dad, and I don't blame her for that. I thought maybe she was so depressed or upset that she needed some alone time. And if she's got a new man friend, maybe she'd be preoccupied with him. It's not like Phillip was a baby, right? And she knew he was safe with me." Which was kind of ironic, now.

"And she hasn't called your brother, since? Her only child?"

When you put it like that. . . . "Okay, so that does seem unusual," I said. "At least, she hasn't called him that I know of. But Phillip didn't tell me everything."

"Did your father ever tell you the name of the man, or where they were living?"

"Well . . . no." For the first time, I wondered if my father had been telling the truth. Suddenly, Betty Jo leaving with another man didn't seem likely.

"All right," Trumble said. "We'll talk to him. We'll see."

I wasn't sure what that meant.

But next, I did something morally ambiguous. I'd been sitting on the news of Clayton's supposed abduction ever since his mother had told me about it. I'd made up my mind I wouldn't tell. And I'd already resisted temptation to tell the detective. But I'd reached the end of my rope. My brother's life might depend on it. I gave Trumble a big clue. "You really need to go talk to Clayton's girlfriend, Connie Bell." I'd been thinking about Katy Bell's face when she'd seen me in Walmart. She didn't think we were all in this terrible situation together. She knew something, and that something could only have come from Connie.

I believed Connie Bell had left the note on my car. I did not think she'd come home right after school was out. I believed she'd stayed in the car with Clayton. I was sure she knew exactly what had happened that afternoon.

"Why?" Trumble said. She looked at me quizzically. "What does Connie Bell have to do with the situation?"

I glanced at Robin, but I couldn't tell if his face was disapproving or not. Suddenly, it seemed clear to me that I should have spoken up earlier, that I should not have kept the secret, no matter what Karina Harrison had said. It was not only Clayton who was at risk. The more I considered it, the fishier it was that only Clayton had been held for ransom. Why not Phillip? My father might be beset by loan sharks or whatever, but I had a substantial amount of money I'd inherited, and Robin had a substantial amount that he had earned. The Finstermeyers weren't hurting, either, and they had two children to ransom. Aubrey and Emily were on a tight budget, I was sure, but it was reasonable to suppose they would mortgage their house to redeem their daughter.

I gave her a direct look. "Didn't Sarah Washington tell you she thought she saw Clayton's car? Didn't Jessamyn tell you Joss mentioned Clayton in their phone conversation? And where you see Clayton, you see Connie. Have you actually talked to Clayton? Face to face?"

"All right, I'll play along about Connie," Trumble said,

getting up. Robin and I rose, too. "I'll go by her house. And I'll ask to talk to Clayton. Though the older Harrisons, the grandparents, are usually gone at Christmas. Colorado, I think. And Karina and her husband often go with them. So the boy may be there."

"Karina says her daughter is in Savannah with her other grandmother," I said.

Trumble looked at me with narrowed eyes. "Meaning?"

"Just saying," I said.

When Trumble had left, there was a long silence. I wasn't going to defend myself to Robin. I felt both justified and guilty. "I might as well have gone ahead and out-and-out told her I thought Connie knew what had happened. Rather than beat around the bush like that. It's dumb to cling to the illusion that I haven't spilled the ransom beans." I felt unhappy. Trying to have things both ways almost never worked out.

"I'm not going to say you were wrong," Robin said. "You did what you had to do. It's not just Clayton's safety that's at stake, not just his parents who are desperate for an answer." He hugged me. "No good choices, here. I wondered if you might not call the police the minute Clayton's mom told you they'd had a ransom demand. I thought about doing it so you wouldn't have to."

I sagged against him. "Thanks, Robin." It would have been devastating if he'd condemned me. And I didn't think I could take much more devastation. "In retrospect," I said, "it seems amazing that I didn't question Betty Jo's absence earlier. Did she really run away with another man? Did loan sharks take her to make my dad pay up? I just didn't ask enough questions. Of course, I didn't know that you knew some of this already."

"I'm sorry, honey," Robin said, his voice muffled in my hair. "Phillip was so worried about what you would think. He knows how angry you are at your father. But Phillip still loves his dad. So I kept his secret."

My irritation collapsed in the face of his reasons, and in the overwhelming issue of more important things. "None of this makes sense," I said. "None of it."

"We must be looking at it wrong."

"I just can't think of any fresh or new way to look at it." It made me feel helpless and stupid.

"Here, let's just sit." Robin and I sat on the couch, and he put his arm around me, and I savored the peace of the moment. But my mind would not let me simply enjoy it. Instead, my thoughts ran around like a hamster on a wheel, and the repetition was surely just as boring.

All those kids missing. Phillip, Joss, Josh, Liza, Clayton. Only a ransom demand for Clayton. The dead Tammy . . . whose funeral was today. We would have to go, though I hated the idea of all those eyes on me, picking at how I looked, guessing how I felt.

Running a far second behind was the revelation that my father was actually a worse man than I'd thought. I'd been giving him some slack. Lots of men were unfaithful, and though that was despicable, it was also fairly common. I could give him a grudging pass on that, since it really wasn't any of my business, now that he wasn't married to my mother.

Or was it? Didn't that effect the whole family?

It had certainly impacted Phillip.

For the first time, I wondered what my life would have been like if my father had not cheated on my mother. Aida Brattle Teagarden Queensland was not going to put up with that for one minute, and she'd divorced my dad as quickly as the lawyer could file. If my dad hadn't foreseen that, he didn't know her at all. My mother had brought me up by herself. Her own mother had been living, then; I remembered my grandmother Brattle vividly. My father's parents had been dead before he married my mother. Or at least, that was what he'd said. For the first time ever, I wondered if that had been the case.

"Wait a minute," I muttered out loud. "I don't want to make this more than it is."

"Mmmmm?" Robin sounded abstracted.

I explained my thought train.

Robin said, "You think his whole life might be a lie? That would be on a grand scale."

"It does seem unlikely. But if you'd asked me a few days ago, all of this would have seemed unlikely, in the extreme."

"True," he said. He scooted down in his seat a little, his arm still around me, and he closed his eyes. I closed mine, too, but I couldn't relax quite enough to take a little nap. Instead, I had a waking dream, the kind where your thoughts pinwheel away and come up with strange situations. I was running on a treadmill that wouldn't slow down. (That was easy to interpret.) I was searching for something in my bedroom, under the bed, up on a shelf in the closet . . . well, that one was not so difficult either.

We sat with each other for half an hour, which was refreshing. What if I had married a man like my father? I was lucky to be with Robin and lucky to be carrying his baby. And I told him so.

"I think we both got very lucky," he said, with a smile. "And some day this will be over, and we can enjoy our lives again."

Chapter Twelve

Funerals. I've been to more than my share, I feel. But nothing is as sad as the funeral of a young person who had a whole life yet to live. Since I'd been to the visitation at the funeral home the night before, I tried to persuade myself we didn't need to go to the funeral. But I couldn't quite make myself believe that.

At the funeral home the night before, I'd paused to look at the picture of Tammy set up by her closed coffin. Tammy had been blond, athletic, a star student; her hair was still long in the picture. She hadn't even had a chance to have her picture taken with her new short haircut. She'd had two brothers, both younger, who looked so lost and out of place at a funeral home that my heart ached.

The Finstermeyers, too, were there, looking just as bad as I was sure I did. But Beth told me, "If Joss loved Tammy, I have to represent her at this."

I admired her very much for looking at the situation that way, and I admired the way she hugged Tammy's mother. Both of them cried, and the dads shook hands in an awkward but sincere expression of commiseration. Joss was missing temporarily, we all hoped. Tammy was missing forever.

The funeral wouldn't be any better. After Trumble's visit to collect the anonymous letter, I had a hard time climbing into my funeral clothes. The promise of rain had been fulfilled. The blustering wet wind made it feel very cold, at least for Georgia; the temperature dipped into the low thirties.

To cap off the morning, the phone rang as we were going out the door. Robin answered, and he looked stricken after a moment. He covered the mouthpiece. "I have a phone conference I'd completely forgotten about. It's with Louise and Gerald." His American agent and his UK agent. I tried not to look tragic as I waved good-bye. I believed he'd really forgotten. He'd put on a suit for the funeral, which he would never have done if he'd planned on dodging it.

So I went by myself in a dark gray dress with a navy and yellow scarf at the neck. I just needed to see some color that day. I belted my lined black raincoat a little more loosely to accommodate my thickening waistline.

The funeral was at the First Presbyterian Church, which had been built in the thirties and added to ever since. It was a lovely old place, with a ceiling so high that the eye was led upward. The simple large wooden cross hanging behind the altar led me to think of what I should be contemplating: making my own soul right to meet with my maker. I had a lot to offer up as I waited for the service to start. I was seated toward the rear of the church, and I'd scooted into the middle of a pew to make room for people to pack in on either side.

I watched the people entering the church. The one I wanted to see most came down the middle aisle: Connie Bell. She was only seventeen but today she looked much older. Her mother was with her, and Katy looked even worse than Connie. She was carrying a burden, clearly, and I didn't think that burden was solely Clayton's abduction. I wondered if Trumble had visited Connie yesterday as she'd said she would. I wondered if she'd learned anything from the girl. Most of all, I wondered why

Connie was at this funeral when she was so obviously emotionally drained.

I was vaguely aware that someone had come in from my left.

"Roe," said a familiar voice, in the hushed tone people use in church. "Hey, how are you?"

"Perry," I said. "Good to see you." I leaned forward to peer over him. "Hi, Keith." Keith Winslow, a financial adviser, raised his hand in a tiny wave. Perry and Keith had been dating only a short time, but they seemed well suited. Perry had had emotional issues for a while, and I'd been a little scared of him, but his therapy had worked, and his admitting to himself that he was a gay man had been a huge breakthrough. "How's your mom, Perry?"

He shook his head. "I'm going to have to put her in a home. She's getting too erratic for me to take care of, she can't work any longer, and I never know what she'll take it in her head to do. I tried having a woman stay with her during the day, but Mama got out anyway. It's going to take someone with training to watch her."

"I'm so sorry. Sally and I were friends for a long time, and it makes me sick this has happened to her." To change the subject, I said, "I didn't know you knew Tammy?"

"She was part of the gay community," he said, with some dignity. "We try to support our own."

I wasn't quite sure how to respond, but I tried to look approving. I found I was curious about the process of discovery, though. When did people understand that about themselves? Was there always a huge conflict? Once Beth had learned Joss was gay, she had stiffened her back and adjusted to it, apparently. Of course, Joss was missing and all her emotional energy had to be invested in that loss. That absence.

"So you knew before her mom did? That Tammy and Joss were a couple?"

Perry said, "Sure."

Keith leaned over him to whisper, "Haven't you ever heard of gaydar?"

I smiled involuntarily. Apparently, this was a real thing.

That was the last time I smiled for the next hour, during the poignant funeral and graveside service. Tammy's little brothers were miserable, her mother and dad were tragic, and I hated whoever had made them look that way. I kept my eyes on Connie, and when she glanced back at me and saw me watching her, she flinched. Connie knew way more than she was telling, and it was so frustrating that she would not talk. She and her mother left the graveside very quickly after the funeral was over, and Connie was crying so hard she could scarcely walk.

My childhood friend Amina Day Price was waiting at my house when I returned. I was shocked to see her, delighted to see her. Amina lived in Texas with her husband Hugh, and their daughter Megan, now in her terrible twos. But today, Amina was alone.

"We're back in town for Christmas, and I had to come see your new house and your new husband," she said. Amina was magnetically attractive, so of course she'd always been popular in high school. I'd met Hugh, of course—I'd been Amina's bridesmaid—but I'd never had the chance to know him well. Hugh worked long hours at his law firm, I knew from my exchange of e-mails with Amina.

"Where's the husband and the baby?" I asked, taking off my coat and hanging it on one of the hooks on the coatrack in the entry. "For that matter, where's my own husband?" Amina was by herself in the living room.

"Robin got a phone call from his publisher about cover approval on the next book, and he had to take it," she said. "He's in his office. Just happened a minute ago."

I saw that Amina had a cup of coffee, so Robin had done his host duty.

"I just came from a funeral," I said. I hoped that would

explain any lack of enthusiasm in our unexpected reunion. I went to our coffee machine and made a cup for myself. The idea of something hot was irresistible.

"That's what he was telling me. In fact, he filled me in on the whole situation. Of course, my mom called me about your half brother. She knew I'd want to know."

I kind of wondered why Amina hadn't called me to tell me she was thinking of me; but after all, she'd known she was going to be back in Lawrenceton. "So how long are you staying?" I asked, forcing myself to look beyond my own problems.

"Well, through Christmas," she said. "Megan and I are staying my mother's."

Even I noticed the big narrative gap. "Ahhhhh . . . what about your husband? Is he joining you in a few days?"

"That's the bad part. We're trying a separation," she said, taking a big gulp of air.

"Oh my gosh! That's so sad! I'm really sorry." I tried to remember if Amina had ever hinted this might be in the offing, but I could not think of anything she'd said that might have prepared me. "This seems out of the blue," I said tentatively.

"I held on as long as I could, because I really do love him," she said, tears rolling down her cheeks. "But he just never felt he could cut back on his hours at the firm, and I could not stand being alone at home all the time." Amina had always been social and outgoing.

"You didn't make many friends in Houston?" I said. "I have a hard time believing that."

"I did make some," she admitted. "But we didn't all have babies at the same time . . . and the other wives of partners at the firm told me I had to suck it up, that him being gone was the price I had to pay for the good lifestyle."

"Gosh," I said, in a neutral voice. I had had the selfsame thoughts when Amina had commented on Hugh's long hours at the firm. Amina had dated Hugh for months before they'd gotten engaged, and I was sure she'd known the kind of hours Hugh would have to pull after they'd married.

"So I have playdates with other moms with kids, but I never get to do anything on my own any more. He's working all the time, and he never keeps Megan. I don't get a break!" Amina's voice was almost scarily passionate and angry.

"You all didn't talk about this ahead of time?" I said.

"No. More fool me! I thought he'd be different from the other go-getters at his firm." She shook her head. "I know he loves me. I know he loves the baby. But having an absent husband is almost like having no husband at all. He comes in after I've gone to sleep, he leaves while I'm still in my bathrobe, and he never shows up in between. As far as he's concerned, I might as well never get dressed."

"So what are you going to do?" This was the last thing I'd expected when I'd seen Amina's mom's car in the driveway. But I was her friend, and I had to rally.

"I'm going to stay with Mom for a while," Amina said. "We'll see how Hugh feels about living without us. I'll see how living without Hugh is for me. If he can think of a way to be a more present husband, I would be happy to work something out."

I remembered that she'd always really enjoyed spending money, had always lived right up to her slender income prior to her marriage, and had reveled in being a lawyer's wife. I'd heard a lot of that when I'd been her bridesmaid. But I bit the words back, because I was sure she really did love Hugh. If she wanted a change, she would have to be prepared to accept the downside of that change. Right?

Amina took another deep breath, and arranged her face in an expression of concern. "So how is the search for Phillip going? Any news?"

We talked about the missing kids for a while, and then my stomach lurched. "I have to eat something," I said, and luckily Robin got off the phone then and came into the living room looking happy. It must have been a good conversation. "Honey," I said, "can you get me some graham crackers?"

"Sure," he said, and in about thirty seconds, he'd brought me some on a little plate. If Amina hadn't been there, it would have been a paper towel.

I ate one in little bites, pushed the coffee away, and drank a glass of water instead. Amina watched all this with a quizzical look.

"Better?" Robin asked, after a minute or two.

I nodded gratefully.

"Roe, are you sick?" Amina asked.

"No, not exactly. Pregnant," I said. If circumstances had been different, I would have made a big deal out of telling her, and I would have expected fireworks and streamers and confetti, but that wasn't going to happen.

But I did not expect that Amina would look unhappy.

"Oh, and you've waited so long," she said. "Well, that's great!"

"Actually, you don't seem very happy," I said, because Robin had that written clearly on his face. Might as well take the bull by the horns.

She had the grace to look embarrassed. "I guess I thought it would be like high school," she said. "I'd tell you all my problems, you'd tell me how sorry you were and that it would all work out, and you'd remind me of the many guys who wanted to date me, and I would feel better. Get my ego back in shape."

"You're grown up now, Amina. So am I. I'm your friend, not your cheerleader." At least I'd thought so.

"I see that," Amina said. "I really do. And I'm very happy for you, Roe. If anyone deserves happiness, you do."

"Because?"

"Because in high school . . ." Then she shut her mouth to reconsider. "But that was long ago."

"I've been married and lost a husband since then. I'm hardly that person anymore," I said.

"I see that," she repeated. "I guess we have to build a new friendship, Roe. Now that I'm home, we'll have time to do that. If you want to."

"Sure," I said, wondering if I really meant that.

"Then I'll take my leave." She stood, and I heaved myself to my feet. "I'm so glad about the baby."

She took her departure a bit hastily.

"What the hell was all that about?" Robin said.

I shook my head. "I think Amina still had this image of me as a teenager, and she cast me as the unattractive friend who was there to provide support for the glamorous one who had all the advantages. Which would be her, of course."

"Weird and stupid," Robin said.

"Looking back, I dated enough," I said. "Not the captain of the football team, or the homecoming king. But smart guys I liked. I didn't sit at home every Saturday night, and I had friends. But I now know that my friendship with Amina was uneven, to say the least."

"To hell with high school," Robin said. "This is a lot better."

"You're absolutely right. To hell with high school. I wouldn't be a teenager again for any amount of money. And I'll tell you another thing. After keeping Phil and Phillip distinguished for years, we are not naming the baby either Robin or Aurora."

"Agreed." Robin sat down with me, and we talked about the funeral, and we talked about Robin's conversations with his agents and his publisher, and he told me how his work had gone today. We just talked.

It was very pleasant, and my dad's absence was a real pleasure, too. I called my mother to tell her that Dad wasn't in residence any longer, though I didn't go into the why of that, and she tactfully didn't ask.

Robin worked that afternoon, and I tried to catch up on the laundry. I also gave Moosie some lap time and stared at the television, not registering anything that was going on on the screen.

That evening, Connie Bell killed herself.

Perry called me at eight thirty to tell me. His friend Jinnie, an intake clerk, had been on duty when they'd brought Connie into the hospital. Apparently, she'd taken her mother's sleeping pills. Katy had found Connie in the girl's bedroom. I imagined it patterned on the rooms of my friends at that age: decorated with dried corsages and pictures of the boyfriend. Connie was unresponsive. Despite everything the doctors and nurses could do to keep the girl alive, she'd died without regaining consciousness. Jinnie, who loved to be the bearer of news more than she respected confidentiality, called Perry from the ladies' room.

I was profoundly depressed. Not only had Connie lost her own life, which was tragedy enough, but with her had died the only source of knowledge about what had happened that day in the alley. I was convinced Connie had been there. I was convinced she was the one who had left the note on my car. But that was just a conviction with no factual support.

Cathy Trumble came by that evening. She was in a grim mood. "I went by and questioned her after the funeral," she said. "And this is the result. She cracked."

"I don't know if you're saying this because you want me to feel guilty, or what," I said. "I also think if Connie'd been questioned even more, earlier in the investigation, she might have cracked and told you everything she knew. She'd still be alive, if she'd gotten rid of the knowledge that made her so hopeless."

"Are you trying to make *me* feel guilty?" Trumble looked angry.

"I'm saying she was the guilty one," I said. "The pressure was too much for her. And since keeping secrets didn't work for her, I'm going to tell you one. The Harrisons had a ransom demand for Clayton." I didn't look at Robin. Even if he disapproved, I had to do this, and I only regretted I hadn't revealed it long before. I was tempted to tell Trumble about our observation of Dan Harrison paying the ransom, but I figured that would pretty much extinguish her faith in us. If she had any. And Robin and I hadn't figured out what that whole episode had meant.

Trumble's eyes got round and wide. "How long have you known about a ransom demand?"

"Three days," I admitted. "Karina pleaded with us to keep silent. But as far as I'm concerned, silence killed Connie. If Karina Harrison hates me for the rest of her life, I'm okay with that. I'm sure they've paid the ransom. So where is Clayton?"

"I've got to call in to the station. You should have told us immediately," Trumble said. She ran a hand through her graying hair.

"I agree," I said. "Though if I truly believed that keeping her secret would keep Clayton alive, I'd stick to it. But I think this whole thing is completely . . . bogus, fishy, out of whack."

"I agree," she said. "And now I have to talk to my boss.This changes everything."

"Will the FBI be called?"

"That's happened. In my opinion, and don't quote me, we should have called them immediately. Especially since Liza is so young."

After she'd left, I turned to Robin. "I felt like I couldn't win, in this situation. And I'm so sad about Connie. But at least this horrible death may shake something loose in the investigation."

"You mean, maybe someone will be horrified enough to tell the investigators something new?"

"Yes. Or maybe the FBI can find something the locals weren't able to find. I think the law enforcement here in Lawrenceton does a good job. But you always hear that the FBI has so many resources. Maybe they'll work some magic that will help us find Phillip."

"Maybe, at least, they can track down Betty Jo, so that your dad won't be a suspect in her disappearance."

That caught me up short. "I don't like my father. But I don't believe that he's a murderer. And it seems really stretching it to believe that loan sharks from California took Phillip to make my father pay up."

"Coming all the way to Georgia just doesn't make sense," he agreed.

That was the truth. "I think my dad would have tried to get the money from me to pay them off," I said.

"I agree, and that's the most solid argument for Phil being innocent I've heard." Robin really didn't think much of my father. I wondered what his own had been like.

If I'd thought things had been bad, the next day was worse. Way, way, worse.

The press arrived. In droves.

Chapter Thirteen

I don't know how we'd escaped so far. I suspect that the sexting scandal in a much larger town had captured lots of interest, and it was much juicier. When teens are sending around nude pictures of themselves, older people take notice. Especially if some of the teens are football players and cheerleaders. Or National Merit Scholars.

Anyway, the story of the missing kids somehow, in its ninth day, blossomed into a sensation. The fact that the youngest of them was the only child of a minister and his wife was news, and that one teen had been left dead at the apparent scene of the abduction was even more sensational, and that a ransom demand had only been received by one set of parents, and that one of the kids had just moved to Georgia from California . . . well, there were just a lot of interesting angles to play off of, and lots of people to interview. Unfortunately, I was one of those people. And when they realized I was married to Robin Crusoe, the best-selling author of many fictional mysteries, that was fascinating, too.

Our landline began ringing early in the morning. After thirty minutes, we unplugged it from the base. When I looked out the front window, I saw three cars I didn't recognize parked on the easement in front of our house. Two strangers came to knock on the door. We didn't answer. Crap. I talked briefly to Beth Finstermeyer, who said that she had at least eight cars at her place . . . "I guess because I have two children missing, instead of one," she said bitterly.

Within the hour I got a call from Cathy Trumble at the police station. She said there was going to be a press conference at the station at eleven that morning, that all the families involved had been asked to send a representative, and that in the sheriff's opinion that was the best way to handle the situation. If all the families gave a statement, the local law enforcement, both city and county, could ask the media representatives to stay away from the homes of the victims.

"Okay," I said, though I was far from sure I was going. "Where and when?"

"Please park in the lot in back of SPACOLEC," she said. "The police parking lot, the enclosed one behind the complex. Come in through the rear door. Be here by ten thirty. Then all of you can go out for the press conference together."

SPACOLEC was the Sparling County Law Enforcement Complex, which housed the police department, the sheriff's department, and the jail. And traffic court. The building was less than ten years old, but it was already bursting at the seams as the urban sprawl of Atlanta engulfed Lawrenceton, raising both the population and the crime rate. I knew the current police chief, Cliff Paley, only by reputation. The newly elected sheriff, David Coffey, a massive man, had been graduating from high school when I'd entered it.

I talked it over with Robin, who was no stranger to dealing with the press.

"I think you ought to go, if you can stand it," he said. "The police are right. They'll come here, if you don't go there."

"Oh. Right." I hated the idea of the news people waiting outside, observing our coming and going, in hopes of catching the moment when something pertinent actually happened. Reporting is a tough job, and has to involve a certain amount of persistence and boldness. But being on the receiving end could be very uncomfortable. "Are you going with me?" I asked, on my way to the bathroom to shower.

"I haven't decided. Maybe I'd be a distraction, because my name is well known . . . if you're one of the few American citizens who reads," he added gloomily. One of Robin's favorite independent booksellers had closed its doors the week before, and he was in a state of pessimism about the future of books. "Not like an actor," he added hastily, lest I should think he was boasting.

"Robin, I know your name is in the public eye," I said. "You don't have to downplay it." He'd always sold well. But after the even larger success of his nonfiction book about the murders in Lawrenceton years before, Robin had spent some time in Hollywood, working on the script of the book. He'd dated an actor whose star was rising, so he'd gotten a fair amount of press . . . even more when she died. And he'd gotten a screen credit on the finished product. The movie had done only moderately well, but any association with the movies threw a handful of glitter on a writer.

"It's up to you," I told Robin. "Of course, I'd be glad if you were there, but if you don't think it would be a good idea, stay home." I really meant it, but it was hard not to whine. I left him to think about it, while I headed for the bathroom.

After showering, I faced a clothing issue. The sweater I'd chosen for the day was just too tight. Maybe someone who didn't know me well would not have seen much difference, but it seemed to me that my body was expanding every day. Since I hadn't finished the laundry, I had one clean pair of pants that fit, a pair I'd meant to give to the next clothing drive. They were brown, heavy knit, and had an elastic waist, and I couldn't imagine how I'd come to have them. But today, I was glad they were still in my closet. I found another sweater, beige and white, and I decided I didn't look horrible. I slapped on some makeup and gathered my hair in a sober braid. A little jewelry, and I was good to go. I made a note to finish the laundry soon. No matter what the crisis was, we needed clean clothes to face it. Robin was not wise in the ways of the washing machine, though he was great at doing dishes. It balanced.

Soon, I hoped, I would feel cheerful enough to shop for maternity clothes. But right now I would scrape by.

There was some time to kill when I was ready, so I turned on the television. I was just in time to get a breaking news update from an Atlanta station. "This just in, there will be a press conference at eleven today about those missing teens in Sparling County," the anchor said, and I snapped to attention. "Stay tuned for more on this story."

I was staring blankly at a game show when Robin emerged to tell me he'd decided to come with me to SPACOLEC. He was wearing his better khakis and a button shirt instead of a polo shirt, so he'd made an effort. I patted my own head to remind him, and Robin pulled out a comb and dragged it through his red hair. We were the messy-haired couple, for sure. I'd never been able to smooth out my wavy brown hair, which fluffed out like a Diana Ross cloud on occasion.

Our baby was doomed to have a flyaway mane. I hoped she (or he) would get Robin's hair color.

"What are you thinking about?" Robin said. He could see me in the hall mirror. "You have the funniest expression on your face."

"I'm hoping the kid has your hair," I said honestly, and he shook his head.

"Bane of my childhood," he said. But he looked pleased.

We bundled up. The weather forecast was not good. It was cold enough for any rain to cause potential problems as sleet, and we might not see the sun for a few days. In the past couple of years, I'd noticed that if we had too many days like that in a row I became moody and a bit depressed.

"We don't have any Christmas decorations out," Robin said, out of the blue.

"Nope, I was waiting for Phillip to be out of school, so he could help put them up," I said. "I thought it would make him feel homier, like he belonged with us." And to my horror, I felt tears well in my eyes. I didn't want to cry. It would be too easy to keep on crying.

My plan to make Phillip feel included in our family seemed long ago and far away. I had a closet full of presents that needed wrapping. I had made meal menus and planned grocery trips to keep the refrigerator from getting too crowded. It seemed like all my planning had belonged to the life of another person, someone who had anticipated a future that now felt incredibly optimistic.

"You're right," I said. "Maybe we can try to get the tree up tomorrow." I didn't sound enthusiastic. I sounded apathetic. "I'm sorry," I said, apologizing for being such a killjoy.

"Putting it up might make us feel better," Robin said. "If anything will."

"I'm ready for *something* to make me feel better." Suddenly, I realized that the Harrisons would probably be at the press conference; the Harrisons, whose trust I'd just violated by revealing to Cathy Trumble that there'd been a ransom demand for their son. "Oh, shit," I said, and told Robin what I was thinking.

"It may not be pleasant," he conceded in a masterly understatement. "But you did the right thing, you know that. If it was just a question of Clayton's well-being, that would be one thing. But there are a lot more people involved than that boy."

"I'm pretty sure the Harrisons won't feel that way," I said. And I wondered how to ask Dan Harrison what he'd been doing the night we'd followed him.

We got into the car so quickly that we only got a few shouted questions from the reporters outside. We ignored them, though something in my Southern soul chided me for being rude. The employee parking lot was enclosed in a high chain link fence topped with barbed wire, and a uniformed deputy was there to open the gate. Robin found a spot some distance from the back door. The other vehicles were huddled close to the building in case it began raining; given the ominous sky, that was a probability. I pulled my gloves on as I got out of the car, and I was glad I'd tucked a scarf around my neck.

Robin put his arm around me and we made our way between the cars to the door. When another deputy (my friend Levon) opened the door to my knock, we entered to find ourselves standing in a holding room of sorts. There were a couple of tables and some chairs, but they were against the walls to leave a clear path in between. Since it was cleaned by trustees, the floor was polished and gleaming.

"The other families are in the room to the right," Levon said. "If you'd join them, we'll get started with the briefing in a couple of minutes."

"Hi," I said, feeling glad to see a familiar face.

"I'm sorry we haven't found them yet," he said, his voice dropping from official to personal.

"Thanks," I said. "I know you all will do everything you can."

He nodded. "We're looking as hard as possible. By the way, your dad's here."

Somehow I hadn't expected that. I was glad of the warning.

Following Levon's pointing finger, we entered a hallway, with the concrete block walls and linoleum floor of a place designed to receive hard use. I could hear a low hum of voices from the open doorway to a room on the right hand side of the corridor. When we entered we were surrounded by familiar faces: Beth and George, Emily and Aubrey, and Daniel and Karina Harrison, who now publicly belonged to our club. My father was in a corner, very much by himself. When we sat down in some of the folding chairs scattered around the room, we received weary nods from all of them.

I didn't know whether to apologize to the Harrisons or not. I wondered if they'd jump on me and pummel me, or curse me out. Karina seemed to read my face. "Don't worry," she said dully. "We paid the ransom and we didn't get him back. And now poor Connie is dead. What is happening in this town?"

I am ashamed to say I felt a rush of relief that I wasn't going to be the target of her hostility, and then I was even more ashamed. Robin and I had had several conversations about what had happened to the ransom money, there one minute and gone the next. Had Dan retrieved it, and returned the next night to replace the money behind the heating and cooling unit? Had we witnessed a dry run?

"I told, too," Beth said, and I felt a flood of relief.

"You had to." Karina shrugged. "You're missing your own kids."

"Not Aurora," Dan Harrison said, his voice heavy. "It's her half brother."

I wasn't sure what to make of that. I started to take him up on the challenge of who was missing a child more, but I didn't have the energy or the righteousness to do it. I dismissed his words and sank back into the bog of unhappiness I'd been slogging through for what seemed like forever. I was thinking, and my thinking was that this forgiving behavior, while a relief to me, was atypical of what I knew about Karina Harrison. I added that to the long list of things I didn't understand about this case.

I didn't look at my father.

The sheriff and the police chief came in together, which was a rare thing. David Coffey and Cliff Paley were not buddies, I'd heard. Coffey had moved into the sheriff's office when his predecessor, Padgett Lanier, had had a heart attack. I heard good things about the job he was doing.

Cliff Paley, the appointed chief of police, had come up through the ranks and was a lifelong resident of our town. When the previous police chief had retired, Cliff had been the overwhelmingly favored candidate for his replacement.

I didn't know exactly why they'd never been in harmony, and frankly, I didn't care, except insofar as it might complicate or impede the investigation somehow. I was anxious to hear if there was any news, and I was anxious about the press conference. I was not much of a public speaker. I gripped Robin's hand and waited in the tense silence that fell over the small group as the two newcomers took their places in front of us all.

"We don't have any big news," the sheriff said directly.

The air went out of my lungs.

"I'll be telling the media all this soon, but I wanted you all to know it first. Josh's car didn't have any prints we could identify as belonging to someone who might be the abductor. Comparing the prints to those we found in their homes, we identified prints from all the kids. The spots of blood were from Jocelyn Finstermeyer. As I've already informed the Finstermeyers, the blood was not sufficient to indicate anything life-threatening."

Emily began to cry almost silently. Aubrey put his arm around her. He looked helpless and hopeless. George and Beth sat straight, eyes ahead, stoic. My father simply looked relieved.

"In conjunction with the police department, we've searched every location connected with the missing kids or their families. We've questioned known felons in the area. We've come up with nothing but some stolen goods we didn't expect to find." Both Paley and Coffey looked grim and unhappy at having to deliver such negative news. "The cell phones of all the kids . . . we've been unable to track them, so they've been destroyed or disabled. On the other hand," Coffey continued, "we haven't found bodies, personal effects, or anything that might make us think that the kids have been harmed."

I hadn't looked at it that way. But it didn't exactly make me sit up and cheer. The absence of negative news didn't make me feel positive.

My cell phone rang, and I winced. I had forgotten to silence it. Everyone turned to look at me as I pulled it out, saw the number calling was unknown. But since every call might be news, I put it to my ear without apology. "Yes?" I said warily.

"Roe," a voice said, low and urgent. The minute I heard it, I put the phone on speaker

"Philip?" I said, my voice rising. "Where are you? Have you escaped?" From the corner of my eye, I saw someone lean forward, absolutely focused on me. Karina. She must hope for news of Clayton.

"Josh is hurt. I can't leave him." Phillip was still talking in that low, hurried voice.

"How is Josh hurt?" I had so many questions I couldn't force them all out of my mouth. "*Where are you?*"

The sheriff plucked my phone from my hand and put it to his ear automatically, as if that might make him hear more clearly despite the phone's setting. "Phillip," he said, in what was meant to be a reassuring voice. "This is the sheriff. Son, give me a clue where you are."

There was a slight pause, voices coming faintly over the phone.

"I can't talk any more," Phillip said. His voice was dull. "He's got a gun to her head."

And the line went dead.

We were all frozen in the moment, eyes wide, terrified, waiting.

But there was nothing more to hear.

It was a terrible moment. And yet, I knew that just a moment before, Phillip had been alive and talking. And he'd somehow made it to a telephone. I could not bear to look at the Finstermeyers or the Scotts. Josh was hurt, and either Liza or Joss had been threatened with a gun.

"Oh, George," Beth said to her husband. Her composure dissolved, and she wept.

"But Josh was alive," George said. "And so was our girl." And he wept with his wife.

The Scotts were staring at each other, too upset to speak, and my father got up and began pacing around the room. His jaw was set tight and he did not look at anyone at all.

The sheriff was still holding my telephone. I asked him, "Did Phillip say anything we couldn't make out? Did you hear any background noise that we didn't hear?"

"I heard only what you heard," David Coffey said.

There was an outburst of protest at this. No one believed him. If I could have, I would have opened his ears and dug out what he'd heard my brother say. But nothing we told him swayed his decision.

When the noise had died down, the sheriff said, "Obviously, this gives us more to go on. And if you'll give me your phone Mrs. Crusoe, I'll take it to our tech guy to see if he can learn anything from it."

Being called "Mrs. Crusoe" was the least of my worries now. He could call me Annie Oakley for all I cared. I surrendered the phone numbly, feeling I was giving up my last contact with Phillip. Levon hurried out with it.

"We can't reveal this at the press conference," Sheriff Coffey said.

The police chief stared at him incredulously. "Are you kidding?" Paley demanded. His face was red. "Why the hell not?"

"If the kidnapper gets too panicked by hearing about it on the news, the repercussions might be considerable," Coffey said. "On the kids, you understand. As it is, the kidnapper may believe that Phillip was simply talking to his sister."

There was a heavy silence while we all considered the implications. After a moment, Paley nodded. "All right," he said. "But for the record, I think we should reveal this." Paley turned to look at us. "The agents are in the building, reviewing all the work done so far. From now on, we'll be assisting them. We'll see which way they choose to handle it."

I looked anxiously from one man to another. We didn't need a divided law enforcement effort. What if the FBI didn't agree with either one? Surely a united front would be more effective.

"In the name of God, please get along," Aubrey said, as if he'd heard my thoughts. "We are all praying for you to solve this, praying as hard as we can, and it doesn't inspire us with confidence to hear you disagreeing about how to proceed."

Both the men looked a little ashamed, or maybe "embarrassed" would be more accurate. "Father Scott, we're doing our best to search as hard as we can," Paley said. "I don't think the different approaches we take to the search will end up in less efficiency."

"We're united where it makes a difference," Coffey said.

Aubrey shook his head silently. I couldn't tell if he doubted Coffey's words, or if he was disgusted that the two men couldn't agree.

"Now, about the press conference. I'll make an opening statement from Chief Paley and myself, giving an overview of the case and the search," Coffey told us. "We'll take questions from the press. Then we'll open it up, and I'm sure they want to ask some of you different questions. Like how you feel about your missing loved one, how you're passing your time while you wait, what you think may have happened to the kids. And if you really want to answer these, of course you can. But we'd like each of you to make a statement, one per family, and leave it at that."

"We don't like the idea of putting ourselves in the spotlight like that," George said.

"They want sound bites for the evening news," Coffey explained. "Our psychologist says it would be helpful if you could say that you know the kids will be returned unharmed, you want them back for Christmas, and you're sure no one set out to hurt them."

Karina Harrison glared at him. "Of course no one set out to hurt them," she snapped. "They're all just kids. But we *paid,* and we didn't get him back."

The Scotts, the Finstermeyers, and my father had not known about the ransom drop, and the knowledge that Clayton had not been released even after the payment hit them like a large brick. There was a volley of questions about the ransom money how the Harrisons had paid, and how long ago that had been.

Robin and I glanced at each other, deeply puzzled. The ransom had been collected by an invisible person, as far as we were concerned. Dan had put it in the designated spot (we supposed), and then it had vanished, at least. Now Karina said it had been paid, and we didn't know for sure to the contrary.

"Please, please, folks, let's get back on track for this press event," Coffey said, holding his hands up to get our attention. "The fact that ransom was asked for one kid is *not* public knowledge, and I don't want it to be. Keep it to yourselves. We're focusing on being positive, on projecting the belief that we do expect the kids to come back soon."

"What good will that do?" I whispered to Robin. He shrugged and shook his head. "Dunno," he whispered back. "I guess it's better than weeping and wailing."

"Did it seem to you that he was less than . . . convinced . . . about the ransom demand?"

"Yes," Robin said. "And I wonder what that's about."

"I wonder if the kidnapper saw us watching Dan, and then called Dan and told him to pick the money back up. To do the whole thing again another time, when he wasn't observed. That's on my conscience."

"Truthfully, Roe, I don't think there was money in the bag at all. I think for reasons best known to himself, Dan dropped off a bag filled with newspaper and then picked it up. Though I can't understand why he would do such a thing."

"You think Karina knows that? Or was he double-crossing her, too?" Just when I thought people couldn't get any more despicable, they'd find a way to do it. I didn't like being so negative. I felt it was being forced on me. *Baby,* I thought, *don't mind me. Your mom is just a little depressed right now.* It was the first time I'd thought of the little cells multiplying in my womb as an individual person, and it flooded me with a new emotion. I couldn't ponder it for long, because we were all getting up for the walk to the front of the station and out the front doors to and the area designated as the press conference site.

"I thought we were going to get to ask Paley and Coffey questions, ourselves. Maybe he wants to keep questions at a minimum," Robin said, as we emerged into the cold.

"Pretty good strategy," George Finstermeyer said. He was walking beside us. Beth was a few steps ahead. She was clutching a tissue, and watching her feet move. "I would have asked him more about the FBI coming in, myself."

"From my book research, I've come to believe that the FBI can make a big difference," Robin said.

"Right now I'm wondering how badly our son is hurt, and if our daughter has been shot. The FBI can't take charge soon enough for me. The more eyes and ears and feet on the ground, the better." And George hastened his steps a little to walk by his wife.

I found myself agreeing wholeheartedly. I didn't doubt that the local law enforcement was trying hard to find the kids, but surely more brains and manpower couldn't hurt? We were filing out the front door of the law enforcement complex, now, and I was shocked by the number of cameras and microphones waiting for us.

My father maneuvered his way to my side. I couldn't outpace him or dodge him. He had a right to be here. I just didn't want to talk to him.

"Roe, I'm trying, here," he said.

"Really?" I kept walking, didn't look at him. That might seem childish, but at the moment I didn't care. "How are you trying?"

"I just want to find my son, same as you," he told me, his voice raised. A couple of people looked around at us curiously. Robin pulled me to a stop, and faced my father, towering over him. "Listen, Phil," Robin said, "I think Roe has made it clear that right now, talking to you is putting even more strain on her. Back off." And then we were moving again, leaving my father standing by himself.

After that, Dad kept his distance.

I squeezed Robin's hand in thanks.

Some thought and preparation had gone into this press conference, I saw. The family members were herded to cluster to the right of the microphones. The law enforcement contingent was to the left, Cathy Trumble among them. Chief Paley and Sheriff Coffey were at the center.

Robin said, "See that woman with the long red hair?"

It was hard to miss her. She had made some bold fashion choices. Her hair, an improbable bright red, was styled à la Adele, and she wore a mustard-colored coat with a full skirt, cinched at the waist. She was also wearing formidable heels. She was the only woman present not wearing trousers. I could only imagine how cold her thin legs were in the chilly wind. "She must be freezing," I said, awed by her determination to present herself according to her own vision.

"That's Scarlet Mabry, a true-crime blogger," Robin said. "She travels to the location of interesting murders, writing blogs about the crimes as they're being investigated."

"And she can make a living doing that?" I was astonished.

"Yes, a good living." He hesitated a moment. "I met her when I was in Hollywood."

"Okay," I said. "Did you date her?"

"No, no, it wasn't like that," he said, unconvincingly. "She interviewed me about the club murders." I'd met Robin when he came to a meeting of the Real Murders club, which had examined old cases and debated who might have been guilty, or if the right verdict had been reached. It wasn't as ghoulish as it sounds. At least, I hadn't thought so at the time.

At that moment, Scarlet Mabry spotted Robin, and gave him a brilliant smile of recognition and a little discreet finger wave. "Uh-huh," I said, trying not to sound skeptical. "Not like that."

Robin looked acutely uncomfortable, and I didn't think it was just the cold wind. To tell the truth, I thought it was just a little funny, but there was a tiny thread of pique running through my reaction. I had to fight the urge to hang on Robin's arm like a spare coat.

Then Sheriff Coffey stepped up to the microphone, and my attention was all for the main event.

"Thanks for coming today," he said, by way of opening. "This is what we know. Five days ago, five young people went missing. Jocelyn and Josh Finstermeyer, ages sixteen, Phillip Teagarden, age fifteen, Clayton Harrison, eighteen, and Liza Scott, age eleven. Found dead at the probable scene of the abduction was Tammy Ribble, sixteen. Three days ago, Connie Bell, eighteen, was found dead, an apparent suicide, in her home. We are operating under the assumption that all these events are related. Josh Finstermeyer's car has been recovered, and there has been no significant evidence found in it. Clayton Harrison's car has not been found." He described the car and gave the license plate number.

"You don't think they've all run away together?" asked a voice from the back of the crowd.

"That theory was considered, but discarded."

"Why?"

"Because none of these kids were in trouble at home or with the law. They had every reason to look forward to the vacation from school and to Christmas with their families."

Emily utterly broke down and shook with sobs.

"Did any of them have debit cards? Have they been used?" Another question, this time from a reporter at the Lawrenceton paper.

"No," Coffey said heavily.

"Did Connie Bell leave a suicide note?" said someone else.

"A very brief one."

"What did it say?"

"Nothing pertinent to the case," Coffey said, stone-faced.

The questions rained on, some of them interesting and some of them retreads of information I'd already gotten. I wondered if some of the reporters hoped Coffey would give a different answer, or reveal something new.

Then Chief Paley had his turn at the microphone, and he described the crime scene behind the hair salon, and the injuries suffered by Tammy Ribble, though in no graphic detail. He emphasized that the two departments were working in tandem because their goal was to bring the kids home safely, not to play one-upmanship.

That was a relief. Robin snorted, though.

Scarlet Mabry asked, "Have any of the parents received a ransom demand?"

"We're not commenting on this at this time," Paley said.

"Does that mean such a demand *has* been received?" Suddenly, she was on point, and the whole crowd of newspeople became more attentive.

"We're not commenting. That's what it means." Paley was trying to imitate a stone wall. He was doing a pretty good job.

"We didn't get any notice of such a demand," he added. Nothing short of an unambiguous "No" would have deflected the crowd now, and I wouldn't have expected it could. Waffling is easy to detect. Paley was not subtle.

"If I may finish," he bellowed, and the questions died down. When he'd glared around to make sure people were listening,

Chief Paley continued, "Since we have limited resources and manpower, we have asked the FBI to step in on the case."

This was a huge piece of news, and temporarily eclipsed the ransom question. I wondered if news conferences were always so adversarial.

There was a barrage of questions that had no answer (as of yet): how many agents were coming, were any technicians coming, how long would it take the FBI agents to get up to speed on the investigation, and so on. By this time, I felt like an icicle, and my eyes were tearing, and all I wanted was for this to be over. It was hard to pay attention when I was huddling close to Robin for warmth, and burying my nose in my scarf.

But it wouldn't be over for a while, yet. The families were scheduled to speak next. We all had messages to deliver, and Paley was anxious to get away from the microphone. But he had a parting shot. "The families will take no questions," he said in an iron voice. "None."

That was fine with me.

Aubrey Scott went first, since Emily was completely unable to step up to the microphone. Aubrey said what you would expect any man to say: that his daughter was very young and needed her parents, and that he and his wife were praying that she would be returned to them unharmed.

Dan and Karina had chosen not to speak.

Beth went next, with George standing silent beside her. She was collected and clear, and I admired Beth even more. She said her children were guiltless of any crime except somehow being in the wrong place at the wrong time. "Even if my children have been injured, even if they have been frightened, I will forgive whoever took them if they will just release Josh and Jocelyn so they can come back to us."

Well said, I thought.

Paley looked from me to my father, asking silently which

one of us would speak. I half-thought my father would take the opportunity to tell the world how much he missed his son, but he made an "it's all yours" sweep of the hand. I had a hard time making my numb legs move, but Robin put his arm around me to get me there. Robin had guessed that morning that I might be making a statement, and before we left the house we'd made some notes, thank God. "My brother Phillip is a newcomer to town," I said, "so he hasn't been here long enough to make enemies. He did make good friends of Josh and Jocelyn, and they are with him wherever he is. He and Liza go to the same church." When I could get Phillip up on time. "They are all good kids. I love Phillip and I want him to spend Christmas with us. Please, please let him go."

As I retreated, I noticed Beth was looking at me with a troubled expression. I wondered if she felt I'd try to distinguish Phillip from the other kids, long-time residents. We'd felt obliged to emphasize that if any local situation had caused the abduction, Phillip had had no part in it. I wasn't trying to throw anyone to the wolves, but I had to do the best I could for my brother. I felt I was compromising myself right and left, and I didn't like that. But my moral purity wasn't the issue. Phillip's life was at stake.

Then Chief Paley stepped back to the microphone. "Are there any more questions before we conclude?" he asked.

"Yeah!" Scarlet Mabry called. "What is the connection between the bullying Liza Scott was undergoing at school and her abduction? Is it true that the three girls responsible were going to be expelled?"

"I can't speak to that," Paley responded. "That's something you'll have to ask the school authorities. All I can say is that at the moment, we have no evidence that the two situations are connected. That concludes our press conference. Please respect the privacy of these families in this stressful and painful time."

The Harrisons were livid. I could understand why. Their daughter Marlea was one of Liza's tormentors, yet their son had disappeared with Liza. They were damned either way. What a position to be in. Looking at it now, it was hard to believe we'd followed him through the sleeping town, and we'd felt almost lighthearted and triumphant about it.

We all filed back into the station. "Wow, that Scarlet is thorough," I muttered, impressed.

Emily Scott was dry-eyed and angry. "I'm glad Sienna is sorry," she was saying to Aubrey. "But Marlea and Kesha shouldn't get away with it! They tore our daughter's life apart." She shot a glare in the Harrisons' direction. But the Harrisons were clearing out as if the building were on fire.

"Emily," Aubrey said, sounding both desperate and pleading, "when we get home, we'll talk about it. Again."

But Emily Scott, that most correct and upright of women, pulled away from her husband and strode out of the back door of the station to their car, her back straight, her eyes burning. Emily's Christian forgiveness had just taken a hike.

As Robin and I drove home, I rummaged in my purse before I remembered the sheriff had confiscated my cell phone. "What if he calls me again?" I said. "What if no one at the sheriff's office answers the phone?" The picture of Phillip, disappointed in me because I didn't answer, because I failed him, was agony. Robin glanced over at me, and I could tell he was scrambling for something consoling to say. "You know they'll sit on that phone like hawks," he told me, trying to sound sure. For the rest of the day, we just went through the motions of living.

The next morning, after a night of no news, we put up our Christmas tree. We couldn't think of anything else to do. Robin said he simply couldn't focus on work. I didn't even call the library. I thought of calling Amina; I'd had a message from her on our landline's answering machine, telling me she'd seen me on television. But I couldn't summon up the energy. I don't think I've ever felt so helpless. I got up once, I threw up, drank some peppermint tea and ate some toast in bed, then tried again. This time I managed to stay on my feet.

I moved through the routine of getting clean and getting dressed. We got the artificial tree out, because we didn't have the heart to go buy a fresh one—though Phillip had looked forward to a real tree. Selecting one at the tree lot seemed beyond my capability.

My mother had been calling every day, and I'd been giving her the "no new information" bulletin. This was not her crisis; she had another family to think about, too. John's sons and grandchildren had grown very dear to her. They were still going to have a Christmas, and it would be a happy one. I didn't begrudge them their holiday. I only wanted the same for myself and Robin and Phillip.

The doorbell rang about ten that morning, and because any caller could be bringing news, Robin hurried to the front door. I was on a step stool putting ornaments on the higher branches. I didn't recognize the voices I'd heard, and I turned slightly to see who was coming into the family room. A man and a woman I'd never seen before were looking around, and the cold outside air hung around them in a cloud. She was a tall woman whose black hair was streaked with gray; and she was wearing a gray coat, making a very striking impression. She was pulling off black gloves. Her partner was less memorable, a slight brown-haired man with narrow features, doffing a rather nice olive wool coat to reveal an equally nice suit.

"Please have a seat," Robin told them, and he zoomed over to me to give me a hand down from the stepstool. "FBI," he said in answer to my inquiring look.

"Do you want some coffee or some water or Coca-Cola?" I asked, feeling a little more energized. "Or maybe we have juice?" I'd lost track of what was in my refrigerator.

"I'd love a cup of coffee," the woman said. "I'm Bernadette Crowley, by the way, and this is Les Van Winkle."

No problem remembering those names, I thought. "I'll just be a minute," I said, and went into the kitchen to put the coffee on. I hadn't been drinking any because of my morning sickness, and I hoped I could get a cup down now. It might pull me out of this malaise.

"It's perking," I said blankly. I found I was back in the living room. "Be ready in a minute."

"Great," said Bernadette Crowley. She tucked her chin-length hair behind her ears and took out a small notebook. "Ms. Teagarden, Mr. Crusoe, Les and I are from the FBI, and we've come to help the local law enforcement with this case."

"Good," Robin said, and I nodded.

"How so, Mr. Crusoe?" Van Winkle's voice was quiet and neutral, an inviting kind of voice.

"Anything that might show us some progress is welcome," Robin said, surprised. "But I don't think we're dissatisfied with what they've done, right, Roe?"

"No," I said, and realized that was open to interpretation. "I think the local guys have been doing everything they can," I explained. "But if there is something you can do to turn over a few more rocks, and give any new leads, of course . . ." and my voice trailed off.

"An investigation like this, we turn over a lot of rocks," Crowley said, with a wry smile. "For example, the gambling debts your father has incurred."

"That was bad news," I agreed. "And we didn't have any idea until just—two days ago? I don't talk to my father very often. And even less now."

"Why is that?" Van Winkle said, only polite curiosity on his face.

"He's a disappointing father," I said. "He behaved badly enough to run Phillip out of the house, and he made Betty Jo's life so unhappy that she ran away, too. Now we know about the gambling." I shook my head. "I've reached the end of my rope with him."

"Please tell us about this," Crowley said. "Because this is the first time we're hearing this story from you. We want to know how your half brother happened to be in that alley with the Finstermeyer twins and the Scotts' little girl, and Tammy Ribble."

"And Clayton," I said. "And Connie. And maybe Marlea, Clayton's sister."

"You think they were there, too?"

"Sure. Clayton's missing, too, right? Connie must have witnessed what happened. And she must have kept what she saw secret. Because otherwise, why would she kill herself? And Clayton had just been seen at the soccer field. Maybe he'd come to pick up Marlea. She was there with her two friends."

"Sienna Andrews and Kesha Windham?"

I nodded.

"Sarah Washington told us about that," Crowley said.

"We're coming back to Phillip," Van Winkle said, "but I'm interested to know why you think Connie was in the alley. And why she wouldn't talk about what she saw?"

That was a good question, and it pulled me up short as though I'd walked into a wall. My brain cleared a little.

"The kids tell me Connie went everywhere with Clayton. I assumed that Connie kept what she saw secret because she feared for Clayton's safety," I said, figuring it out as I spoke. "Or maybe she had been threatened by the kidnapper that something would happen to Clayton if she talked."

Robin murmured that he'd get the coffee and came back in minutes with everything we needed on a tray except spoons. And I retrieved those.

"Or maybe," Robin said after he put the tray on the coffee table, "Connie knew the kidnapper and couldn't bear having that knowledge."

I looked at my husband in some astonishment. I'd never thought of that. I should have, though. The FBI agents certainly weren't surprised. I felt like I was shaking off cobwebs from my brain. I hadn't been thinking. I'd only been sinking deeper into a quicksand of misery.

"Let's hear about Phillip, if you don't mind," Crowley said. "Tell me how well you know your half brother."

"I used to babysit him," I said, and explained that my father and Betty Jo had lived nearby until Phillip had had a scary thing happen to him. While he'd been staying with me. So my father and Betty Jo had decided that he needed to deal with it by moving to California.

"We started e-mailing each other when he got old enough to get on the computer by himself, though," I said, smiling as I remembered how glad I had been to hear from him.

"So your father kept you two apart?"

"Yes, he did," I said. "I flew out to see Phillip a couple of times, and we went out by ourselves. During my first marriage, Martin and I flew out to California to spend time with Phillip. It was great. But Dad wouldn't let him come to Lawrenceton."

"So how did Phillip come to be here with you?"

"He hitchhiked here," I said. "It scared the hell out of me. I had no idea he was coming. I would have sent him some money, or gone to get him. And he had some very tense moments along the way, he told me. I was scared all over when I thought of what could have happened. But he made it here, and he showed up at the library where I work." I smiled and shook my head, remembering. "I didn't even recognize him for a second, he was so grown-up."

"And then what?"

"Well, I called my father and Betty Jo, of course, and told him that Phillip was here, and safe. And that Phillip had asked to stay with me."

"Quite an adjustment for you, a newlywed, to have a teenager living with you." Van Winkle was stirring his coffee, looking wise and understanding.

I wasn't buying that, not completely, but I was sure going to tell them the truth. I didn't know what might turn out to be important, and what might not.

"Oh, yes," I said. "But in the end, I didn't mind."

"Why is that?" Crowley looked only quizzical.

"Because I love my brother," I said. "And Robin was willing, thank God. We weren't married at the moment, but we got married."

"Late last month," Robin said. I could scarcely believe it.

"And I understand you are expecting?" Crowley said, nodding at my middle.

"Yes," I said, and felt a little smile curl my lips up. "We are."

"So did Phillip feel that he'd been edged out by the baby?"

"He didn't seem to. He was pretty excited. But he had barely learned about it before he was gone."

"So how was Phillip's schooling arranged?"

"Well, he'd been taking these classes in California, at some kind of joint classroom for home-schooled students," I said. "I didn't know anything about it, but as it turned out, this system is nationwide."

They both nodded, as if this was a well-known established educational mode. I'd had no idea.

"Phillip took off from California before the end of a semester, but after about a million phone calls and e-mails, we worked it out so he could finish his semester from here, which he did. In January, he was going to go to the high school here."

"Because he'd already made friends," Crowley said, nodding.

"Right," I said. "I knew Josh from the library, he was a frequent patron and a good kid, so I asked him to come by to meet Phillip. I didn't want Phillip to be stuck with me all of the time."

"Or you didn't want him to be around all of the time," Van Winkle suggested.

Oooooh. A snake in the grass. "Phillip is nice to have around the house," I said. "He's even reasonably helpful. But teenagers need to hang around with other teenagers, and they need a social network. So of course I was hoping he'd make friends."

"Of course," Crowley said smoothly. "And did that work out?"

"Better than I'd ever imagined. He and Josh really hit it off, and Phillip liked Jocelyn, too. Joss and Josh are very close, naturally, so that made it a good match."

"Your brother had romantic feelings for Jocelyn?"

I smiled. "He thought Joss was pretty, and he admired the fact that she was a good athlete," I said. "He did like her. But Phillip found out fairly quickly that he wasn't what she was looking for."

"In fact, Jocelyn is gay," Van Winkle murmured.

"Yes, that's what Phillip told me," I said. "That she and Tammy Ribble were girlfriends."

"Who did you tell about this?"

"No one. It wasn't my business."

"Did it disgust you?"

"Disgust me? It's not my business to be disgusted," I said slowly. "I've known girls who liked girls before. I don't think that's really big news these days, do you?"

"Did Phillip take it hard, that his crush didn't give him the time of day?" Van Winkle said. He looked so kind and understanding!

I laughed, for the first time in forever. "No, he didn't take it hard," I said. "Phillip is an optimist, and he's blessed with good looks. I understand he and Sarah Washington were 'talking.' Phillip was content to be a friend of Joss's. Which you'd have to, to be friends with Josh."

"So the twins were devoted to each other?" Crowley asked.

Robin and I nodded simultaneously. "They seemed to be," I added cautiously. "We didn't see as much of Joss as we did of Josh."

"Close, despite being so different?" Crowley inquired.

"Are they so different?" I considered. "Well, I guess so. Joss is more athletic and really direct. Josh is more of a reader, and Phillip said he makes all A's. But they're both popular at school, and both very involved in activities."

"What about Tammy Ribble?"

"I only knew her by sight," I said. "I had never talked to her."

Crowley looked inquiringly at Robin, who shook his head.

"And Liza Scott?"

"I've known Liza since she was a small girl," I said. "When her mom moved here and started coming to church, Liza came too, of course, and then Emily married Aubrey, our priest, and Aubrey adopted Liza. He's always adored her. So I still think of Liza as a little kid, though she's eleven now. Little enough," I added, feeling a wave of sadness.

"And I understand she was fond of Phillip?" Van Winkle said gently.

"That's what I hear," I said. "I wasn't aware of it, but Sarah mentioned that."

"Did Phillip discourage her?"

"Not by being *mean,*" I said instantly. "Liza was in a vulnerable position, because of the situation at her school. Maybe she was looking for a champion?" I thought of Phillip's drawings, now in the hands of the police. "Phillip did feel a lot of sympathy for Liza. And he was always nice to her, as far as I know." I remembered being a teenager, and I remembered that impatience could get the better of someone who wanted everything to happen *now.* Plus, I knew it must have been not a little embarrassing for Phillip . . . right? To have a preteen hanging around with pleading eyes?

They asked me to talk about the bullying, but I had no

firsthand knowledge. I hadn't known the full scope of the problem until Phillip had gone missing. I did tell them about Tiffany Andrews' visit.

Then Crowley and Van Winkle took me over Phillip's call of the day before, in exhaustive detail. At least at that moment, I reminded myself, Phillip had been alive and able to talk. It broke my heart that he had called me, and I hadn't been able to help him. Though Van Winkle and Crowley took me over his words again and again, I could not wring any more meaning or information out of them.

"The call came from a cell phone," Crowley told me. "That makes its location impossible to pinpoint exactly in a semi-rural area like Lawrenceton, though we know the call originated from the area to the west side of the town, and a little farther out. Before you ask me, he didn't call again. The only calls on your log are from your family and one of your coworkers."

My heart sank. She returned my phone. I looked at it, longing for it to ring again, to hear Phillip on the other end.

But while I spoke to the FBI agents, hoping against hope that they would find something new in my words, or be set off on some investigative angle they hadn't visited, I had my own new thought.

Liza Scott's three persecutors weren't the only bullies who played roles in the tumult surrounding our missing kids.

Clayton Harrison had a reputation as a bully, too. And he was something of a classic bully, if the stories I'd heard about him were true: that he dominated everywhere he went, that he was quick to gibe at kids who had less, were different, were smarter or dumber. He liked to snap towels at other guys in the locker room, and if he didn't like something, he proclaimed it "gay."

So why had he been seeking out Josh, Phillip, and Joss? After all, they were more-or-less two years younger. Or had he just come to the field to pick up his sister? If that were the case how had Marlea and the other two girls gotten home?

Tammy Ribble had encountered the other kids not thirty

minutes later. And ended up dead. The kidnappers had appeared and forced all the teenagers, and Liza, into coöperation. Some terrible confrontation had taken place, something so bad that Connie had killed herself rather than live with it.

I'd been assuming that that "something" was the forceful abduction of the kids in the car. That Tammy, coming out the back door of the beauty salon, had witnessed this crime and been killed because she knew the abductor, or at the very least could give information leading to his (their?) arrest.

I could at least understand that.

But I sure couldn't understand Connie's drastic action. Had she been on the scene? Had the girl been so fragile that seeing Tammy die had unhinged her? It couldn't be the mere absence of her boyfriend that had precipitated her death. She would hope for his rescue, right? Connie had to know something about where Clayton was, who had taken him. I thought again that Connie must have been threatened with Clayton's murder if she talked.

The picture we'd been looking at (all the kids in one car, all abducted) did not make sense, like so many things about this crime.

Lost in my own thoughts, I didn't notice my visitors had gotten up to leave until Robin touched my shoulder. "Sorry," I said, with an effort. "Can I ask you something?"

"I'll answer if I can," said Crowley. She waited with brows raised for me to speak.

"Connie really died from the pills, right?" I asked. "Nothing suspect about it?"

Whatever they'd been expecting, it hadn't been that. Both the agents looked just the slightest bit disapproving. Perhaps they thought I was asking out of ghoulish curiosity. "Yes, she took all of her mother's sleeping pills," Crowley told me.

"But why?" I just couldn't understand it.

"The assumption is she despaired of her boyfriend's ever

coming back, since his parents paid the ransom and he never showed up," Van Winkle said.

And the way he said it told me that the two agents also had their doubts about Connie's motivation for such a drastic act.

"So the Harrisons told Connie, from the get-go, that they'd gotten a ransom demand for Clayton?"

Crowley looked surprised. And thoughtful. "Maybe since she'd told you and George and Beth, Karina figured she ought to tell Connie," she said. "But that wouldn't have been my choice."

"There's no doubt she took the pills voluntarily?" I said.

And they were both looking at me with quizzical gazes now.

"No doubt," Crowley told me. "She was alone in the house. Her father was at work and her mother was visiting her own mother's nursing home."

"She was lying on her own bed, and the pill container was beside her, along with a bottle of water," Van Winkle added. "The autopsy has shown she took the pills, and she hadn't sustained any bruises or other injuries."

"Okay," I said slowly. That seemed conclusive. I still could not understand why it had happened. "There was a note, I hear?"

"A very brief one." Les Van Winkle was looking at me funny. "Do you have a theory about Connie Bell's death?"

"It just seems so unlikely," I said. "Unlikely and unnecessary. Based on the facts as we know them."

"Any kid's death seems unnecessary," Crowley said. She and her partner pulled their coats on.

"Can you tell me what *you* think happened in that alley?" I said.

Van Winkle smiled cryptically. "No," he said. "We can't share our speculations with you."

And then they were gone.

Two hours later, the tree was up. Robin and I had a lackluster lunch while we looked at it and tried to feel a spark of optimism. Robin had also wound lights around the bushes in front of the house and then told me our lighting was complete. I had hung an artificial wreath on the front door. That was as much as we could do, and more than we had heart for.

Though the visit of the FBI agents had given me food for thought, all that thought didn't lead anywhere. Robin went to his office and tried to work. I sat and held a book in front of me, though I could not have told you what I read. Instead of staring at a book, sometimes I stared at the television. I missed work more than I ever thought I would, yet I was sure I couldn't get through a whole day at the library.

My mother came by after showing a house in my neighborhood.

"You shouldn't have gone to that press conference," she said. "Roe, you look awful."

"Maybe I should have stayed home," I said listlessly. I wanted to tell her I'd talked to Phillip, but after my recent experiences, I was obediently keeping my mouth shut. "All I seem to be able to do is sit here."

"You and Robin need to go out and be around people," she said firmly. "Is your Christmas shopping done?"

"There doesn't seem to be any point," I said. I'd been telling myself to go to my laptop and at least order some things, but that hadn't happened. In the back of the linen closet, I'd stashed two pairs of jeans for Phillip, two shirts, and a coat (he needed everything), and a couple of shirts for Robin, some books he'd been wanting, and a leather jacket, plus some gift cards. That might constitute our Christmas gift exchange.

"If nothing happens by Christmas," Mother said, and paused to pick her next words. "If nothing is discovered, please come to our house for Christmas dinner."

"Can I tell you later?" I said. "I'm really grateful for the invitation. Right now, I just don't think I'm up to it."

"For goodness' sake, just go ride around," Mother advised. "You need to look at something besides these four walls, honey."

My mother wasn't much one for endearments, so I made the effort to smile. "I'll try, but I'm not promising."

"I saw your father," she said.

"Where?"

"At the Piggly Wiggly," she said. "I don't go there often, but I had to get some of that granola I like so much, and it's the only store carrying it. And there he was, buying some TV dinners. I assume his hotel room has a microwave in it."

"I guess. I don't know where he's staying."

This really shocked her. "You don't?"

"No, I got really mad and I'm shunning him," I said, trying to smile.

"My gosh, what's he doing in town, then?" She was genuinely bewildered. "With his wife missing, too, you'd think he'd be back in California."

"Dad said she was with another man. I don't know whether to believe him or not."

"If she is I certainly don't blame her," my mother said with some asperity. "But with his son missing and his wife missing, I'm surprised he's not sitting in a jail cell somewhere being interrogated. That's a lot of missing family . . . two-thirds!"

I hadn't put it that way to myself. I started to tell her about the gambling, but it seemed like too much trouble to open my mouth. When Mom got up to leave, she said, "I'm going to just say hello to Robin," and walked back to his office without waiting for a yea or nay.

I don't know what she said to my husband, but we got out that day. Robin made sure I was bundled up, and we just drove around and looked at Christmas decorations. We walked through the town park behind the courthouse. We went through the drive-through at a fast food restaurant.

It did make me feel better.

I felt sharper. I regained my curiosity.

Late that afternoon, I ran into Levon Suit inside the post office, where I'd gone to buy some stamps. Robin was waiting outside. Levon was wearing his off-duty clothes and he smiled when he saw me, so I stopped to speak.

"Good to see you out and about," he said.

"How are things at SPACOLEC?" I said.

"Keeping busy. Of course, the missing kids. I'm so sorry, Roe. But lots of other stuff, too. Crime doesn't stop for the holidays. In fact, sometimes it seems it picks up. Family quarrels sure do." He shook his head.

"I know there must not be any news," I said. "You would have told me."

"The FBI agents are lighting a fire under everyone," Levon said. "Now that we know about the ransom being paid, the Harrisons not getting Clayton back . . . that has us all worried." Then he looked chagrined. Okay, maybe that hadn't been the most tactful thing to say, but I had other fish to fry.

"There's no doubt the Harrisons actually paid ransom?" I asked, as casually as you can ask a question like that.

"The money is missing from their account," Levon told me. "Dan came into the bank and drew it out himself. The bank president was pretty worried, letting Dan walk out with that much cash in a duffel bag, but Dan insisted."

"Ooooh," I said. Frankly, I was stunned. I'd wondered if the whole thing had been staged. "How much cash?"

"Three hundred thousand," Levon said.

That was a lot of money. And yet, in another way, it wasn't. By my standards, that was a huge chunk of change. But in today's world, where the rich were getting richer, I was astonished the kidnapper hadn't asked for more.

"Keep up the good work, Levon," I said. "We're all counting on our law enforcement people."

"We were all wearing out, but we're getting reenergized. If anyone can help us find your brother, the FBI can. The whole situation is something we've never faced before, in this county."

"I haven't ever faced anything like it myself," I agreed.

"Oh, there is something else I can tell you," Levon said. "The Fibbies tracked down your dad's wife."

"Great!" I hadn't really been worried about Betty Jo, but it was something of a relief to hear she was living and breathing. "Was she really living with another man?" I asked belatedly.

"No." He looked surprised. "She's living in a commune in Northern California. She said she figured Phillip was safe with you now, and she had to get away from your dad or kill him. Or be killed. She told us a pretty frightening story on the phone. I'm sure she'll share it with you."

I hardly knew which part of this to respond to first. "A commune! I didn't know there were any still around." I gave him the surprise and amazement he deserved.

"Me either."

"She always seemed so down-to-earth, that's hard to picture." I had an image of prosaic Betty Jo in her polyester pants, planting seeds and making bread.

"My oath on it." Levon was tickled. "She had given up watching the news or reading the papers because she wanted to cleanse herself of negative feelings."

"I wish her good luck with that," I said darkly.

"Your dad was some kind of relieved to hear where she really is, because the FBI had been asking him lots of questions about her whereabouts. Some pretty bad people are mad at your dad."

"I'm not really talking to him right now, so thanks for letting me know," I told him.

He looked interested. "Any reason you can share with me?"

"I don't like what I've learned about him lately," I said. "And despite his massive life screwups, he was trying to make me feel responsible for Phillip's disappearance. I would do anything, *anything*, to find my brother."

"I believe that," Levon said hastily, because he could see the tears welling up in my eyes.

"Thanks, Levon. At least I know for sure Betty Jo is okay. Is she coming here? She knows about Phillip?"

"She said she was sending positive energy his way, according to the woman who interviewed her. But I bet she'll be on the road, after she's had time to absorb it."

I couldn't think of anything to say to that. "I hope so," I said finally. Betty Jo seemed to have reinvented herself. Levon patted me on the shoulder awkwardly before he left. I bought my stamps, dropped Robin off downtown for a haircut. Instead of bringing a book into the shop and reading while he was being shorn, once again I returned to the alley behind the hair salon. If I could only get these walls to speak to me, I would know what had happened. I sat there and moved cars and people around in my head, trying to create a scenario that made sense. It seemed like I'd been playing mental chess with all these pieces forever.

In my imagination, Josh's car came to a stop in the alley. His sister had texted Tammy to tell her she had arrived. But something might have happened to prevent Joss from going right into the shop. So Tammy walked out the back door of the salon to check on her. What if Josh had had a car malfunction—maybe his foot slipped from the brake to the accelerator—and the car surged forward, killing Tammy? In a panic, all the kids in the car decided to run away. Somewhere. Towing an eleven-year-old.

But I remembered Josh's car had no traces of having collided with a human being, or of receiving any more of a collision than bumping a tree in the grove where it had been found.

Okay, another possibility. As Josh's car pulls in, an unnamed person gets into a car in the little parking lot. Maybe a hairdresser, running late to pick up a kid. She doesn't realize Tammy is behind her, and she backs into the girl, killing her. She snaps and forces all the kids to . . . do what? Vanish themselves? And of course the other employees would have told the police that someone had left at the crucial time.

Try again. Tammy is out in the parking lot before Josh and company arrive. An unknown enemy, or a careless driver, speeds down the alley and hits her. When the kids get there, they see Tammy's body and . . . *don't get out to check on her or call an ambulance*. I discarded that idea right away. That just wouldn't happen.

Fourth attempt. Josh's car arrives, but right behind it is Clayton's car, with Clayton driving and Connie as passenger. Maybe Marlea is in the Trans Am, too? Clayton hops out and comes forward to confront the kids in the first car. I didn't know what their offense could have been, but I had to assume there was one. Maybe they'd cut him off in traffic, or insulted Connie in some way. Clayton yells at them.

And at this point, I had to assume that someone who wanted to kidnap Clayton had followed them there. He was armed. Had to be. Otherwise, they could have overcome him.

This individual forces Josh to drive away, and somehow gets the Trans Am to follow. The only way I could think of for the kidnapper to do that was to tell the kids in Car 1 that a kid in Car 2 would be killed if they drove off. Tammy comes out of Shear Delight, sees what is happening, rushes to rescue her friends, and is hit by the Trans Am, either on purpose, to eliminate a witness, or by accident in the heat of the moment. And this haunts Connie so much that she kills herself.

Okay. So why had Connie remained free? Why had she been left, and who had come to get her? She could have revealed everything to the police.

I ran over that several times in my head. There were huge gaps in this scenario. But it was the only sequence of events covering the few facts that we knew.

I knew I was hardly the smartest or most crime-savvy of the people investigating this case. Surely the police and the FBI had reached some version of the same conclusion. In that case, what would they be doing about it?

Searching for the place the kids were being held prisoner, of course. Like everyone else. They were all over it. What could I do any better?

I didn't know, but I had to do something.

After I'd picked up Robin at the barber's and we'd stopped at our mailbox, Robin sat at the kitchen table to sort the mail while I sorted dinner. I put in a chicken casserole to heat, and I sat in the chair opposite Robin.

"Here's what I've been thinking," I said, and outlined it all for him.

He took a while to mull all that over. "One of those pretty much has to be correct," he said.

I relaxed a little. I hadn't known I was so tense waiting for his opinion.

"Why can't they find the kids?" I said. "They have to be here, right? Can you construct a narrative in which they aren't in Lawrenceton?"

"Or in this immediate area," he said cautiously. "No, I can't. If it had been just Josh, or Josh and Joss, I could understand it. But not three able-bodied teenagers. And why would anyone sane take the chance of abducting Liza? She's hardly self-sufficient. Any time a child that young is snatched, the press coverage ratchets up a notch."

"Liza asked the wrong person for a ride," I said sadly. "If only she had been willing to wait in the parking lot for her mom. But not with those three little savages there."

"Why were they there?" Robin asked.

"What?"

"Why were they there? I understand that Joss had been giving Liza a private lesson. Why were the tween girls there? The last day of school before Christmas break? They should have been home planning what they were going to be doing over the holidays. Or helping their mothers make cookies. Or texting all their other friends to find out where a party was. Something. And we have to know if Marlea was with her brother, or not."

"How can we find out the answers?"

"Ask 'em."

I screwed up my nerve to call the Windhams' house. I knew Kesha's mother better than the other two. "Hi, Sandra," I said when she picked up the phone. "This is Aurora. How are you?"

"I've been better," she said. " And I know you must be feeling terrible. I'm so sorry."

"About that. Would you mind very much if I came over and asked Kesha a few questions?"

"Listen, Roe, I know she's done a bad thing, and she's getting punished. But I hate to keep drumming her badness into her. She's ashamed of what she did."

"I don't want to accuse her," I said. "And I'm relieved to hear she's standing up to it. You and your husband are good parents. I just want to hear from Kesha's own lips what happened at the soccer field that afternoon."

There was a long silence. Then an audible sigh. "Okay," Sandra said. "I guess that would be all right. But just you. And you can't try to tell her how bad she is for being a bully. We've been all through that, believe me."

"That isn't my responsibility," I said, though such a conversation would be deeply satisfying.

"With that understood," Sandra said, after a significant pause. "You can come over."

Robin wanted to go with me, but I thought any deviation from the guidelines Sandra had chosen might cancel my interview with Kesha.

The Windhams lived in a very nice neighborhood, Fox Creek Hills, not far from the Harrisons' house, in fact. It was a lovely area, next to open country. The Windham house was at the base of the hill, and the Harrison house farther up; and I believed Dan Harrison's parents' was at the top. In Fox Creek Hills, property got more valuable according to the altitude, my mother had told me. The lots were large, the houses very large, the yards well kept. The whole subdivision had been established in the past ten years.

Webster Windham was a dentist, like his father. They were in practice together now. He had an excellent reputation. They were nice people. But I hardened my heart a bit, because I was going to have to make at least one of them uncomfortable.

It was a workday, so I didn't expect Webster to be home at five o'clock. It was dark, but I could see that there was only one vehicle in the garage. Sandra answered the door. She was wearing jeans and a long-sleeved T-shirt with coordinating necklace and earrings. Casual but nice.

"Hi," she said, trying to give me a welcoming smile, but failing.

"Sandra," I said. "Sorry about this."

"I know." She stood aside to let me in.

I hadn't realized that Sandra was an antique buff, but most of the pieces of furniture clearly had some history. I'd expected neutral chic, but I got an eclectic blending of ages and designs. "Gosh," I said. "Sandra, this is so pretty. I bet you decorated it yourself?"

She looked pleased. "Yes, I did," she said. "I tried to use an interior decorator, but she aggravated me so much that I had to fire her. She kept telling me what I couldn't do. I disagreed."

I almost laughed, and only the serious nature of my errand stopped me. "I'd love to have you tell me the history of these pieces sometime," I said. "When we're all happier."

"I'd be glad to."

"Your house is so sparkly. I haven't felt like cleaning, and boy, can you tell it."

"Oh, I use that maid service. Helping Hands. Just about everyone in this development does. Give them a call. They're great about trying to work people in."

We walked together into the huge family room, which had a ceiling extending up through the second floor. Kesha was sitting on the couch, looking like she'd been called to the principal's office. She was a pretty little girl, with huge brown eyes and toasted-almond skin. Her ears were pierced, but she wasn't wearing makeup, and her clothes were age-appropriate, at least as far as I could tell—bright aqua slacks and a cream-colored sweater, and UGG boots.

"Kesha," said Sandra, and Kesha got up and said, "Hello, Ms. Teagarden."

"Hi," I said. "Kesha, I'd like to ask you a few questions."

She nodded glumly and sat down on the couch again. I perched on the matching ottoman so I could sit directly opposite her. Sandra hovered.

"Kesha, can you tell me exactly what you saw the afternoon the kids went missing?" I tried to sound sympathetic and warm, and to my relief, she responded to that.

"We were hanging around at the soccer field," she said.

"Why?"

"What?"

"Why were you hanging around at the cold soccer field, when school had just let out for Christmas vacation? I remember not being able to get away fast enough."

Kesha looked sullen. "Because we knew Liza was going to be having her lesson with Joss."

The words *And you wanted to torment her some more* were stillborn on my lips. No accusing, her mother had stipulated.

"What happened during the lesson?" I couldn't help it: my voice was less friendly.

"Well, Liza wasn't doing too well, and Marlea said something about it." Kesha smiled. It was much more genuine than her pretense of sorrow.

I did my best not to look at Sandra. My jaw tightened.

"Joss tried to tell us to leave, but we had a right to be there. It's our school, too. And Marlea told her no big old lesbo was going to tell her what to do."

I literally had to hold my breath. I could feel my hands shaking. I glanced over Kesha's head at Sandra, but she'd turned her back and her face was to the wall. I didn't blame her.

"After Marlea insulted Joss, what happened?" I said, when I could keep my voice level.

"Joss said she might be gay, but we were bitches, and she'd rather be gay than be like us."

I made a "go on" gesture when Kesha stopped dead.

"Well, then that new guy, Phillip, and Josh pulled up. They were there to pick up Joss. But Liza was scared to be alone with us," Kesha said with some pleasure and some scorn. "She begged them to take her with them."

"Was anyone else there besides the people you've told me?"

She looked surprised. She actually gave it some thought. "I saw Coach Smith walked by," she said. "But he didn't talk to them. I think he was making sure the equipment shed was locked up."

"No one else? While you were in the parking lot?"

Kesha looked confused. "Marlea called her mom to come pick us up."

"So you were waiting in the parking lot. And no one else walked by."

She nodded, giving me a look that showed me how dumb she thought I was for asking.

"Did anyone else *drive* into the parking lot after Joss left with Liza?"

"Yes," she said promptly.

"Who?"

"Clayton, Marlea's brother. He's so cool. And his girlfriend was with him, that Connie who just killed herself." For the first time, Kesha looked genuinely unhappy.

"You didn't tell me that," her mother said, turning around.

"That FBI lady asked me. You were out of the room," Kesha said.

"Did Clayton talk to you?" I asked.

"He said hi," Kesha said with a smile, basking in the remembered coolness of talking to Clayton Harrison. "His car is red. And Connie was driving."

"Did he talk to you?" I was holding on to my patience with a thread. "Did Clayton say anything else?"

"He talked to Marlea. He wanted to find out where Joss was. Marlea said they'd just left, and told him Josh and Phillip were with Joss. And said Joss had a hair appointment. Then Marlea asked him if their mom had told him to pick us up. He said no, he needed to talk to Joss. And Marlea said . . ." Kesha abruptly cut off her narrative. After a second, she said, "Well, Clayton told us to keep cool and he'd see us around, we should call someone else." Kesha smiled a secret sort of smile. "Connie didn't say a word."

I cast around trying to think of some way to get Kesha to tell me what she'd just withheld from her narrative. "No one else came after that?"

"Sienna's mom," Kesha said. "We called her, and she came quick. She was going to take all of us to Sonic to get a milkshake. She'd already called my mom and Marlea's. Ms. Tiffany wanted to know why we'd stayed after school and what we were doing at the soccer field, and we told her, and she laughed and told us we really needed to quit teasing Liza."

"Teasing," I said.

Kesha shifted. "Well, yeah."

I tried to think of anything else I could ask her, while I could still stand to speak with her. "Kesha, tell me," I said, "why did you three decide to target Liza?"

"Because she told on us last year for taking some makeup from Walmart," Kesha said. "And our parents made us take it back and apologize to the manager. It was so embarrassing. What kind of girl tells on other kids?"

I rubbed my hand over my face. "Well, I guess you showed her," I said.

"Yeah," Kesha said, with simple satisfaction. "We did."

So much for Kesha being contrite and learning from her mistakes. I felt sorry for Sandra and Webster, and sorrier still for the people Kesha would encounter throughout her life. I looked at the girl bleakly. She met my eyes for a minute, but then she looked down. Really, there was nothing to say to her that would put a dent in her armor. I'd never had my own twelve-year-old; I didn't know whether or not Kesha was retrievable.

I couldn't bear to look at Sandra's face. It must be one of the worst things in the world, to see your child revealed as a selfish little sadist.

Being a mother scared me, suddenly, the huge responsibility of making sure your child did not turn out like that. Sandra and Webster had not taught these values to their daughter. Was Kesha bad by nature? Had the other two girls polluted her with this gross selfishness, this lack of empathy?

"Good-bye, Kesha," I said, trying to sound neutral. I stood up. "Thanks, Sandra, for letting me come over and talk to your daughter."

I nodded at Sandra without looking at her directly, and went to the front door. She came up behind me in a flurry of steps, and her hand landed on my shoulder. I turned to face her. "I'm so sorry for your troubles," she said. "If I can help, I will."

"You've already helped," I said. "I hope . . . well, I hope

that . . ." I struggled with an ending to the sentence that wouldn't be overwhelmingly negative. "I hope things get better," I said, and then I left.

Kesha was a liar. I was willing to bet good money that there had been more conversation between Clayton and the girls. Otherwise, why would Clayton and Connie follow Josh's car? But at least I knew that Marlea had not been with her brother behind Shear Delight.

I was left wondering why Clayton had wanted to catch up with Josh. I felt I had taken a baby step farther to getting the big picture, but it was still far from clear.

Maybe if I could talk to Clayton's parents, I would get a better idea. But I was confident that the Harrisons were not in any mood to speak to me. And it made me feel weird to remember that we'd followed Dan. I hoped he never knew about that.

It was making me desperate, knowing that Phillip had gotten the chance to talk to me, and had not been able to let me know where he was. My brother was being held hostage by an armed and dangerous person. Phillip had asked me to help, and I had failed him.

I was so worried it made me sick. Literally. My stomach lurched like a ship in rough waters, and I thought about pulling to the side of the street and trying to vomit discreetly. I made it home, just barely, and sped by Robin on my way to the bathroom.

He gave me privacy for upchucking. I appreciated it.

After I brushed my teeth and scrubbed my face with cold water, I made my way to the living room. I lay down on the couch, and Robin regarded me from one of the armchairs. "Tell me about it," he said, and I did.

"There's no way we could have a child like that," he said immediately.

"I'm sure Sandra and Webster felt that way, too." I sounded as dismal as I felt.

"Roe, I have a little news. It's not good."

My heart actually stopped for a moment. "Tell me," I said.

"Less than a half mile from where they found Josh's car, they spotted a shirt in the ditch. It was Josh's. It was really bloody," Robin said. "They're testing the blood to find out whose it is."

"Phillip said Josh was hurt."

"Yes, he did. The spots of blood in the car were Joss's. So maybe this blood is hers, too. But since the shirt is Josh's . . ."

"Not so much blood that he might die?"

Robin shook his head. "Not that much. But not a few drops, either."

"I don't want to sound like a coward, and I know I don't have an alternative to handling this," I said. "But sometimes I don't believe I can take any more. That's stupid, I have to." I sighed. "Where was the shirt found? In relation to Josh's car?"

"Just out of the first search radius, whatever it was. It was thrown down in a shallow ditch. And since it was a dark-colored shirt, it didn't stand out until the search widened," Robin said.

Why not in the car? I shook my head. "Robin, like everything else about this, that doesn't make sense."

"I know."

The doorbell rang. I'd never thought I'd hate that sound. Lately, I had not wanted to see anyone who came in through our door. And today was no exception. Betty Jo Teagarden bustled into our house, with an airplane carry-on bag hanging from one shoulder.

"Why didn't you take better care of your brother?" she demanded, dropping the bag on the floor and stepping toward me, completely ignoring Robin, who was staring at her with his mouth open. I saw the moment when something in him snapped.

He came around to stand between me and Betty Jo, and he said, "You apologize to my wife, or you turn around and leave." I'd never heard him sound so angry.

Betty Jo's eyes opened wide and she stared at Robin as though she'd realized he was green. "Who might you be?" she snarled.

"I might be Roe's husband, and I might be the one who agreed with Roe that we should take Phillip in and support him, because his parents weren't doing a very good job."

There was a long moment of silence.

"All right," Betty Jo said. She straightened up, and her face ironed out. "All right. I'm sorry. I had the whole plane ride to think about Phillip and how scared I am, and I tried to find someone to blame."

"Okay," I said wearily. Robin moved aside. "Excuse me for not getting up, but I'm nauseated."

"Do you have the flu?"

"No, I have a baby." She looked puzzled. "I'm pregnant," I said, with none of the joy I'd had initially.

"Oh, that's wonderful!" she said, but then the weight of the burden of Phillip's disappearance descended on her shoulders. "Roe, what's happened to my boy?" She sank down onto the ottoman, her shoulders slumped.

It had been a long time since I'd seen Betty Jo. She'd never been what you would call a pretty woman—she was built for endurance rather than style—but she'd always been healthy and energetic. The woman I was looking at now was haggard and thin.

"You've been living at a commune?" Robin said, since there was no way I could answer Betty Jo's question.

"Yes." She sighed heavily. "The day after Phillip caught his dad with the whore on our couch, two men showed up at our front door. Phillip was at school—or so I thought, but he was actually on his way over to you. Phil had gone to work, to get away from our epic argument, of course. Why stay and try to talk to me, to patch things up? I was doing laundry and trying to figure out what I would do next."

"Two men?" I said, to get her back on track.

"It was so scary, Roe. They were really bad men, and they were really determined that Phil repay them."

"Oh my God," I said. "They were like Mob men? Really?"

"They were," Betty Jo said. "And they told me that if Phil didn't get them what he owed them, they'd come back and rape me and make Phil watch."

"Good God almighty," Robin said. "Did you call the police?"

"I did not," she said. "And I've regretted it ever since. Instead, I decided I would just leave, because then I wouldn't be there and they couldn't use me to leverage Phil into doing something stupid. Well, stupider. And I sure didn't want to be at their mercy. But I couldn't watch out all the time, you know? I have to go out sometimes. So leaving seemed safest. Then I found out that Phillip hadn't been to school, and I knew he'd run away. I had to stay around so I could find out where he was, if he was safe. When you called, I was so relieved. So I packed my bag and took off, because by that time I was so scared I could hardly stand being in the house."

"Did you tell Dad what had happened? With the Mob men?"

"I was so angry I didn't say a word," she admitted. "I just wanted to get out of town. And if they came back and beat the shit out of him, well, that wouldn't make me cry. I'd visited the Harmony commune before, when I was a girl, and I'd liked it then. I'd been exchanging e-mails with them about staying there, at least for a month. Like a retreat. A breather. So I could decide what to do with my life."

Sounded like she, too, had been at the end of her rope.

"Why didn't you tell Phillip what you were going to do? You could have called him. Or texted him." I tried not to sound accusatory. I don't think I succeeded.

"He would have tried to get me to call the police," Betty Jo said frankly. "I love Phillip. But he has a streak of . . . righteousness, I guess. I was feeling stifled. I just had to get away or die. The bone busters showing up at the house just made me more determined."

"You couldn't have left Dad a note?"

"I did," she said. "I attached it to Phil's coffee cup with Scotch tape. But I didn't tell him where I was going, just that I would get in touch with him when I felt safer. I thought he might pester me, so I left my cell phone and bought a prepaid. I tried to call Phillip, but I guess he didn't recognize the number and he blocked it."

"Dad said you had run away with another man."

"Roe, Phil is quite a liar." She looked at me as if I'd told her I believed in Santa Claus.

"I'm getting that picture." I closed my eyes.

You can't really turn your back on the world. Betty Jo had tried that at the commune, but it hadn't worked. The world will track you down with bloodhounds baying at the bottom of your tree.

I'd extended that metaphor as far as I could, and I abandoned it.

"I wondered if I could stay with you," Betty Jo said.

"No," I said immediately, and caught a flash of relief on Robin's face. "Dad stayed with me, and it was a disaster. He's at a hotel now. You can stay with him, or in another hotel, or ask one of your friends here. But I just don't feel well enough to have a houseguest."

I could see that she wanted to argue with me, perhaps to tell me she wouldn't be any trouble. Fortunately for us all, Betty Jo decided to beat a dignified retreat. "I understand," she said. "I have a rental car. I'll go to the sheriff's department to see what I can learn, and then I'll find a place to stay."

I nodded, unable to get up, unable to care about her plans. "You do that," I said. I closed my eyes. I heard a murmur of voices as Robin showed Betty Jo out.

When I heard the door close on her back, I was delighted.

"What do you want to do now?" Robin asked.

That was a good question. I held up a forefinger to let him know I'd heard him. "Thinking," I said. But I couldn't come up with a single thing, a clear idea, a direction. Instead, I fell asleep.

Chapter Fourteen

When I woke, I was completely disoriented. I couldn't understand why I'd been so tired, why I was so upset, and where I was. After a moment, I was sure I was on the couch in my own living room. The room was dark and gloomy with twilight. I couldn't hear anyone moving around in the house. Where was Robin? Working in his office? Phillip must be over at the Finstermeyers'. I'd have to ask Josh to dinner soon, because Phillip was probably eating Beth out of house and home.

Then I remembered I didn't know where Phillip was. The situation tightened around me once again. For some reason, I found myself thinking about an incident years ago, just after I'd inherited Jane Engle's house and property. Jane had left a message for me. She hadn't wanted it to be available to other people. Taking her cue from Poe, she'd left it in plain sight, in a letter rack. It had looked like a letter and been in the right place, and I'd only thought to check out that it was what it seemed to be after days. Almost too late.

My brain was trying to give me a clue by throwing up the memory of this incident. But what could it be?

Who could hide Phillip in plain sight? Clearly, that wasn't

literally possible. But since Phillip hadn't been seen since his disappearance, and neither had his friends, there must be a connection. Since I knew my brother, I discarded all the wilder theories floating around Lawrenceton, theories Robin had seen posted on a chat site: that all the kids were drug users and their disappearance was due to a deal gone bad, that Phillip and Josh had owed drug dealers and had traded Joss and Liza for debt forgiveness. That Phillip was in love with Joss and Josh with Liza, and they'd all eloped to Mexico. That the kids had come across a meth lab in the woods and been killed by its owners. And on and on.

Sure, any of those things *could* have happened . . . but I knew the teens involved, and those things *hadn't* happened.

I went over the same knowledge again, searching for some insight.

Phillip and Josh had picked up Joss and Liza had asked for a ride. Fact.

Soon after they'd departed, Clayton and Connie had driven up, and after some conversation with his sister, he'd wanted to know where they'd gone. According to Kesha, he'd left Marlea in the parking lot and followed the black Camaro. Fact . . . maybe. Kesha was withholding something, but it didn't have to be anything significant.

But almost certainly, Clayton had directed Connie to follow Josh's car to the hair salon. In response to a text (probably) Tammy Ribble had walked out the back door to see Joss. And then, Connie had seen (or done) something so awful that a few days later, she had taken her own life.

Josh's car had been found out in the country. A shirt, maybe Josh's, had been found in another location, with an alarming amount of blood on it. And there was that terrible phone call from Phillip, not from his own cell phone, when he'd told me they were being held prisoner and that Josh was hurt.

Because of the car and the shirt, and the call, I was sure that the missing kids were being held in the country somewhere. God knows, there was still enough farmland around Lawrenceton to conceal a few people. But I'd seen evidence that the police and the sheriff's deputies were combing the area for remote structures. It seemed reasonable to conclude that if the kids had been hidden in a farmhouse or barn or some kind of shed, the law enforcement people—now including the FBI—would have found them. Or gotten a lead on them. Something.

I thought, *Then they're in town.* Or was that an absurd idea? How could four kids be concealed in a relatively close-knit town like Lawrenceton?

Okay, then. How could they?

Garages. Basements. Storm shelters. Toolsheds. Hothouses? (No, that was ridiculous.) Barns. Empty storefronts, which had been plentiful in the past five years; though they were beginning to come back to life now. But I was not thinking about the economic recovery today.

The most likely three candidates were a garage, an attic, or a basement.

This whole ordeal had been riddled with liars.

For the first time, I thought, *If Clayton isn't a victim, he might be a perpetrator. What if the Harrisons are liars, too? What if there never had been a ransom demand? What if they knew all along where Clayton was?*

How could I get into the Harrisons' house? And then I remembered that the older Harrisons were in Colorado. Their house would be empty. My brain caught fire with excitement.

I called my mother. "Didn't you sell the Harrisons their place?" I said. "I seem to remember that."

If she was startled, she didn't let on. "Yes," she said. "The mansion on Overbrook. And further up the hill, I sold the older Harrisons their house, too."

"Do you remember the features of those houses?" I asked, keeping my fingers crossed. My mother was a walking encyclopedia of real estate in Lawenceton and its environs. She never forgot a property.

Though she sounded puzzled, she complied. "Okay," she said, warming up to the task. "Dan and Karina's house is a four-bedroom, two living areas, chef's kitchen with eat-in area, dining room. There are, hmm, five bathrooms? And an entertainment room in the basement."

I closed my eyes. *Thank you, God,* I said. "What about the older Harrisons' house?"

"It's about the same size. But instead of an entertainment room, they have a pool room in their basement for visiting grandkids."

"Right. How big is that pool room?"

"At least twenty by sixteen, if I'm remembering correctly," Mother said. "But I don't believe Dan's parents have talked about selling, and I would have heard. Do you think the baby will need that much more space?" I could tell she was smiling.

"So you think the basement room in Dan and Karina's house is that big?" I asked.

"Larger," my mother said. "There's a huge storage closet for Christmas and holiday stuff down there, and there's the movie room. Roe, I'm getting worried. What's on your mind?"

"I was just thinking."

"About what?"

I didn't want to show my hand, but I owed her that much. "I wonder if our missing kids are being held in a basement," I said. "I was thinking of all the people involved in the case who might have a basement. Voilà!"

She drew in a sharp breath. "How could they be?" she said. "Right in town!" There was a moment of silence. "Well, the nearest houses are not close," she said slowly. "Both lots are maybe three fourths of an acre."

"How many people in residence in those houses?"

"Karina and Dan, of course. And normally, Clayton and little Marlea. The older brother, Bobby, is at college at Auburn. He's engaged to a girl from . . . oh, well. There's a cook. Comes every day. Not live-in."

"And the other Harrison house?"

"Just Dan's folks. They travel a lot. They don't have a live-in maid, and neither do Karina and Dan. Right now, Lena and Tate have gone to Colorado to ski, like they do every winter," Mother said. "Their other son and his family live out there."

"So what help do the Harrisons have?"

"I actually know the answer to that!" My mother sounded pleased to find her knowledge was so thorough. "They use a maid service. The same company I use. I recommended them to Karina when she and Dan bought the house. Helping Hands," Mom said. She added helpfully, "The ones with the pink smocks. I think Dan's mother Lena uses them, too. Just about everyone in that subdivision does."

"Do they use anyone else, regularly?"

"They use one of the yard services, I'm sure," Mother said promptly. "Either Garcia and Sons, or Landscaping Magic. Roe, it sounds to me like you're going to do something stupid. The police are competent, you know. Don't go acting like you have to rescue Phillip yourself."

I didn't look as though I worked for Garcia and Sons or Landscaping Magic, but the maid service . . . I could do something with that. "Mom, don't worry," I said. "I just have to find out everything I can about everyone involved. You know how I am. I like to have all the facts. If I ever learn anything that's really decisive, I'll call the police in a jiffy. Thanks, Mom, I have to—"

"Have you decided if you all come to us for Christmas dinner?" she asked quickly, stopping me right before I could hang up. I knew I owed her some conversation. So for what felt like an eternity, we chatted about the Christmas meal, when John's sons were arriving with their families.

"Mother," I said, "I'll let you know in a day or two." I knew that was shabby. But I couldn't even think about Christmas without my brother, burdened with the overwhelming uncertainty about his whereabouts and well-being.

"By the way, Betty Jo is in town," I said. I didn't want Mother to run into the woman somewhere in Lawrenceton without being warned.

"Where did the police find her?" Mother had been really intrigued that no one could lay hands on my father's wife.

"On a commune," I said. It didn't seem right to tell Mother Betty Jo's reason for taking off like she had.

"A commune," my mother said with delight. I'd made her day.

"I have to go," I said, trying to suppress my excitement at actually having something to do. I might have known I couldn't fool my mother.

"Roe," Mom said sharply. "Don't go doing anything foolish. You talk to Robin right now, before you go running off alone." She was serious as a heart attack.

"I'm going to talk to him right now, or at least as soon as I see him." And I did.

After I'd hung up, I felt like getting off the couch. In fact, I felt a rush of energy. I went to our bedroom and picked up the strewn clothes and shoes. I realized that what I'd told Sandra Windham was true. Our house looked shabby and forlorn after a more than a week of neglect. When I'd picked up and made the place look tolerable, I went to my own laptop at my own small desk in the corner of Robin's office.

Where was he? I hadn't seen a note, and I hadn't checked to see if his car was gone. I'd do that next, I decided, after I retrieved the phone book to look up the older Harrisons' address. Lena and Tate Harrison. They were listed.

Turning to the Internet, I tracked down the maid service. Helping Hands was not an uncommon name for both temporary help services and cleaning operations, but I finally tracked down the right one. It was complete with pictures of smiling women holding mops and dusters. I realized I'd seen their zippy green cars around town, the distinctive logo on the side. After studying their pale pink smocks, I called the office number.

"Helping Hands," said a woman briskly. "How may we assist you?"

"I'm picking up Lena Harrison's mail while she's on vacation," I said. "She asked me to check with you. Lena's worried that she told you the wrong date to resume service."

"Let me see," the woman said, without a single hesitation. I could hear the keys clicking on a computer. "I have January third?"

"Great, that's right. I'll let her know."

"Sure. Thanks for calling."

I began to make a plan, but it was so risky that I hesitated.

I called Detective Trumble. When the switchboard put me through to her, she sounded distracted. "Hi, Aurora. What can I do for you?"

"Any news?"

"You'd be among the first to know," she said.

"I figured. Listen, I know you all have searched every nook and cranny around Lawrenceton . . ."

She sighed heavily. "Believe me, we have."

"But have you searched the homes of everyone involved?"

"Like whose?" she asked bluntly.

"Like the Scotts, the Finstermeyers, the Harrisons, the Bells. Or even the two other bullies . . . the Windhams' house, or Tiffany Andrews' place." I thought I was clever, just easing in the Harrisons like that. But Trumble was suspicious.

The silence she kept had a texture to it. "Do you know something you're not telling me?" she demanded.

"You know everything I know," I said, which was the literal truth.

"That's good, because I'd really hate it if you didn't give me every little fact you have."

"Nope, you have all the facts." *I only have suspicions.*

"We've searched the rooms of all the missing kids," Detective Trumble said. "Josh's, Joss's, Liza's, and Clayton's. Just like we searched Phillip's room. But there was no credible reason to search all the houses. And the little bullies? There was no legal basis at all for getting a search warrant for their rooms, or their homes."

"I understand."

"What's on your mind?"

"Nothing," I said mendaciously, joining the ranks of the liars without a qualm. "I just wanted to be sure that you searched everyone's room, not just Phillip's."

"For what purpose?"

"To make sure you had no special reason for picking him out," I said.

"Let us handle this, Aurora," Cathy Trumble said, after a fraught pause.

"Hmm. Sure thing."

"Call me if you have any new information."

"And you call me, likewise." We both hung up, equally unsatisfied with our conversation. My phone buzzed, and I picked it up quickly, hoping it was Robin. But my caller ID read "unknown." "Phillip?" I said, my voice wavering.

"Ms. Teagarden?"

I slumped, deflating with disappointment. I didn't recognize the voice, but she was young.

"Yes," I said.

"This is Marlea. Marlea Harrison?"

"Marlea, what do you want? Why are you calling me?" I really wondered how she'd gotten my number, but I'd already asked two questions. "I thought you were out of town with your mother's family."

"I am. Kesha was lying to you," Marlea said. She sounded pretty happy about that.

"Oh, I can't *believe* that," I said with heavy sarcasm. "And I guess you're going to set me straight?"

"Yeah. She told me that she told you that Phillip was just friends with Liza Scott."

"And?"

"And he was having sex with her," Marlea said coolly. "Your brother was having sex with a *child*."

I thought my head was going to explode. I knew this girl was lying, but the fact that a child could call me and say something so horrible, so calmly . . . it was disgusting. "You make me sick," I said, seeing no reason to mince words. "Why are you saying this?"

"All I have to do is tell people that," she said, clearly drunk on her own power. "And some of them will believe it."

I was talking to a twelve-year-old who believed she could manipulate the world. Was there any possible thing I could say to puncture the balloon of her ego?

"I wonder what you told your brother," I said. "You're a small person, Marlea. Mentally and emotionally. You'll always be small. And if I can send you to the juvenile detention center, I will be happy to do it." I hung up, leaving her to think of that what she would. Could I really charge her with anything, like slander? I didn't know. I doubted it. But I was willing to find out.

I couldn't understand how someone so young could be so twisted. Had her parents beaten her? Had she been molested by a cousin? Had the three girls formed a toxic pool by their very chemistry? Was she born that way?

I didn't have any answer. But now I'd talked to two of Liza's tormentors, and I'd taken their measure. I was older and smarter and meaner—at least, I could be. And I planned to be.

My phone rang again. This time, it was Robin. "Hey, honey. I decided to go Christmas shopping while you were asleep. I want to put something under the tree. Anything you need while I'm out?"

"I don't even know. Isn't that pathetic? Someday we'll be back to normal." Maybe. "Listen, I've had an idea. When you come home, we'll work it out."

"Okay," he said, pleased. "I'll be home in a few minutes."

I felt better the minute I saw Robin. He had several mysterious bags in tow, and he looked something other than worried for the first time in days.

"Anything happen while I was gone?" he asked, while he stuffed his loot in the extra bedroom.

The nursery.

"I had some ideas," I said, "and Marlea Harrison called me."

"The third girl," he said.

"Yeah. She's a piece of work. She threatened to start the rumor that Phillip was having sex with Liza Scott."

"She said this to you?" Robin was horrified. "I didn't think I believed in corporal punishment, but I may reconsider."

"I told her I'd take legal action if she did that."

"I doubt that's enforceable."

"Look, Robin, I had to threaten her. She can't keep ruining lives. Someone's got to take her in check."

"Umm. Well, what's this idea you had?"

I took a deep breath. "To my mind, there are very few places the kids could be," I said.

He listened to me intently as I told him what I wanted to do.

"That's a dangerous plan," he said. "Let me."

"There's no way you'd get in," I said. "But I can do it. And after I verify they're there, this will all be over. The police can come in."

We talked some more, and though Robin was reluctant, he finally agreed that if he were nearby, with the police on speed dial, he'd go along with me. With a safeguard or two.

Finally, I had something to do.

That evening, I walked into the local uniform shop, Work Togs, right before it closed. I'd never had cause to go there before, but I'd vaguely remembered it for its location, right by the Hallmark store where I'd bought gift paper and bows. The small shop was absolutely crammed full of smocks and scrubs in all kinds of fabrics and some really startling colors and patterns.

Did any nurses, anywhere, still wear white starched dresses? Or caps?

My mother had described these to me with great nostalgia. But then, she hadn't had to wear them.

There was a young clerk, who was glad to let me search on my own while she attended to the urgent business of filing her nails. I was the only customer. At the back of the store, I found the pale pink smocks I'd been looking for. And there was a small. I tried it on just to be sure it would fit. I felt like I became invisible the minute I put it on, exactly what I wanted.

I paid for it and took it home. The clerk did not look at me the whole time she rang up my purchase.

Robin and I spent half the evening going over and over the plan. I had a hard time getting to sleep, because I felt excited at the prospect of action. I was tired of reacting.

Early the next morning, after Robin had left to get into position, I brushed my wayward hair vigorously, put product on it to slick it into a ponytail, and twisted the ponytail around in a bun. I picked my glasses with care; nothing too frivolous. My little tortoiseshell ones, the most anonymous frames in my glasses repertoire. Since I looked like hell on wheels anyway, I actually did have a natural disguise: big dark circles under my eyes, white as a sheet, drawn and pinched-looking, thick through the middle. Yeah, I was a knockout, all right.

And pink was definitely not my color.

Now that we were doing something, we both felt so much better—as if the very act of *trying* to solve the problem meant we *had* solved the problem.

I knew that wasn't so. I knew I might be completely wrong.

But at least I had a plan. Robin had protested the evening before, but he knew better than to try to forbid me to do something. He understood I wasn't going to be reckless. I just wanted my brother back.

My car was a staid color, less notable than Robin's, so we'd decided I'd take it.

On the way up, I passed the Windham house just past the Fox Creek Hills sign. What would the Windhams' Christmas be like this year, in their beautifully decorated house, in this affluent suburb? I had no idea if there were foxes resident, or if there was a creek; but there was definitely a hill, and I was driving up a steep one.

First I went all the way up to the most likely place, the home of Dan Harrison's parents, Tate and Lena. It was supposed to be empty, and I was sure I'd be able to tell if it really was.

Robin had preceded me in his car. As I drove past the mansion at the top of the hill, one of three on a cul-de-sac, he was parked at the Harrisons' front door, knocking patiently, a large folder under his left arm. He waited, and knocked again.

No one was going to answer the door, but I hoped someone inside was pretty alarmed. I made a slow circle and passed by again, this time seeing Robin get in his car.

I'd expected that. I was sure this was the more likely place to conceal the missing kids. My heart began beating faster.

I drove down the other side of the hill, circled around, and drove up again. This time I turned in to Tate Harrison's driveway and drove to the back, where a garage and a back door were on the same level. I left my car and walked unhurriedly to the back door, which had some glass panes. As I knocked lightly on the doorframe, I looked in. I saw an empty kitchen. There was absolutely no sign that anyone had been using it. No dishes, nothing out of place. Total order. I glanced around, but I didn't see a soul out in one of the tidy yards who might be watching me, even in the grounds of the houses below me, though the day was warm enough to be tolerable. So I opened the garbage can, a large rolling one that could be wheeled out to the curb. It was not only empty, but clean. (Whose garbage can was *clean*?) Just as I was considering going part of the way around the house to peer in a window, a thin man in a blue long-sleeved jumpsuit walked around the corner of the house.

It took every ounce of self-control I had not to shriek.

"Hey," he said, and I could tell he was startled. Maybe not suspicious, but he was waiting for an explanation.

"Hi," I said. "I was supposed to come check on the job my cleaning team did yesterday, but this house seems to be empty. I need the Harrisons' house?"

"There are two Harrisons living up here," he said readily. He was glad to help me. "This place belongs to the older couple, Tate and Lena. The place down there," and he pointed to a roof below and to the west, "is the other Harrisons, Dan and Karina. That help?"

I did my best to look embarrassed. "Dang it, I'm supposed to be at the other one," I said. "I'm glad you came along. Otherwise, I wouldn't have anything to fill out on my form." I lifted the arm cradling a clipboard. There was indeed a form clipped to it, one I'd designed and printed out on Robin's computer last night. There were boxes to be checked, and lines for signatures. It looked very real.

"Gotta fill out those forms," he agreed. "Well, I'm glad I was able to set you straight."

"Same here. Thanks a lot. I'll see you," I said and climbed back into my car. I maneuvered the car into facing the opposite way, and I zoomed out. As I stopped at the mailbox to check for oncoming traffic—of course there wasn't any—I saw the yardman's pickup parked at the front of the property. Sure enough, it was labeled "Garcia and Sons."

I drove down to a 7-Eleven at the foot of the development

and waited in the parking lot to get the green light from Robin. I only had to wait for thirty minutes before Robin called to say he'd seen the Harrisons leave. I turned my key in the ignition, with a rush of excitement. But my cell rang again.

"Another car just pulled in," Robin said. "I don't know the driver. She's a middle-aged woman in a uniform. Not a pink one."

I decided to risk it. I said, "I'm coming up."

Dan and Karina's driveway led down at a sharp angle and then split in two. The right-hand section swept in a semicircle around the front yard, while the left descended to a paved apron outside a three-car garage. It was the first time I'd seen the back of the house. I got out of my car on the apron. The windows in the garage doors faced west, and would get some evening light. I didn't see how there could be any windows, for that floor, to the east. It would be part of the hillside. There were two stories above that. Of course, the ground level would be the public floor, for family and entertaining, and the next level would be the bedroom floor. I glanced over at the garage again. All the doors were down, which wasn't a surprise.

There was another car parked on the apron, a neatly kept but aged Malibu. I pulled my jacket almost closed to hide the fact that I didn't have a name embroidered in black on my left chest, since all the women employed by Helping Hands wore their names on their chests. With my clipboard in my hand, I went across the apron and up the steps to what should be the kitchen door, and I knocked.

The Harrison cook opened the door. She was a brawny woman in her forties; I'd never seen her before. No one else in Lawrenceton had a cook, either full-or part-time.

"Yes?" she said. "Can I help you?" She wasn't irritated, but she wasn't interested, either.

"Hi," I said, full of cheer. "I'm the supervisor of the Helping Hands team that cleans this house. I'm supposed to check the job the team did for Mrs. Harrison."

"Oh," the cook said, somewhat surprised. "Why didn't you come yesterday right after they cleaned? I wasn't here, but the maids always come on Thursday."

"My car broke down," I said, rolling my eyes. What you gonna do? "By the time I got it fixed, it was too late. But I have to fill out the form." I waved the clipboard. "Is that possible?"

"I guess so," the cook said. "I haven't been here in a week. I have a lot to catch up on. They gave me a paid vacation week, if you can believe that. Before Christmas! I guess you better come on in. I'm Gina Ruffin." She was wearing scrubs, too, a tan outfit. Scrubs appeared to be a universal uniform.

Gina stood aside to let me enter, and I suddenly realized I had no idea if she was responsible for cleaning the kitchen or if the maid service did it, something I ought to know. Crap.

"I'm Rose," I said. "Hey, I don't want to disturb the family. Are they home?"

"Mr. and Mrs. Harrison aren't," she said. "And who knows where Clayton is?"

Did she truly not know that Clayton had vanished? "If he's in the house, should I warn him I'm here?" I said, feeling my way.

"No, I haven't seen him," Gina said, shrugging. But then she looked uneasy. "But you don't need to go downstairs. The Harrisons got the maids to skip the fun room yesterday. They're having some electrical work done down there, and it's not safe. They left a message on my phone."

"Must be nice to have a fun room," I said with a faint smile.

Gina smiled back. "Oh, that's just what they call the big room downstairs." On the garage level. "There's a Ping-Pong table and big TV for watching movies. It's really a hangout for the teenage son and his friends." I was growing anxious; Gina seemed to be having second thoughts about letting me do my inspection. "How long do you think this will take? Maybe you should come back when Karina is at home."

"I'd rather not explain to my supervisor why I was late getting it done, if I can help that," I explained. "If I can just take a quick look, that would sure be great. I can just go down my checklist?"

I held my breath while Gina thought it over. "All right. You're already here, and I have a lot to do. I can tell you your team did a good job in here, so you don't need to check it. But the garbage cans are already full again. I don't know how the Harrisons generate so much garbage. Only two people!" Again, she seemed uneasy. I judged it was better not to comment.

"Then I'll skip the kitchen," I agreed. "And there's loose electrical in the fun room. So, I'll start upstairs and work my way down." I spoke as matter-of-factly as possible.

"What do you check for?" Gina asked, just as I was wondering where the stairs to the "fun room" might be.

It occurred to me Gina was glad to have company. In fact, the cook seemed anxious. I sensed she would shy away from a direct question about what was making her so jumpy. I had to be careful. But I was burning with impatience. What if the Harrisons came back?

"I check the details," I said. Of course, I'd thought about this when I was cobbling together my plan . . . such as it was. "The corners of the bathrooms, the cleanliness of places that aren't immediately visible, whether or not the pictures were straightened on the walls, the frames dusted. If the baseboards are clean, the headboards. Then I rate the team. Their bonus depends on my rating."

"Wow. I guess they're pretty scared of you!" Gina smiled to indicate she was teasing. "I have some prep work to do for lunch and dinner, so I'll let you go about it."

"Thanks for being understanding," I said. "See you in a few."

Aside from the door to my right, which must lead down to the garage, luckily there were only two other options, one a swinging door that logic dictated went to the front part of the house, and one open doorway that led onto stairs. A back way up to the bedroom floor, for sure. I walked over to it confidently, the clipboard clutched to my chest in an official-looking way . . . at least, I hoped so. I didn't look back, because I was scared I'd catch her staring after me, or picking up the phone to call the police, or doing something else that would show she'd cottoned on to me. But instead, I heard water running in the huge farmhouse sink, She'd gone straight to her food preparation.

First hurdle successfully cleared.

I knew Robin was keeping track of me, since my phone was on and in my front smock pocket. "I'm starting up the back stairs to do the bedroom floor," I said quietly. "Trying to be authentic."

When I thought of what trouble I might get into if I was discovered doing this, I broke out in a cold sweat. I would lose my job at the library, and everyone would look at me out of the corners of their eyes for a long time afterward. I might go to jail—the Harrisons would have every right to press charges against me.

But when Cathy Trumble had told me the police were not going to get a warrant to search the Harrisons' houses, I'd had to do something. This intolerable strain had to end, life had to return to something approaching normalcy. I had to get Phillip back.

I hadn't realized how much I loved my brother until he was gone.

He could be as stubborn and uncommunicative as any teenager. I was sure he'd tried most of the things teenagers try. And sometimes I had to ask him more than once to do things around the house, especially unpopular tasks like taking the garbage out or picking up his room. But the fact that he was human and fallible didn't matter. Phillip was my brother.

When I got to the room that must be Clayton's, I looked around carefully. Sure, Clayton's room was bigger and more luxurious than Phillip's. Sure, the furniture was more expensive. But it was still the room of a teenage boy.

And it shouldn't be. Clayton was taken the same time as the other kids, nine days ago. And the maids had come yesterday.

This room should have been pristine. But there were signs that someone had used it: a sweatshirt was on the floor beside the clothes hamper in the bathroom. A drawer was pulled out a little. But the textbooks on the desk were piled neatly, and you could have bounced a dime on the bed.

The maids would never have made the bed and ignored the sweatshirt. At the very least, it would have been picked up and folded.

I looked in every corner. The wastebasket was empty. The bathroom was clean, but it was not perfect. The towel had been hung crookedly. I touched the toothbrush. It was faintly wet. There were beads of water on the shower door, though it was almost dry.

So someone had been visiting this room to shower and change. And who, if not Clayton?

I relayed all this over the telephone to Robin, trying to speak quietly and without emotion. I took pictures of the small signs of usage and sent them to him. I didn't want Robin panicking and forcing his way into the house before I could go downstairs to check out the situation.

I left Clayton's room and headed east to the main staircase, grandly visible in the morning sun streaming in the two-story entry. I went down the carpeted stairs quickly and stood looking around, trying to decide where to go next.

Then, elsewhere in the house, I heard the *beep-beep-beep* that signaled a door monitored by the alarm system had been opened. I gasped. Though it was possible that Gina was doing something like taking out the garbage, chances were just as good that the Harrisons had returned.

I had only minutes to finish my search. The Harrisons might not recognize my car, but they were sure to ask who else was in the house.

I abandoned any pretense of "checking" the main floor. I spotted a hall, and it seemed to lead back to the kitchen; yes, there was the swinging door at the end. There were two more doors to my left. I opened the first one, as silently as I could. Coat closet. I moved on to the second. I stood, listening.

I caught the voices in the kitchen. ". . . didn't expect you back today," Karina's surprised voice said. She sounded displeased.

Mumble, mumble. ". . . week is up," Gina was saying, her voice artificially bright.

I turned the handle silently and stepped inside, closing it just as carefully behind me. There was a pulse of sound when I opened the door, but I hoped I'd closed it quickly enough that it hadn't penetrated to the Harrisons' ears.

The fun room was soundproofed.

"I'm going downstairs. There's someone here in basement," I said to the telephone. "They call it the fun room."

The stairs were dark down to the landing. Below that, I could see from the glow that there was an overhead light switched on below me. It's impossible to go down wooden steps silently; if there's a way to do it, I haven't discovered the technique. Taking as many precautions as I could, I gently laid down the clipboard just inside the door, to leave my hands free. I also slipped off my Pumas.

Hugging the wall, down I crept, excited and frightened. My heart was beating in a way impossible to ignore, and I hoped that was not hurting the baby. I hadn't even considered my physical response to the situation.

Gina's unexpected week off had made me even more suspicious that the Harrisons knew more than they'd ever let on. Who let their cook off the week before Christmas? I remembered how frozen the couple had seemed at the press conference (which felt as though it had been years ago, instead of days). I would have expected them to be angry, or grieved, or stricken, instead of silent and rigid. They had refused to make a statement. And then they'd rushed out as soon as they could . . . after Phillip's phone call.

I reached the landing, and peered around the corner to spy out the situation.

Clayton Harrison was sprawling on a red leather couch, his back to me, blasting away with an electronic gun at the huge television.

Playing a damn *video game*.

I had to make myself hold still, and take a deep but silent breath. I said some words to myself that had never passed my lips. I hated Clayton Harrison with the heat of a thousand suns. I hated the older Harrisons just as much. All this time! *All this time* he had been here, safe and sound!

The ransom, a sham. The search for him, a mockery.

While Clayton was intent on the screen, I scoped out the room, once I could focus on anything other than my rage. There were two doors off the large room, one to the left of the television on which the game images flashed and made noise. That door had two padlocks on it, freshly installed, from the yellow of the wood around them.

The other door, to the right, was half-open. A bathroom. Closer to the east wall was a Ping-Pong table, with a wall rack of equipment. Against the left wall was a bar—Of *course,* I thought—and a refrigerator, a microwave, and a few cases of soda. I could see a bed pillow propped on one end of the couch. Clayton had been sleeping down here.

I didn't know what to do. I wanted to describe what I saw to Robin. I was certain that the police could come in now. Someone they were searching for was sitting in front of me. Right? But if I spoke loud enough to be intelligible to Robin, Clayton would hear me. I didn't want him to have time to do anything.

Then I saw the gun on the table by the couch.

I'd anticipated there would be a gun. How else could one boy make a herd of kids do his bidding? But seeing it made everything suddenly much more clear and drastic. As silently as a mouse, I crept back up the steps. I took my phone out of my pocket and put it to my mouth. "Robin," I said, very softly. "Clayton's here. He's in the basement. He's got a gun. There's a padlocked room."

"I'm calling the police right now," Robin said. "I'll have to hang up for a minute to do that."

"Okay," I breathed. But I felt cast adrift when he was off the line. I sat down on the top step to wait. I figured the padlocked room was Karina's holiday storage closet. I didn't think there were Easter eggs in it now.

Below me, the noisy computer game suddenly went silent.

I sat up, every nerve on edge and screaming with tension. What now?

I listened intently. Finally, I heard what must be bothering Clayton. There were faint voices, and a rhythmic thudding noise. "Shut up!" Clayton screamed, and I jumped. "I've had it with you, assholes!"

But the thudding continued, unabated. What was happening? I didn't know what to do. I crept down a few steps. I could make out a voice, very muffled. It was a male voice, and it was saying, "Let Joss out! She needs the bathroom!"

Phillip's voice.

Relief flowed over me like a river of honey. A future that included a safe and rescued Phillip was *just out of reach*. I clapped a hand over my mouth to keep from exclaiming out loud. My heart began to pound more quickly than ever.

While I was exulting, things had been happening in the big room below me. I heard Clayton unlocking the padlocks. He called, "Stand back. I've got the gun. Only Joss can come out. If you make another move, I'll shoot her."

"We understand," said a little voice. Liza Scott. I went down the remaining steps to the landing and peered around the wall.

"Hands up!" Clayton ordered. And below me, Joss came into sight.

She was a wreck. In my imagination, I'd been picturing the

kids as they were when they'd vanished. But of course, Joss was wearing the same clothes she'd had on that day. She hadn't been able to wash. And she hadn't eaten much. The change in her was dramatic. There was a large scab on her right arm.

When Clayton and Joss crossed in front of the television to get to the bathroom, I was within their sight in my perch on the stairs if they looked right. Something alerted Joss, and she turned her head to see me. I had my finger across my lips in the universal gesture for "Shhh." She jumped a little, but she recovered much more quickly than I would have. She turned the jump into a sideways movement, pretending she'd been turning to face Clayton.

"Listen, asshole, you've got to let us take showers," she said. "We can't stand being around each other any more. And Josh needs a doctor."

"That's not going to happen," Clayton said. He sounded both tired and at the end of his rope, which was disturbing. "Don't argue any more."

"What do you think is going to happen?" Joss said, ignoring him. "Do you think there's any possible happy ending to this?"

Clayton was too close to snapping to bear any added pressure, but Joss did not see that; or maybe she had simply reached her own snapping point. Her glimpse of me on the stairs had given her heart, since she assumed help was coming.

"Shut up!" Clayton screamed.

I stood, because clearly something was about to happen, and it wasn't going to be anything good.

And just then the cook opened the door to the stairs. "What are you doing here?" she said, in a voice that was anything but soft. "We're not supposed to come down here, remember?" Then Clayton came to the foot of the stairs and looked up. I was caught between them.

"Clayton? What's going on down here?" The gravity of the situation seemed to hit Gina all at once. "I thought you were gone? What . . ."

"Stay up there, Gina!" I could see Clayton pointing the gun to his right, at Joss. And Gina could see the gun, but not the girl.

Joss yelled, "Clayton is keeping us hostage down here! Do you want to go to jail with him?"

I looked up at the cook. Gina's face was a picture of conflict. There was a long moment of frozen silence. We had a four-way standoff.

Clayton's face relaxed, the longer it took Gina to respond. He thought he had her on his side. "Gina? Who's up there?" he said, more calmly. I realized I was in the shadows at the top of the stairs. He couldn't risk moving closer to the stairs to see me better.

"A woman from the maid service," Gina said. She was clearly torn. I shook my head at her emphatically. *He has a gun,* I mouthed silently.

"What's she doing?" Clayton was trying to keep his eyes on Joss, but he kept glancing toward the stairs.

Gina said, accurately, "Nothing." She went back up a step. She was clearly on the verging of cutting and running, and that would be absolutely disastrous.

"Where are Mom and Dad?" Clayton called to Gina. "You listen to them! You want to work here, right?"

Gina said in a normal voice, "I'm not going to jail for you." And she backed away from me as if I were the Devil, and then turned and ran into the kitchen, leaving the door open.

"Who's there?" Clayton yelled.

I went down one step to see Joss resolutely not looking up at me, Clayton backing away from her, the gun held in a shaking hand, and I heard a barrage of pounding and thudding from the makeshift prison.

A few minutes would see us all safe. Just a few minutes. I

tried to figure how many had passed since Robin had hung up to call the police, and I could not even hazard a guess. And maybe it would take them ten minutes to get someone over here? Or maybe they would wait for a SWAT team to assemble? Oh, God, I hoped not. I should probably follow Gina out of the house, but Joss was by herself, facing down a murderer. I couldn't abandon her. I was torn between securing safety for my baby and acting a witness to whatever was going to happen.

Wisdom suggested I beat a retreat.

"Who's on the stairs?" Clayton screamed. "Answer me, bitch!" He lunged toward Joss and hit her across the face with the gun.

She yelped with pain, and blood ran from a gash on her forehead. I couldn't think what to do. "Clayton, put down the gun," I called. "Put it down and it won't be so bad on you." I had no idea what I was saying or if it was true.

"Who are you?" He sounded less hysterical but more determined; that was probably a bad thing. I didn't want him calm. I wanted him thoroughly rattled and scared. Or did I? Would he be more likely to shoot someone if he thought all was lost? Or would he surrender? I was not adequate to meet this situation.

"I'm Aurora Teagarden, Phillip's sister," I said. "And the police are on their way, Clayton. This is over. Your parents aren't here," I lied. "It's just you."

"I heard the door beep," Clayton said, though uncertainly.

Maybe the Harrisons had gone upstairs, because they hadn't appeared yet. Maybe they wouldn't.

But then there were footsteps on the hall floor. "Gina?" a woman called. "Where's the woman from the maid service? Did she come out this way?"

Sometimes I just couldn't catch a break. Launching myself up the stairs, I felt the doorknob urgently. There was a little press-to-lock button. That would buy me a little time.

"Clayton?" This time it was a man. "What's happening? Where is Gina?"

I held on to the doorknob with both hands. Someone outside tried to turn it.

"What's wrong with the door?" Karina asked, from just a few inches away.

Thanks, universe.

"I think it's locked," Dan said.

"There's one of those skinny keys around here somewhere," Karina told her husband. Though I didn't hear one inserted, I gripped the knob so ferociously that I would fall down the stairs if the knob came loose. Again, someone tried to open the door, with no key but more muscle. Probably Dan Harrison. But I was determined to keep my grip: nothing good could come from adding two more people to the equation.

Especially two adults who were letting their son hold hostages in their basement.

I don't think I've ever been more scared in my life. Clayton was at my back and his parents were at my front. It couldn't get worse than this.

Then I heard footsteps on the stairs below me and I knew Clayton was coming up behind me.

I looked over my shoulder and saw him almost at the landing, half-keeping the gun trained on Joss, half-glaring in my direction. If he shot me in the back, all his immediate problems would be solved. And the gun was beginning to swing around when Joss did an incredible thing.

She tackled him.

The gun flew out of Clayton's hand to land on the floor. He wriggled free from her and dove for it, but she was there ahead of him.

Clayton froze. He was stomach-down on the basement floor, and Joss was sitting up, still bleeding profusely from her forehead, the gun pointing steadily at her captor.

"You won't shoot me," Clayton said.

"I would be so happy to shoot you," Joss said. "Don't tempt me."

I don't know about Clayton, but I believed her.

Now the older Harrisons were doing their own pounding and yelling, the door reverberating with their blows. If they found a key, I didn't know how much longer I was going to be able to hold on to the knob. I wondered if I would hear sirens any time soon. Like, *now*?

But the police did not arrive with sirens. They came in quietly and heavily armed. I heard Karina scream when she saw them. That came through the door loud and clear. And the rescuers began yelling very specific orders at Karina and Dan. "Step away from that door!" was popular, as well as "Hands up!"

Dan Harrison began to bluster immediately: "Why are you in my house? Do you have a warrant? I'm calling my lawyer!"

"You do that," said one recognizable voice. I felt glad all over. Cathy Trumble. Another woman said, "I'm going to read you your rights." Bernadette Crowley. God bless her.

"Get them away from the door," she added. "We've got hostages down there."

Finally, I was able to let go of the doorknob. I felt like sagging to my knees. I turned the knob to unlock the door, but I didn't open it, not knowing the situation on the other side.

"I'm in here!" I called. "It's Aurora and I'm in here! Clayton has been holding the kids hostage, and Joss just got the drop on him. So there's a gun down here," I added. An important point.

"Okay, steady, Aurora. Steady. Open the door and stand back against the wall."

I wasn't quite sure how to do this since the stairway was narrow, but I turned the knob and pulled the door open, flattening myself against the wall. Just for insurance, I put my hands up. Cathy Trumble's was the first face I saw. She had a gun pointed at me.

"I'm stepping back," she said to me, her voice level and steady. "When I do, you come out of there."

I could only nod. Several times.

She did step back, revealing a hallway which had become a narrow corridor lined with men and women and guns.

Clayton was clearly out-armed. "Who's down there?" Crowley demanded.

"Joss is the only hostage loose," I said. "She's taken Clayton's gun from him, and she's ready to shoot if he tries to get it back."

Crowley propelled me forward down that corridor, hustling me toward the back door, and, barely registering the fact that the paved apron was now solid with law enforcement vehicles, I hurried through the kitchen and started down the steps. And then I kept on going because my husband was there waiting, his face tense with fear. His arms opened and I flew in, wrapping my arms around him like a monkey. Robin didn't say anything, just hugged me very tightly. That was enough. After a moment of feeling safe, I peered around Robin to see Gina, talking excitedly to Levon Suit, clearly beside herself.

After a minute, I noticed that Bryan Pascoe was standing back behind Robin. He looked very lawyer-like in a full suit and a starched shirt and subdued tie. "Bryan, I'm so glad you're here," I said. "I don't think Phillip is going to need you, but it might be really, really handy."

Bryan said, "I wouldn't have missed this for the world." Bryan was not a smiley kind of guy, but he was delighted, no two ways about it.

Then there was quite a bit of yelling from the house, but I couldn't understand it. Joss shot out of the kitchen door, bleeding but triumphant. Two officers hustled her to the waiting ambulance. In short order she was loaded in on a gurney and sent off to the hospital with sirens wailing.

Next out was Liza Scott. I don't know who had called Aubrey and Emily, but they appeared walking down the driveway just at that moment. They ran across the apron to hold their daughter. Emily was weeping and laughing at the same time. Aubrey picked up Liza and began to carry her up the driveway. He brushed aside an EMT. "We're taking her to the hospital ourselves," he said firmly.

I unwrapped myself from Robin to wait for my own hostage. And he was out next. Like Joss, Phillip was filthy and thin, but his back was straight and his face was hard. He came right into my hug willingly, though. He said, "I was never so glad to hear anyone's voice in my life, Roe. Oh, thanks, thanks, thanks." His voice broke into something suspiciously like a sob.

"Hey," I said, and then I couldn't say anything else, because it was my turn to cry all over him. And he didn't demur. He smelled awful. But I was so glad he was alive and intact, I'd have hugged him if he'd been skunked.

I missed a lot of the ebb and flow and the commands, but an EMT crew ran past me. After a few long minutes, Josh was carried out on a stretcher. I had a moment of wondering if we'd really have a happy ending when I saw Josh. He looked terrible, and he was clearly very ill. "Call the Finstermeyers," I suggested to Robin. "I'm sure they've already heard, but they could go to straight to the hospital, skip this confusion." Robin extricated his cell phone. After a moment he said, "Beth? They're taking Joss and Josh directly to the hospital. They're safe."

I could hear her scream over the phone. Phillip grinned at me. It was so good to see him smile. I grinned back.

"Yes," Robin said. "We just got them out of the Harrison house. Clayton was keeping them hostage. We'll tell you later."

He dropped the phone back in his pocket, and did some beaming of his own. He turned to the nearest uniform, who was (I saw with some surprise) the chief of police, Cliff Paley. He was talking to his shoulder, which was explained when he turned toward me and I saw some kind of communication rig attached to it.

"Chief," I said, "can we go home? You all know where he will be."

"Let me check," he said, and talked to his shoulder some more. He said, "Roe, you can take Phillip home if you don't let him call or talk to anyone else until we get his statement. Pascoe?"

Phillip nodded emphatically. "I just want a shower," he said. "And food. I don't need an ambulance."

"My client will stick to those restrictions," Bryan said. "Though we hope you'll interview him sooner rather than later, so he can tell his friends he made it."

Chief Paley nodded. "Done."

"But wait a moment," Robin said. Down the kitchen steps came the Harrisons, Dan, Karina, and Clayton. And they were all in handcuffs. I'm sure it was wrong of me, but I was absolutely delighted. Phillip had a broad smile on his grimy face. It was all I could do to keep from spitting at them as they walked by. Karina turned to look at me, but her face was blank with shock. Then they were in separate police cars and going to jail.

"Okay, we're going home," I told Chief Paley, smiling. "No talking or calling." And just like that, we started to Robin's car, which he'd parked at the house across the street while he waited for my instructions. I would not be able to move mine for hours, it was clear. As we hiked up the driveway to the street, we passed the Scotts. Phillip stopped, so we did, too.

Liza wriggled gently from her mother's grasp and hugged Phillip without reserve. "Mom, Dad," she said. "Phillip saved my life."

Phillip hugged her back, but he looked embarrassed. "Oh, naw," he said. "Liza was brave all the way through."

"I think Clayton would have killed me right away if it hadn't been for Phillip," Liza said.

"Liza, what are you going to do with those girls the next

time you see them?" Phillip asked, looking down at her. He was obviously going through a ritual.

"Punch them in the nose," she said stoutly. "I promise I will."

Aubrey looked a bit shocked, but Emily, after a moment's hesitation, said, "You do that, Liza. Turning the other cheek isn't working with them."

There were going to be some interesting discussions in the Scott household in the next few days, but that was not my concern. I let it float away on the outgoing tide of tension. I was replacing that with well-being and relief. It was amazing how the world had changed in less than an hour. I said good-bye to Bryan, who told me to call him if we wanted him present when the police interviewed Phillip. I promised him I would, and I thanked him.

Once in the car, we could not think of anything to say, which was odd. There was too much . . . or not enough. "Phillip," I said. "We want to know all about it, but you don't need to tell us now. We just want you to feel clean again, and we want to feed you."

"I'll eat *anything,*" he said, as if he were swearing on a stack of Bibles. "Even asparagus. Even salmon croquettes." He had not liked my salmon croquettes to an extreme degree.

"I have to tell you that your mom and your dad are both in town," I said. The bliss of anticipation disappeared from Phillip's face. But I had to warn him, or perhaps prepare him would be more accurate.

"They can wait," he said, pushing his problems with them away. "For now, shower, shampoo, and soap. And food. Any food."

Though Phillip had no coat on, he did not seem to be feeling the cold at first. But halfway home, he began shivering. We turned the heat on high, and I tossed him a lap robe Robin kept in the car in winter, but he couldn't stop. "I'm not cold," he said. "I don't know what's happening."

"It's a reaction," Robin said. "In a while you'll be fine."

"What day is it?" Phillip asked suddenly.

"It's Christmas Eve," I said, surprised to realize it, myself.

"I thought so," he said. "I tried to keep track of the days. I was scared I might have miscounted. I was scared we'd be in there for Christmas. Or he'd kill us all before then."

I couldn't imagine how scary it must have been.

But in two more minutes we were home and hustling Phillip into the house. He went to his room briefly to grab clean clothes. Then he vanished into the hall bathroom. The water started thundering down in the shower before he could have taken off his nasty clothes, and I smiled to myself. I had been afraid I'd never hear Phillip wasting hot water again.

I began pulling food out of the refrigerator. Now the food friends had brought us would be put to good use.

Chapter Fifteen

An hour later, Philip was sitting at the breakfast bar in the kitchen. He had consumed lasagna, creamed spinach, cheesy carrots, and a bowl of bread pudding, all with a truly inspiring single-minded intensity. His hair was clean, he'd scrubbed and shaved, and he was wearing clean clothes. He'd asked me to throw away the clothes he'd worn all during his captivity. I'd put them right in a trash bag and tossed them out in the garbage can.

Phillip hadn't wanted to talk.

But now he sat back on his stool, sighed, and looked about ten years old . . . for just a second. "That was the best food I ever ate," he said simply. "We didn't get fed much. I'm so full I think my stomach will pop."

Robin and I both perked up, since we were finally going to hear what had happened.

The doorbell rang at that moment, of course. Not at all to my surprise, the callers were the FBI agents. Bernadette Crowley was impassive, but Les Van Winkle gave me quite a steely look.

I did not quiver in my shoes.

My brother was home. If I hadn't done what I did, he'd still be in the basement.

"We're here to talk to Phillip," Crowley said. "Phillip, it's good to meet you face-to-face after looking for you. I'm Special Agent Bernadette Crowley, and this is Special Agent Les Van Winkle."

"The FBI? Wow," Phillip said, impressed. He slid off the stool and shook their hands, I waved everyone to the two big couches and the armchairs. Robin and I flanked Phillip, while the agents took the other couch.

"First off, do I need to get our lawyer here for this?" I asked.

Van Winkle looked surprised. "No, this is just a preliminary interview to get Phillip's story down."

"I'm afraid you're going to have to repeat it a few times to law enforcement bodies," Crowley said, after she and Van Winkle had turned down my offer of coffee or a soda. "But we need to hear it."

"Okay," Phillip said. "What do you want to know?" He had tensed up again.

"Let me ask a question or two first." Crowley smiled. "Why did Clayton Harrison keep you prisoner for so long?"

That was an odd question, I thought, but I suddenly found myself wondering the same thing. Why, indeed?

"He was waiting for his passport," Phillip said, with no hesitation. "He'd lost his a month ago. He'd already applied for a replacement since he was going on a trip to Peru in June. Since he was leaving the country as soon as he got it, he was waiting for it to come."

The agents glanced at each other. "He told you this?" Van Winkle asked.

"Yeah, he did. He said as soon as his passport came he'd be gone out of the U.S., and his parents would 'discover' us in the basement and let us go."

"Did the older Harrisons come down there at any time? Did you see them?"

"No," Phillip said. "But Clayton went upstairs to shower

and change clothes. Just not when the cook or the cleaning crew or whoever was in the house. Because he was supposed to be missing," Phillip added, in case the agents hadn't registered that crucial point.

"Do you know for a fact that his parents knew you were in the basement?"

"They had to know," Phillip said. For the first time, he began to get excited. "For one thing, though they didn't feed us much, we did get food maybe once a day. And he sure didn't fix it or go to buy it. He was only out of the basement at night, when he went up to shower or whatever. And we were locked in, of course."

"How did Josh get hurt?" Van Winkle asked.

"He got a little hurt when we were taken," Phillip said. He looked ashamed. "If we'd all rushed Clayton then, none of this would've happened, and maybe Tammy would still be alive. We all jumped out of the car when Tammy got hit. Josh was slow getting back in the car to drive. Clayton clipped him on the side of the head with the gun."

"And Josh was hurt a second time?"

"He lunged for Clayton on a bathroom break, and the gun went off. I can't believe the Harrisons could miss that," Phillip said.

Even in a house as large as the Harrison mansion, and in a soundproofed basement, I thought a gunshot would be audible.

"But you don't know that they were in the house at that moment," Crowley suggested.

"They might not have been. They didn't come down. Clayton made us drag Josh back into the storeroom. Later he threw in some first-aid stuff."

I put my hand over Phillip's and squeezed. I tried to imagine being fifteen and handling the shooting of my friend without any expert help or any adult backup. My hat was off to Phillip. For the first time, I believed my brother would be fine . . . not because we would help him, but because he was innately strong.

"Just to be clear, you did not see Clayton's parents with your own eyes at any time?"

Phillip looked taken aback. "No," he said slowly. "I did not."

"Does that mean they're going to get away with this?" Robin said. He was not bothering to repress his anger.

"They may," Crowley said. "They can pretend they didn't know Clayton was keeping hostages, that they were only concealing their son because he was in trouble. As his parents, they were determined to keep him from harm."

"From prosecution," I said.

"Yes. From prosecution."

"Knowing that he had committed murder and kidnapped four people?"

"Clayton says that Connie killed Tammy Ribble." Van Winkle looked off into the distance as if he could not even dignify that statement with the slightest appearance of belief.

"She did," Phillip said.

I gasped out loud, and warned myself to be still. Phillip didn't need an audience to react to the drama. He needed us to hear what had happened in a factual way.

"So tell us what happened that afternoon," Crowley said. "I'll record it, if you don't mind."

"No," Phillip said. "I'll only be telling the truth." He took a deep breath. "I was with Josh," he began. "We were supposed to pick up Joss at the practice field after she'd given Liza her private lesson."

"How well did you know Liza?" Van Winkle asked very quietly. He didn't want Phillip's stride to be broken.

"I had met her at my sister's church," Phillip said. "She was just a kid, four years younger than me. But Josh and Joss had told me what was happening to her at school, and I thought that was shitty. Those girls were just bitches in training, as far as I'm concerned. Liza is a *nice* kid. And she couldn't stop them. No one could."

Phillip looked sideways at me, and I saw the memory in his eyes. He'd hitched a ride with a trucker, who had made such forceful advances that Phillip had been forced to abandon his backpack and run to hide in the woods. Phillip knew about not having control over circumstances.

"So you were at the field . . ." Crowley murmured.

"And the three witches walked over from the school," Phillip said. "They were trying to make Liza cry. I gave them a talking-to. They can't do anything to me."

Marlea had said she was going to try, however. I wouldn't forget that.

"And then?"

"Liza didn't want to be left at the field with them, and her mother was late coming. Sarah had finished up with the girl she was coaching, and she'd be leaving soon, too. Liza left a message on her mom's phone, and Josh said we could give her a ride. We all got in the car. Josh and I were in the front seat, and Joss was in back with Liza. We thought she'd be more comfortable sitting with another girl."

"We heard she had a big crush on you?" Crowley asked.

"Uh, yeah." Phillip turned red. "But she wasn't clingy and obnoxious. Just . . . she was pretty cool for an eleven-year-old."

"All right. So you four were in Josh's car and you went to the hair salon?"

"First we went by the Scotts' house," Phillip said. "But her mom and dad weren't there, or at the church."

The agents both made notes.

"So after that, Joss started freaking out because she had to be at the salon to get her hair cut, and she was late. She was texting Tammy on the way."

"Why?" Van Winkle asked.

"Just to tell her we were almost there. Tammy's sister had dropped her off. She was waiting."

The agents nodded.

"So we were in that little road behind the beauty shop," Phillip said. "Joss said she could go in that way." His words came slower and his face showed stress. "And Tammy came out of the back door and ran over to the car to hug Joss. You know . . . ?"

"That they were a couple, yes," Crowley said.

"Okay. So Joss was about to get out of the car after talking to Liza a second more, to make sure Liza was okay about . . . well, about Joss not being in the car with her. Josh and I hadn't even thought about that." Phillip shook his head. "But Liza said she'd be okay, that she'd told her mom who she was with in her message." He stopped and took a long, shuddering breath. It was obvious he was coming to something he didn't want to relive. I was scared to put my arm around him or hold his hand. I wanted him to know that I was there for him, but I didn't want to undermine his independence when he needed to be strong.

"Just then, Connie and Clayton pulled up in Clayton's car. Connie was driving. I don't know why. Clayton was about to explode. He has a bad temper," Phillip said. "He jumped out of the car and started saying this awful stuff to Tammy and Joss. His little sister—Marlea—had told Clayton that Joss had made a pass at her! What a stupid thing to believe. I don't know why Clayton was so crazy. It was like it was a personal slap in the face to him, somehow." Philip took another deep breath. "Joss wouldn't do anything like that. She's not a child molester. She loved Tammy. But somehow Marlea had made Clayton believe that shit."

"What happened after he started yelling?" Van Winkle said.

"So Clayton slapped Joss in the face—she was out of the car—and Tammy jumped him. She was beating on him." Philip smiled faintly.

"With her fists?" Van Winkle kept writing.

"Oh, yeah, none of us were armed for riding around in Lawrenceton," Phillip said with elaborate sarcasm. "But Clayton punched Tammy in the face, and we all started to get out of the car to help her and Joss—it just all happened so fast. When Clayton hit Tammy in the jaw, she kind of staggered back in front of Clayton's car, and Connie pressed the accelerator and she hit her."

There was a long moment of silence.

"And Joss screamed, or she tried to, but no sound would come out. Connie had stopped the car and she was just staring at nothing. And Tammy was dead." Phillip didn't seem to know that a tear was rolling down his cheek. "Clayton ran to his car and got a gun."

"He had it in the car?" Crowley murmured.

"I think in the glove compartment. He told Connie to leave, to drive back to his house without stopping or phoning anyone. Then he got in the backseat of Josh's car and put the gun to his head, and said if Josh didn't drive, he would shoot him. Clayton would shoot Josh," Phillip said, so we'd all keep it straight.

"So we got to Clayton's house. He got us all to go downstairs, and Connie helped him. He handed her a little gun, too. I don't know what kind. When we were all herded into the little storeroom off the rec room—he got Connie to throw out a lot of the holiday stuff to make room—Clayton shut the door and locked it."

"It had a lock already on it?"

"Yeah. The Harrisons kept their extra liquor in there, and they kept it locked because Clayton had thrown a party once and his friends had drunk up a lot of it, Josh told me. But Clayton knew where the key was, and he locked us in. Later, he put another lock on it, a padlock. So there we were, in the little room, and Joss was, you know, crying like hell because of Tammy and she was bloody, Liza was scared and missing her mom and dad. Josh and I didn't know what to do. Josh didn't feel good, because he'd taken a smack with the gun."

Phillip looked ten years older by this time. "And there we stayed," he said eventually. "Clayton would throw in some

McDonald's bags every now and then that his parents brought him, I guess. He could hardly go out to get them, right? Or there would be homemade sandwiches."

"Can you remember when you ate the McDonald's food?"

It was evident to me that the FBI agents were trying to pin down the Harrisons' involvement in the crime. They were anxious to be able to prove that the couple had known exactly what their son was up to. Surely, buying a large bag of hamburgers and fries meant that they'd known there were other people to feed.

"The day after we got there, and a couple of days after that," he said, after some thought. "There was bottled water in the room, too, so we drank that. But food, we didn't get enough, and he'd only let us out twice a day, one by one, to go to the bathroom. Pretty horrible."

"When did Josh get injured?"

"Oh, the day I called you," he said to me. "We had it all planned out. We were going to rush him, and then I'd make it up the stairs to a telephone while Josh and Joss pinned him down. When he unlocked the door, we went for him."

"He had the gun?" I said quietly.

"Oh, sure, he had it all the time. But we had to get out. So I plowed past him, and Josh and Joss jumped him. I made it up the stairs and saw a cell phone on the kitchen counter. I dialed you, and I heard your voice." Phillip closed his eyes. "I don't even remember what I said to you, Roe. I saw the gun in Clayton's hand, and I had to hang up. Clayton was yelling, telling me that he'd shoot Joss if I didn't come back."

"Did you think about running out right then?"

"I never wanted to do anything more in my life. But I believed Clayton. So I went back downstairs. That was the worst moment." He nodded, definite. "The worst."

Robin patted Phillip's shoulder. Phillip sat forward and put his head in his hands. "How is Josh?" he said, his voice muffled. "Clayton took his shirt for something."

"His parents, I assume, planted it out in the country to draw attention away from town. Josh has an infection from the gunshot," Crowley said. "But since it grazed him instead of lodging inside his body, the doctors are pretty certain he'll recover after some stitching and a lot of antibiotics. He has a mild concussion, too."

"And Joss?"

"She's bruised, but otherwise doing okay."

"Liza?"

"With her mom and dad. Physically fine."

"Clayton?"

"Being questioned, with a lawyer present, and his parents in other interview rooms with their own lawyers."

"What about Connie? Why hasn't she been arrested? She knew what he'd done. She *helped* him."

There was a long silence. I said, "Honey, I have to tell you something. Connie killed herself."

Phillip dropped his hands and I could see his face. "Good," he said. "She murdered Tammy. She should have felt bad about it. I'm glad she did."

I tried not to look shocked, though I was, a little. But how could I blame him? He'd seen something awful.

"What about Clayton's car?" Crowley asked. "Do you know where it is? We haven't been able to find it yet."

"No idea," Phillip said. "He was upset at having to get rid of it, though."

Van Winkle said, "I think it must be close, Bernadette, because it's so conspicuous they wouldn't risk driving it far." (In fact, a very surprised fisherman found it in a pond about three miles from the Harrison house the next week.)

Phillip talked a while longer, giving the agents some more details and elaborating on Clayton's threats. And his plans to leave the country, because his dad had a cousin in Europe. Clayton didn't ever tell Phillip what country, he was canny enough for that. "He tried to keep us quiet, telling us that he'd be gone, and his parents would pretend to be shocked we were in their own basement." Phillip shook his head. "I didn't know if he was telling us the truth or not, but I tried to believe he was. I don't know if the Harrisons would have let us go." He looked too bleak for a teenager, and I ached for him.

"Did you know his parents claimed they paid ransom for him?" Van Winkle said.

"Oh, sure. I heard him talking to his parents about it. Sometimes if he got bored, he'd call them, though he was in the basement and they were upstairs. They all used burner phones to talk to each other, so it wouldn't be traceable. They told Clayton if they claimed they'd paid ransom, Clayton would have the cash to take with him. Untraceable."

We hadn't seen Dan Harrison go through a rehearsal for delivering the ransom money. He'd been doing the motions in case he was being watched—which he was, but not by law enforcement, but by a librarian and a mystery writer.

"Did Clayton ever say explicitly that his parents knew you were downstairs?"

Phillip thought. "No, but when he said 'discover' he practically said it with quote marks, you know?"

"If you find all the burner phones, surely you can prove they were talking to each other," I said. "One of those phones must have been on the counter, and that's what Phillip used to call me. And if the Harrisons withdrew the false ransom money, they had to know all about what Clayton had done." I would be very, very angry if the Harrisons were not punished for their complicity.

Van Winkle and Crowley left soon after, without committing to any certainty that Clayton's parents would stand trial. They told Phillip he'd been really brave, and that they were relieved he was okay. No sooner had we turned away to clear the dishes from the breakfast bar, than the doorbell rang.

This time it was my father. And his wife.

Betty Jo was defiantly dressed in a long black skirt and a fuchsia and black blouse. Phil wore his usual—khakis and a plaid shirt. They were both angry with me, of course.

"I had to find out from a reporter that my son had been found," Dad said to me, venting some of his anger before he even looked at Phillip, who was standing back and looking unhappy.

He was justified, this time. He should have been the first person I called. In my defense, I can only say that it had been years since I'd thought of calling my father with any news at all.

"She saved me," Phillip said. "So don't get onto her. Mom, where have you been?"

Betty Jo looked self-conscious. "Well, I haven't been with a man, if your dad told you that. Honey, I couldn't live with the humiliation your dad had dealt out. There was a lot of other stuff wrong, that I can tell you later."

"You mean Dad's gambling habit? I picked up on that a long time ago."

My father looked away, angry.

"I tried to call you once along the drive north," Betty Jo said. "You didn't pick up. I just had to take the time to put my life back together. At the commune, we couldn't use electronics."

Phillip was pretty angry, himself. "Ever think about writing me a letter?"

This family drama was eclipsing Phillip's homecoming, and I wouldn't have it.

"Shut up," I said to Betty Jo and Dad. "This is not your day to hash out your mistakes and your differences. This is Phillip's day, because he was lost but now he is found. Tell him how glad you are about that." I spun on my heel and walked away, washing my hands of them. I had to put physical distance between us.

Robin kept a tight watch on the reunion, while I put dishes in the dishwasher and listened to some phone messages I'd gotten. One was from my mother, who sounded genuinely delighted that Phillip was safe. "We're ready to throw a party over here!" she said. I called her back right away.

"As soon as we can get your first husband to leave," I said, not bothering to lower my voice. "And Betty Jo, too."

My mom commiserated with me some, and then hung up. Beth Finstermeyer had called next, to rejoice with me. She told me that Josh would have to stay in the hospital on IV antibiotics, but he was already eating and talking about Christmas Day. Joss, she added, was glad to be out of the basement, but she was grieving over Tammy. "I've never had to console a child about the death of someone they loved," she said heavily. "It feels a little strange, talking to Joss about her girlfriend. But as long as she's home . . ."

"Yes, as long as she made it home," I said. "I'll see you soon, and we'll both be happier."

"George says thanks," Beth said, and hung up before I could ask what for.

A couple of hours later, I got a similar call from Aubrey Scott. He was gracious enough to tell me how much Liza had depended on Phillip's kindness to get through her imprisonment. "I know Phillip is a lot older than Liza, especially as kids reckon it," he said, "but I know they're fast friends now, as strange as other kids may think it."

"I don't care what anyone else thinks," I said. "I only care that they all came through it well. The law will take care of the rest. But I'm afraid the Harrisons won't get convicted . . . if they even get charged."

"From the questions the woman detective asked when she interviewed Liza, I think the same thing," Aubrey said grimly. "There is no way in the world they didn't know what was going on under their roof."

"I agree," I said, and on that angry note, we hung up.

I heard later that Aubrey's Christmas Eve service was very

emotional, that many tears were shed, that despite the absence of Emily and Liza, who stayed home, it was a very touching event.

I didn't go. I couldn't stand one more emotional passage. I thought maybe Liza just didn't want all the attention.

I'd never wrapped gifts on Christmas Eve before, or tried to imagine what I'd have for Christmas dinner the night before. I gave myself yards of slack, and we had a beautiful and peaceful morning after Phillip finally woke up on Christmas Day. We opened some presents. We enjoyed being together. My mother renewed her invitation to Christmas dinner but we turned that invitation down with little regret. None of us were in the mood for a barrage of questions, nor yet for ignoring what had happened the past few days. Ham and sweet potatoes out of a can and some traditional green bean casserole, plus biscuits, made a perfectly adequate meal, as long as we were together.

"How's the baby?" Phillip asked. "How are you feeling?"

He seemed a little shy, as if there was something a little embarrassing about having a pregnant sister.

"I feel so much better now," I said honestly. "The doctor is going to check me over tomorrow, she's coming into the office specially so I can have some peace of mind, but I think I'm right as rain."

"That's what I want," Phillip said. "I was scared—when I had any time to be scared of anything besides Clayton killing us—that you would be so upset that something would go wrong with the baby."

"I can't believe you could spare the energy to think about me," I said. "You had plenty to worry about."

He grinned. "Yeah, I did, didn't I? But it's like that play, *All's Well That Ends Well.*"

You couldn't say it better than that.